For the dogs who brighten our days

At Christmastime we all
need a friend...

FLORENCE McNICOLL

First published in Great Britain in 2020 by Trapeze
an imprint of The Orion Publishing Group Ltd
Carmelite House, 50 Victoria Embankment
London EC4Y 0DZ

An Hachette UK Company

1 3 5 7 9 10 8 6 4 2

A CIP catalogue record for this book is available from the British Library.

ISBN (Paperback) 978 1 4091 9268 8
ISBN (eBook) 978 1 4091 9269 5

Typeset by Born Group
Printed and bound in Great Britain by Clays Ltd, Elcograf S.p.A.

www.orionbooks.co.uk

Author's note: While the novel is inspired by the fantastic work of Battersea Dogs and Cats Home, it is a work of fiction and I have taken some liberties with exact procedures. What I hope is reflected in the novel is the great care that Battersea takes in ensuring the best care for all of their beautiful dogs, whether that's in the Battersea Dogs and Cats Home itself or with their incredible fostering team. For more information on Battersea's operations, see www.battersea.org.uk

Chapter 1

Christmas Day, and Kathy Brentwood's stomach was tight with nerves. Excitement, she told herself firmly. She surveyed the living room: perfect. A sparkling Christmas tree, adorned in smart, matching red and white decorations, a mound of presents underneath. She knew that her son, Alex, was a grown-up now, very much so, but she couldn't help buying endless presents for him. It had been harder to think of the perfect gifts for Alex's girlfriend, Jacqui, and her fourteen-year-old daughter, Becs.

Jacqui was one of those women who never seemed to need anything, thought Kathy, and her taste was impeccable. She always looked perfectly put together, lipstick in place, some little accessory brightening up a plain jumper or blouse. Kathy had been unsure what to buy her – Jacqui was a lot more fashionable than she was, let's face it. And for Becs, well, Kathy didn't have a clue about what teenagers liked these days. She'd been a primary school head teacher before her retirement, where little ones were delighted with pretty much anything.

She found herself hoping that they liked their gifts, that this might be the day where she finally got along with Jacqui. A little Christmas magic, a little Christmas drink, and surely they'd be laughing together over the washing-up. She swallowed her nerves. Think positively, she told herself.

Kathy plumped the cushions one more time and straightened one of the Christmas cards on the mantelpiece. They were perfectly spaced out. Once upon a time, the mantelpiece had been full of precious family photographs. Holding her breath, she went to the cupboard under the stairs and pulled out a box. Here were those framed photographs, carefully stored, gathering dust.

Her fingers brushed a photo frame. She picked it up out of the box and traced her fingers over the photo within, exhaling softly.

'Happy Christmas, darling,' she whispered. 'I miss you.'

The photograph was of her husband, John. He'd passed away five years ago from cancer. This photo was of them both before he'd got ill. His blue eyes were still bright and full of mischief, and there beside him, smiling too, was their beloved old Labrador, Buddy, grey and grizzled around the mouth by then. And her, look at her – full of confidence, beaming beside him, wearing a bright beaded necklace that one of her favourite pupils had given her. She'd known her place in the world, then. John's wife, Alex's mum, Buddy's sometime favourite, dependent on how many treats she gave him, and firm-but-fair head teacher of Woodlands Primary. She should wear that necklace more often. John had always loved it.

She wiped the dust away from the photo and put it away carefully. The memories were too difficult, reminding her of what she'd lost. She went upstairs and found the colourful beaded necklace, putting it on, hoping to feel a little boost from it. But it felt like a relic from another time. What was she supposed to do with herself? she wondered. She was only sixty. She still had energy, felt like she had things to offer. But it was so hard now, to feel like she had a place in the world, to know exactly what to do with herself. Kathy sighed and felt the sadness creeping up.

Stop it, Kathy told herself firmly.

Everyone had told her how well she'd coped after John's death. How she'd kept busy, kept fit, taken up new hobbies, like Zumba. Everyone kept saying it's what he would have wanted. She deserved this time to herself, after his illness, people said. He'd been ill for three years and they'd seen the prognosis gradually slide from a very positive one, to the kind where doctors no longer talked in numbers or percentages, but shook their heads and struggled to find the right words. Kathy had taken early retirement when things began to slide that way. She'd nursed John herself when things started to get bad. She'd kept up their normal routine as much as possible, helping him in and out of the car to get to the countryside, pushing his wheelchair around Battersea Park or Clapham Common, insisting on dinners out when they could. But, oh – the pain, the long nights watching him suffer. The endless hospital visits. The sickness. No one in their right mind could claim that was normal. What she wouldn't give for one more cup of tea with John. One more glass of wine, together in the garden, not saying very much at all. One more Christmas morning.

She was off again – dwelling. She pushed it all down and took a deep breath. It was Christmas Day! A time to be happy. Alex would be here before she knew it.

*

Spending Christmas morning waiting on your own was a little strange, Kathy reflected, a half-hour later in the kitchen, over yet another cup of tea. She was an early riser and it was now only 10.30. All being well, Alex would arrive at 1 p.m. Preparation was well under way with the food. Kathy would have to be careful not to get so far ahead of herself that she'd be serving up a roast turkey at 11.30 a.m. She had done another whizz round with the hoover. The kitchen was forensically clean. Carols were playing on the radio.

'*The hopes and fears of all the years, are met in thee tonight*,' a choir sang out, and Kathy shut her eyes. That had been John's favourite carol. Hopes and fears. She knew all about those. She reached out a hand and snapped the station over to a commercial one, blaring out Christmas pop tunes. Better.

As she peered out of the window in the back garden, she could see the colourful Christmas trees of her neighbours. She imagined their noisy, bustling Christmases and felt a jolt of envy. The Christmases she'd spent with John when Alex was young had been some of the best days of her life. Days of laughter – when they'd bought Alex a remote-control car, and she'd literally had to wrest the control out of John's hand and tell him to give Alex a go, she and her son both giggling at John pretending he was 'checking the battery', when he clearly just wanted to keep buzzing the little car around the patio. And then the next year, when she'd bought him a car of his own, sharing the secret with Alex, so the two of them were bursting with impatience for John to open his 'big present' and see the look on his face.

They must have had Buddy by then. Yes, she remembered the gorgeous black Labrador joining in the fun, really just a puppy then, unsure whether the car was for him to play with as well. Kathy hadn't forgotten him – she and Alex had made Buddy a special stocking, crammed with Christmas toys and treats. Oh, Buddy. He'd been their adored dog for twelve years, seeing Alex through from when he was a boy to university, and keeping Kathy and John heading out for their daily walks together. She'd loved those walks. It was so easy, so intimate, such a good part of life together. Walking on your own was different; it just was.

Only another half an hour had passed and Kathy was twiddling her thumbs. She glanced up and saw an old waxed coat hanging on the hook by the back door. Her newer one was upstairs, a fancy thing made of Gore-Tex. This one was John's. She couldn't get rid of it. She decided she'd head out for a brisk walk around Battersea Park – it would be nice to see a few people on Christmas morning – and then she'd have worked up an appetite for lunch. She paused and then shrugged on John's old coat, comforted by the familiar smell of the waxed cotton.

*

'Happy Christmas!'

'Happy Christmas!'

Kathy smiled as she returned the greeting from a passing family bundled up against the winter chill in their colourful scarves and hats. It had been a good idea to come out. She watched children run around, working off the excess energy from chocolate coins, no doubt, and parents watching them proudly. She loved Christmas, she really did.

She kept walking on, towards an area of the park that was a little less busy, enjoying the feeling of the crisp air on her face, a hint of winter sunshine struggling through the clouds occasionally. She shoved her hands in her pockets to keep them warm and her fingers alighted on something. She pulled it out and had to laugh. A squeaky ball! Who knew how long this had been in there? John had had an endless store of treats and toys in his coat pocket; it had been a joke between them. He'd usually included a piece of chocolate or mint cake for her as well, teasing her and saying 'Sit!' before giving it to her. He was the only person who'd got away with teasing Kathy like that, the only person she'd been silly with.

And then, the sound of barking!

She turned round to see a dog galloping towards her, tail wagging, clearly excited to be out and about, lead trailing behind. She looked around for an owner, but there was no one in sight.

Kathy acted by instinct. She pulled the ball out and raised it, giving it a squeak. The dog's attention was caught. He came galloping over to Kathy, slowing down and looking up at her, pleading for the ball.

'Sit,' said Kathy firmly, hoping the dog knew the basic commands.

To her relief, the dog scrambled to sit down, tongue lolling, head cocked to one side. What a gorgeous fellow! He looked like a spaniel cross, judging by those ears. Kathy bent to pick up the lead before giving the dog the ball and a generous pat.

'Who's a good boy? Who's a good boy?' said Kathy as the dog pressed against her legs, keen for more attention.

He was wearing a blue collar, she noticed, with a matching blue lead. She tried to get a look at the tag, the dog wriggling and licking at her for attention.

'Battersea . . .' she murmured, seeing the name printed on his tag. 'You must have come from the dogs' home there, hey, boy?'

Kathy knew Battersea Dogs & Cats Home well. The centre was a twenty-minute walk or so from her house and when she walked around Battersea Park, as opposed to her more usual Clapham Common route, she often saw the Battersea dogs out and about. After Buddy had died, she and John had wondered about getting another dog. They'd even gone so far as to visit the home a few times, their hearts breaking, wanting to give each and every dog there a second chance. But then John had been diagnosed. And all thoughts of another dog had gone out the window.

'Thank goodness you found him!' A very red-faced man, his hair all over the place like a scarecrow, was jogging towards Kathy.

He arrived at her side and bent forwards, holding his knees, catching his breath. The dog yapped happily to see him, tail wagging. The man knelt next to him, fussing the dog, who put his paws up on his shoulders and licked his face, causing the man to chuckle.

He stood up. Kathy guessed he was in his late fifties, a little younger than her. His hair, which was now blowing in every direction, was rather more salt than pepper. He was tall, with long, gangly arms, each ended by a different-coloured glove. His coat was buttoned up the wrong way, a shoelace trailed behind him. She had the urge to sort him out – get him a pair of matching gloves and – oh, Lord! the socks were clashing, as well.

'I can't thank you enough,' he said to Kathy, with just a trace of a northern accent.

She noticed his eyes; sea-green. Unusual colour. He smiled at her, a warm, crooked smile that made the lines around his eyes deeper, and she noticed one of his teeth was a little chipped.

She cleared her throat. 'It was nothing, really.'

'It wasn't. This one is a bit of a Houdini. We call him Harry, actually.'

'Is he yours?'

'I wish. I work at Battersea, the dogs' and cats' home. This one's currently enjoying a little stay there before he goes home.'

'Goes home?'

He nodded. 'It's what we say when a dog leaves for that forever home they've been waiting for. That they've gone home. But they're very well-looked-after until they do.

And of course, the dogs still need a walk and some love on Christmas Day. So, I'm volunteering.'

'That's very good of you.'

He smiled again. 'Well, to be honest, there's no place I'd rather be. It's practically a second home to me now. Let me find a treat for Harry, hang on.'

He reached into his pocket for some dog treats, and bits of receipts, sweets and a pencil fell out. Kathy stooped to help pick them up.

'What a disaster zone I am!'

Kathy couldn't help but agree. She couldn't abide disorder. The dog clearly adored this man, though, looking up at him and wagging his tail.

'How did he get away?'

'My fault. I was tying my shoelace and must have only had hold of the lead loosely, when he saw something and whipped it out of my fingers, and he was off.'

Kathy felt irritated by his cavalier attitude.

'You should be more careful,' said Kathy. 'There are roads near here. He could have run in to one of them.'

The man chuckled. 'Yes, you're right. But it didn't happen. The roads are quiet today, anyhow. Thank you for catching him; he'd have been off the other side of London by now if you hadn't, the way he runs. You got a dog of your own?'

'Not any more,' Kathy said.

Something in her voice must have betrayed her sadness, because the man reached out and gently squeezed her arm.

'I'm sorry,' he said, and he sounded like he genuinely meant it.

A lot of people had said they were sorry to Kathy over the last few years and she'd thought the words had lost their power. She was surprised to find herself a little choked up.

'He was gorgeous,' she said, clearing her throat. 'Black Lab. Called Buddy.'

'Oh, I love a Lab,' said the man. 'Here, I'm Ben. Just so we don't do that classic thing of knowing the dogs' names and not each other's.'

Kathy had to smile at that. She introduced herself.

'Well, happy Christmas, Kathy,' said Ben. 'What are your plans for the rest of the day?'

'Oh, I've got family over,' said Kathy, putting on her brightest face. 'Actually, I should be getting back. I need to put the finishing touches to lunch.'

Ben shook his head admiringly. 'That's impressive. Finishing touches! I'd probably only think of starting Christmas lunch at about three and serving it at eight.'

Kathy tried not to shudder visibly.

'Although, that does make it more of a dinner, doesn't it?' Ben was musing. 'Continental. Which way are you walking? I'll come with you for a bit. It won't matter if this fellow is out for a bit longer; do him good to burn off some of the energy. Want to take his lead?'

Kathy found that she did. She took it back from Ben and set off in the direction of home, enjoying the feeling of the dog's happy energy ahead of her. They passed a few more families and wished them happy Christmas, their voices sometimes chiming in unison. Kathy wondered briefly if anyone thought she and Ben were a couple. Oh, to be walking side by side with your partner, a dog surging ahead of you. Briefly, she felt almost dizzy with nostalgia.

'Are you all right?' Ben said. 'You look a bit pale.'

'Yes, fine, fine,' Kathy said. 'Just thinking of all the tasks ahead.'

'Don't worry,' said Ben. 'Honestly, glass of bubbles and a few mince pies, and they won't notice what you serve up.'

She nodded, wishing she could feel a little more relaxed about the day ahead. But she wanted it all to be perfect, so planning was essential.

'I was going to say,' Ben continued, 'they're going to be looking for kennel support volunteers at Battersea in the new year. You should think about applying. You've clearly got a way with dogs.'

Kathy felt her interest stir. 'What kind of things do they do?'

'They're a really important part of the work Battersea does. They help with the day-to-day care of the dogs – lots of cleaning and grooming and kennel socialisation time. After a few months, they also get trained in walking the dogs. I'm sure you'd do a better job of that than me,' he added with a wink.

Kathy's heart leapt. She'd love that! Being around dogs all day long. Then a wave of fear rose up. *Could* she manage it? It suddenly seemed like a lot of unknowns.

'Oh . . . maybe . . .' she said.

'I think you'd like it down there. We're like one big family. We're all having a Christmas lunch together today, after we've finished with the dogs. It's lovely.'

'It sounds it,' said Kathy. 'Look, this is my turning. I'll leave you to it.' She handed Harry's lead back to Ben, their gloved fingers brushing. 'Have you got that held tightly?'

He grinned at her. 'Yes, miss.'

Kathy resisted the urge to roll her eyes. The dog could have dashed off into the road if she hadn't been there!

'Well, have a happy Christmas,' she said to Ben. 'And you, too,' she added, stooping to pet Harry. He was lovely, she thought, his eyes bright, his tail wagging.

'Merry Christmas to you, too,' said Ben. 'I hope you have a great time with your family. And think about the volunteer role, eh?'

Kathy nodded as she turned away from them. This was actually a little earlier than she needed to part ways with Ben, but there was something about him that got under her skin. The truth was, she'd lost her confidence and Ben talking about the volunteer role brought it home. There was a time when she'd have put her hand up for anything, but that was a long time ago. A time when she couldn't walk down the street without being stopped for a chat about such and such a committee, or to ask if she'd help with a fundraiser.

With Ben gone, she thought she'd be relieved to be alone again, but was suddenly horribly aware of the space beside her and the absence of a dog tugging against her hand. She shivered and pulled the coat more tightly round her.

*

It was 1 p.m. and Kathy was worried. Where were they? She had the turkey in the oven, all the trimmings ready, and the plan had been for Alex, Jacqui and Becs to arrive at 12.15 for a Christmas toast. The fizz was still chilling in the fridge. Kathy had lit a fire, and the living room was sparkly and cosy, ready to be shared with other people. Had something happened? An accident? It didn't bear thinking about.

Her phone rang and she jumped to answer it.

'Hello?' she said.

'Mum?'

'Alex? Yes?'

'Mum, I'm so sorry. We're not going to make it.'

Her heart fell. She could hear noises in the background, the chatter of voices, cutlery clinking, orders being shouted. Alex must be calling from the kitchens. He and Jacqui ran a pub together, where Alex was the chef and Jacqui the manager. It was how they'd met, when Alex had taken over the ailing business about eighteen months ago and had decided to bring in an experienced business manager.

They made a formidable team. Alex was a whizz in the kitchen, recruiting a crack team to help him whip up delicious pub classics and a few lighter, more modern dishes. Jacqui had redecorated the pub and set about giving it a new lease of life, planning a roster of events from quiz nights to wine tastings. Business had boomed, with people even travelling in from elsewhere.

'Why?' she said. 'What's happened? Are you all all right?'

'Too many staff have called in sick and we're rushed off our feet. I'm sorry we didn't call you before now. I didn't even notice the time; we've been so busy.'

Kathy's heart sank even further. She knew they'd planned to open for Christmas lunch, but Alex had assured her that they had enough staff to cover it and would set off for Christmas at his mum's as soon as they'd checked that everything was running smoothly.

'But . . .' she began. 'I've got the turkey in the oven. It's practically done. And all your beds are ready and presents and . . .' She shoved her hand against her mouth. She felt like crying.

'I'm so sorry, Mum,' said Alex, breaking away from the phone to yell, 'Table four!' at someone.

'Is there really no one who could come in?' said Kathy. 'What about Sasha?'

'She's with her family in Poland,' Alex said. 'And Kev has flu, properly, and those two are our safe hands. It wouldn't be fair to the rest of the team to get them to carry on without them.'

'Well, could you come later?' said Kathy. 'For the evening?'

'Alex, come on. We need you,' came a woman's voice down the phone.

Jacqui.

Kathy felt her hackles raise.

Alex cupped the phone to speak to her, but Kathy could still hear the conversation.

'It's Mum. I'm explaining why we can't go.'

Jacqui sighed. 'Well, tell her we're very sorry. But these are circumstances beyond our control.'

She didn't sound very sorry, Kathy thought.

'She's saying could we go later?'

'Alex, we're not going to be finished here before six and we'll be exhausted. Even Becs is washing up. The last thing I want to do is drag her on some car journey.'

'Or Alex could just come,' Kathy said to herself quietly as they muttered between themselves. That would be her preferred option. To have her son all to herself.

'OK, OK, I get it,' said Alex and turned back to the phone. 'Mum?'

'I'm here, darling,' said Kathy brightly.

Jacqui cut in again. 'Happy Christmas, Mrs Brentwood!'

Kathy thought Jacqui's voice was high and false. She'd heard the terse tones Jacqui had used before. And what was with the Mrs Brentwood? She'd told her to call her Kathy the few times they'd met.

'Oh, happy Christmas, Jacqui, to you and Becs,' Kathy said in her most sugary voice.

Then it was just Alex again.

'Mum, we'll come up tomorrow, OK, for Boxing Day. Pretend it's Christmas Day. I really am sorry. We'll be there. I have to go, I'm sorry. You will be all right, won't you? You're OK?'

She heard the edge of anxiety in his voice.

'I'll be fine, darling,' she said firmly, although she certainly didn't feel that way.

And with that, Alex said a brisk goodbye and hung up.

Kathy stared around, the phone in her hand, stunned. This had to be a joke. She had to spend the rest of the day alone. She realised she had no one else she could call – what was she going to do, pick up the phone to one of her and John's friends and say her family had abandoned her on Christmas Day? They'd feel so sorry for her! And if there was one thing Kathy couldn't stand, it was being pitied.

They didn't have many friends as a couple, and she'd let contact slide. She'd felt John's absence too sharply on the few occasions they had met up, had dreaded the enquiries about how she was doing. She'd felt so exposed. It wasn't that she didn't long to talk to someone, but she wanted the intimacy of family. You couldn't spill your guts out to someone you hadn't seen for a year. That just wasn't her at all.

She'd also been well known in the community: that went without saying if you were a head teacher. She'd kept up with people as much as possible when John wasn't seriously ill, but then all of her focus had turned to looking after him. And then, after John died, her focus had been on rebuilding a devastated Alex.

He'd moved back in with her for two years and clung to her like a life raft. His grief came first, that had been the order of things. Of course, they'd cried together and comforted each other, but she'd wanted him to know he could rely on her, that she wasn't going anywhere. It had come as something of a shock when one day Alex had mentioned leaving home again and had started to rebuild his life, although of course that's what she wanted. He'd been preoccupied with whether or not she would be OK if he was abandoning her and she'd reassured him to the contrary. She was fine. She was getting on with things.

Kathy switched on the television and immediately turned it off again. Too many festive programmes, full of noise and chatter.

Her only hope was to forget it was Christmas. Do what Alex had suggested and pretend Boxing Day was Christmas Day. She took out the turkey and hacked a piece off, nibbling at it gingerly while it cooled down. She'd wrap everything up and hope it saved all right until tomorrow. Meanwhile, she'd make something else, something that didn't remind her of Christmas.

She assembled a cheese sandwich and some salad, and sat in the living room, the Christmas tree lights turned off, curtains drawn, trying to focus on a book. The hours inched past. The silence in the house was deafening.

Eventually, it was early enough to go to bed. Kathy took herself upstairs, cleaned off her make-up and climbed into bed. It was only when she'd put the light out on her side – she could never sleep on John's side – that she let the tears come. She knew everyone thought she was getting on with things, that she was capable. But it was so lonely, going to bed by yourself and waking up by yourself, especially at Christmas, when it seemed like everyone else in the world was cosy and loved.

Memories of John, of Christmases past when Alex was a little boy, rose up in her mind. John had been so good at buying presents for her. Silly, thoughtful, beautiful – he always got it right. She remembered when he'd presented her with a wrapped frame on Christmas Day. Puzzled, she'd opened it. It was a painting from a street artist they'd passed in Barcelona that summer, which she'd briefly stopped to admire.

John had sneaked back while she was taking a siesta and bought it for her, and had hidden it for six months. She'd been stunned when she'd opened it. It took her right back to the summer, when they'd wandered the streets of the city and swum in the sea, and eaten delicious seafood, giggling over white wine. She'd put the painting away after John had died. It was under the stairs, as well. Sometimes the memories were too painful to bear.

Kathy heaved a shuddering sigh and told herself to calm down. Tomorrow would be another day to get it right. As she tossed and turned, she thought about Ben and Harry. She wondered how the rest of their Christmas Day had been, imagined the Battersea team joking and laughing and pulling crackers. And then she thought, right before she fell asleep, did Ben not have anyone to spend Christmas Day with, either?

Chapter 2

'We're here!' called Alex through the letterbox.

Kathy rushed to open it and embrace her son.

Tall, blond, handsome – Alex was the spitting image of his father and she adored him. It had been difficult for she and John to have children, and they'd almost resigned themselves to it being just the two of them, when Alex had turned up.

'Hello, darling,' she said, hugging him tightly. 'And Merry Christmas! Take two!'

Kathy had woken up with a determination that Christmas Day 2 would be absolutely perfect. She was an organiser by nature, a believer that you just had to step up and sort things out. She'd put the tree lights on and thrown the curtains open. Then she'd turned the happiest Christmas jingles up loud and made up her face carefully, applying a streak of bright lipstick and making herself wear the colourful beaded necklace, after all. She *would* be happy, she told herself. It's what John would have wanted.

Jacqui and Becs were coming up the path, Becs scowling.

'Sorry,' said Alex quietly. 'Been a bit tense in the car.'

Kathy didn't want to hear this. This was a day for happiness.

'Hello, Jacqui!' she called. 'Do be careful to stay on the path; there's bulbs planted just nearby.'

Was it just her, or did Jacqui keep her head down? Maybe she hadn't heard her.

'Mum,' Alex muttered. 'Stop it.'

'Stop what?'

'Correcting everyone. She wasn't going to stray off the path, anyway.'

Kathy bit her lip. She knew she could be a bit of a busybody. But it was hard when, deep down, she just wanted to be useful again. She knew she came across badly sometimes and it had never been like this before – she'd always been the one to know exactly what to do, and people had been grateful for it. The funny thing was, it came from a lack of confidence – she felt pressure to show people that she knew what to do, when on the inside she felt lost.

'Happy Christmas,' she said to Jacqui warmly.

Should she have reached to hug her? It was hard to know what to do – Jacqui always seemed so tough, her wiry, strong frame dressed in immaculate denim jeans and a neat jumper, her dark hair perfect, not a trace of fatigue on her face.

'You must be exhausted after yesterday. Here, take your shoes off and come and sit down.'

'Oh, no, I'm fine,' said Jacqui. 'Absolutely fine. A very merry un-Christmas to you, too. Just let us know what we can do and we'll get on with it.'

Jacqui made her way into the hallway and took off her boots before bustling through to the kitchen with armfuls of bags. Alex was already in there, no doubt nosing through the fridge.

Kathy turned to Becs, who was scowling in a parka, hood up so Kathy could barely see her face. Kathy didn't have a thing to say to Becs, she realised. She'd only met her once before and she'd been glued to her phone the whole time, answering Kathy's questions with monosyllables. Kathy knew it was a tough age for kids, this transition between childhood and adolescence. She'd always found the little ones easier.

'Merry Christmas, Becs,' Kathy said. She eyed Becs' clompy boots and thought of her immaculate carpets. 'Do take your shoes off, dear.'

Becs sighed loudly. 'Where can I plug my phone in?'

Jacqui was coming out of the kitchen and overheard. 'Becs! We talked about this in the car. You are *not* sitting on your phone all afternoon.'

Becs stomped her way into the kitchen.

'And take your shoes *off*!' yelled Jacqui. 'Honestly, what's got into you? You were so good yesterday, helping us out in the pub.'

'Yes, because you *said* that today I could go and see Lauren and Tamsin! And instead we've had to drive all the way up here, to see *her*!'

'Don't be so rude!' said Jacqui.

'It's going to be fun!' said Kathy. This wasn't how she'd imagined their day going. 'It's like Christmas Day! We'll have Christmas dinner soon.'

Becs groaned. 'I already *had* Christmas dinner yesterday, loads of it. And I don't want to eat more meat.'

Kathy had no problem at all with that. She and John had adopted a mostly vegan diet during his treatment, hoping it might make a difference. But she did have a problem with this grumpy attitude.

'I beg your pardon, young lady,' said Kathy, putting on her frostiest head teacher voice. 'I will not be spoken to like that!'

Jacqui turned round sharply. 'No need for that tone. She's tired. It *was* a long drive and a long day yesterday.'

Fortunately, at that moment, Alex came out of the kitchen, clutching a bottle of Prosecco.

'This looks lovely, Mum. And I've rustled up a few snacks with that smoked salmon. Shall we have a toast?'

Kathy had been saving the smoked salmon for brunch, but never mind, Alex could do what he liked!

'Absolutely, let's go into the living room,' she said, showing them into the bright room.

'Lovely tree,' said Jacqui. 'Ours is a bit more of a jumble.'

It gave Kathy a strange pang to think of Alex having a Christmas tree with someone else. She knew they lived together now, of course she did. She'd even visited, once or twice. But a Christmas tree. That was significant. That was a home.

'Are the decorations new?' said Alex. 'Where's all the old ones?'

'I thought a change might be nice,' said Kathy. The old ones were tucked away, in the cupboard under the stairs.

'It's so perfect,' said Alex. 'Look how everything matches. Trust you, Mum!'

'Well, I prefer jumbled,' said Jacqui.

She was *so* competitive, thought Kathy.

Alex popped the cork and poured them each a flute of fizz, a tiny sip for Becs.

'Happy Christmas!' they chorused, ignoring Becs' protests that it was Boxing Day.

Kathy gulped down the fizz gratefully and Alex passed round the smoked salmon canapés he'd made, little biscuits with a dollop of cream cheese and a tiny piece of smoked salmon.

'Oh, Alex, they're perfect,' cooed Kathy. 'So delicious!'

'Bit too salty for my liking,' said Jacqui. 'Becs, go and get us a glass of water.'

'I'll go,' said Kathy, but Becs was already standing up.

'She'll go,' said Jacqui. 'It's fine. Do you need anything from the kitchen?'

Kathy shook her head. Becs left the room and she could hear her rummaging around for glasses. Now she was stressed.

She got up. 'Becs! Use the ones in the cupboard to the right of the sink. And there's a jug of water in the fridge.'

'Honestly, I'm sure she can manage,' said Jacqui.

Kathy bit her lip. She just couldn't get on with Alex's girlfriend. She felt like they knocked heads about literally anything and everything. Why was Jacqui always so keen to assert herself? To assert her dominance, that's what it felt like. See, there, she even had a hand on Alex's knee. He'd had girlfriends before, at uni, and Kathy had never found them quite so difficult.

'How's the pub, then?' said Kathy.

'It's going really well, thanks,' said Jacqui. 'Isn't it, love?'

Alex nodded. 'Yeah, it's great. The new menu's quite something – people are loving it.'

'And the quiz night! It's brilliant. You should come down sometime, Kathy.'

'Oh, isn't it on a Thursday?'

'Yeah. But you're retired, so should be OK for you?'

Kathy bridled. Was that a dig? She felt self-conscious that they thought she had acres of free time.

'Oh, yes. But still very busy.'

'Oh, what have you been up to, Mum?'

'Reading a lot. Walking. Keeping fit, Zumba classes. Nothing new. The usual.'

She didn't want any further questions on that front. In between the activities, she spent an awful lot of time alone, but didn't want Alex to be worrying about her. Kathy got up and bustled into the kitchen, where Becs was scrolling through her phone, having unplugged the kettle and plugged it in.

Kathy felt cross. 'Didn't your mum want some water?'

'What? Oh, yeah.'

But the girl didn't move. 'Never mind,' said Kathy. 'I'll do it.'

She got the glass, added a slice of lemon and poured some water from the jug in the fridge. She walked back through to the living room, hearing Alex and Jacqui giggle at something, and suddenly felt left out.

'Here we are,' Kathy said, handing over the water.

Jacqui raised her eyebrows. 'Thanks. Although madam was meant to do this. You shouldn't be running around after her.'

Personally, Kathy agreed, but managed not to say anything.

'So, presents?' said Jacqui.

'Oh, after lunch!' said Kathy. 'Sorry, that's just how we've always done it. Isn't it, Alex, darling?'

Alex nodded and squeezed Jacqui's knee. 'Yeah, it is. Let's stick with what we know. I'm starving, anyway.'

Kathy led them into the dining room, the table still laid out from yesterday. She lit the candles and directed them to their seats.

'There's only four of us, Mum,' laughed Alex. 'As much as we appreciate the seating plan.'

Only four of us. Her heart jolted. This would be so much easier with John here. She could share a wry look with him at Becs' behaviour. He'd whisper something to make her laugh, he'd break the tension. She wondered what he'd make of Jacqui. He'd have a way of calming Kathy down, of making her relax and enjoy the day. Without him, she felt like she wound herself up, more and more, determined that everything would be perfect. But she didn't know how to stop it. Sometimes she couldn't believe it was five years since he'd died. She felt like she'd been on pause while time went by on fast forward.

'You've gone to so much effort,' said Jacqui politely, before looking back into the hallway. 'Becs! Get in here! And put that phone away!'

'Coming,' said Becs, trailing in.

Kathy held out a cracker to her. Becs sighed and pulled the other end reluctantly.

'You win!' said Kathy as Becs peered at the joke. 'Put the hat on!'

'I don't want to,' said Becs.

'But it's Christmas! It's a time for silly hats!'

'Honestly, just leave her, Kath,' said Jacqui. 'Here.' She reached over to Alex and offered him the other end of her cracker.

They pulled it, and Alex won the hat. He unfolded it carefully and put it on Jacqui's head, kissing her nose.

Kathy didn't know where to look. She glanced away and saw that Becs had also seen the sweet gesture, her face unreadable. Kathy bustled into the kitchen to get the starters out of the fridge – prawn cocktail, with slices of brown bread.

'Prawn cocktail, retro!' said Jacqui as she brought them in.

'I prefer to think of them as classic,' said Kathy stiffly.

'They were Dad's favourite, weren't they, Mum,' said Alex, and Kathy nodded.

'Ah, that's lovely,' said Jacqui. 'You must miss him at Christmas time.'

Kathy knew she was trying to be nice, to give a moment for her to talk about John if she wished, but the words wouldn't come. Part of her wanted to nod, say yes and mention some of the silly things she and John had done each and every Christmas, but she was worried she'd burst into tears if she started talking about him, and maybe Alex would be upset, and the words wouldn't come. So, she simply smiled and nodded, and said, 'But you just have to get on with things. Bread?'

They tucked into the prawn cocktails and chatted more about the pub, about their plans for it, tried to engage Becs in a discussion about school, caught up about some of Alex's old school friends.

'Hey, aren't he and his girlfriend in Australia at the moment?' said Jacqui when she recognised the name of one of Alex's pals.

'Yeah, they are. Melbourne, I think.'

Alex had spent a few years in Australia after university, working in restaurants, learning his trade and generally having a whale of a time. Though they hadn't met till he was back in England, he and Jacqui had been introduced by a mutual friend they both knew from Melbourne.

'I'll have to give them some tips,' said Jacqui, looking wistful. 'Honestly, Kath, it looked so great over there yesterday for Christmas. My family were on the beach! You should see the Christmas brunch we do, with all sorts: fresh fish, fresh fruit. My dad makes these kinds of breakfast tacos and oh my God, they're so good.'

'It doesn't sound very Christmassy to me,' said Kathy.

Alex looked at her sharply. 'Mum.'

'Well, everyone has their own Christmas traditions, of course,' added Kathy.

'You'll have to come out one year and then you'll be converted,' said Jacqui.

Kathy froze. Why hadn't she thought of that before? Jacqui was Australian, all of her family were there, so surely she'd be thinking of going home, at some point. She knew that Jacqui had been in the UK for a long time. Becs had been born here, the result of a short-lived relationship when Jacqui was twenty, but Alex had said they'd barely any contact with her father. And home was home, after all. It sounded like Jacqui really missed her life in Australia and Alex had loved the time he'd spent there. So if she went back, she'd take Alex with her. Kathy's stomach lurched.

She reached for more wine, her hand trembling, and took a sip.

'Must just . . . do something in the kitchen,' she muttered.

She busied herself preparing the vegetables and putting on a pan of boiling water. Alex came through.

'I can do this, Mum. You go and relax with Jacqui and Becs. It's nice you're getting to know them.'

He hugged her and she melted at his touch. She missed being hugged, the comforting presence of another living being. They'd become such a tight unit after John had died – each other's world.

'What's this?'

Alex was reaching towards the noticeboard where she kept letters pinned, a frown on his face. He was looking at a letter she'd received from the hospital.

'It's just a regular check-up.'

He unpinned the letter. 'It says it's for breast cancer screening.'

'Yes, they offer it to all women of my age, every few years.'

But she could see the fear in his eyes.

'Are you sure?'

'Yes.'

'You're not keeping something from me, Mum?'

Her heart felt like it could break, seeing Alex like this. And it was her fault. Hers and John's. When he'd been diagnosed, Alex was on the cusp of setting out in life. Things had looked perfectly manageable then and they'd encouraged

Alex not to worry, said it was just a little operation and he should get on with his plans. For a time it looked like they'd been right, as the treatment seemed to be working. Alex had gone to travel around Asia, then spend time in Australia. When the cancer came back, John had insisted they keep it secret.

'I'm not having him abandon his life for me,' he'd said firmly. John was a gentle man, but Kathy could see how adamant he was about this. 'This is his youth. It's his time to enjoy himself, free from responsibility. We'll look after each other. And anyway, I'll beat this again. No point worrying him.'

Kathy had gone along with it, even though she instinctively felt it was wrong. John got sicker and sicker, and it was harder to pretend all was well, to tell Alex convincingly what they'd been up to when their time was taken up with hospital visits.

'No!' John had said when she raised it yet again. 'Seeing those emails from him, his photos, how happy he is when he calls with his stories – it's getting me through. I want him to have his adventures. Please, Kathy. Please don't.'

But eventually, they had. Which meant Alex had been back home in twenty-four hours, arriving on their doorstep pale with shock and exhaustion under his tan, rushing straight to his father's bedside. Kathy felt wracked with guilt at the thought of it. No wonder he was reacting like this now.

'Alex,' she said gently, 'don't worry. Look, it says here that it's routine.'

He looked at the letter.

'Will you let me know? As soon as you have the results?'

'Yes. I will. But you're not to worry. I'm completely fine.'

She turned into him, still marvelling at how her baby had ended up taller than she was, and pressed her face into his shoulder, wrapping her arms around him. He hugged her back. She felt emotion well up, but she wouldn't let it show. She needed to be strong, for Alex.

'Sorry,' he whispered. 'I just worry.'

'There's no need to,' Kathy said briskly. This is why she couldn't let on that she was lonely. He had to lead his own life, didn't he? And he'd worry if he thought she wasn't coping.

'We'd better get lunch out,' she said, smiling at him.

'I'll give you a hand.'

How nice it was, working in the kitchen with her son by her side, expertly finishing off the vegetables and loading up the plates together. She wished she hadn't done as much preparation so they could be there for longer, just the two of them, but all too soon the plates were full and ready to be served.

'The signature Brentwood presentation style!' said Jacqui as they set the plates down. 'Looks fantastic.'

They tucked in, Becs poking her food around her plate reluctantly before announcing she was finished.

'But you've not touched it!' said Kathy, the words springing out of her mouth.

'Can't you eat a bit more, Becs?' said Alex. 'Come on, it's lovely.'

'We had all this yesterday,' said Becs. 'I'm sick of Christmas dinner.'

'There's Christmas puddings to come,' said Kathy, trying to cajole her along. 'And surely no one can be sick of pudding.'

'I can,' said Becs huffily. 'Leave me alone. I don't have to eat if I don't want to.'

Kathy gritted her teeth. She thought Becs needed a good talking to, but she could sense the tension around the table rising. This day had to be a good one, if it was to compete with Jacqui's family extravaganza in Australia.

'Get up to anything yesterday?' Alex asked her.

What, after I'd been stood up by my family? thought Kathy before checking herself. She had to put on a good show.

'Enjoyed having the remote to myself and eating whatever I wanted!' she said brightly, as if that was different from any other day. 'Oh, and I went for a walk in the park. Actually, I bumped into this man and his dog . . .'

She told them about catching Harry, about meeting Ben – and about the prospect of volunteering at Battersea. She wanted them to be impressed by the fact Ben had asked her, but instead, her heart sank as she saw Alex frowning.

'Volunteer there? Doing what, looking after the dogs?'

'Yes. Spending time with them, cleaning, eventually helping take them for walks.'

'It sounds rather a lot, Mum. Can't the dogs there be difficult?'

Kathy hated that classification, putting a label on a dog without seeking to understand *why* they had challenging behaviours, which most often meant looking at the way dogs had been treated by the humans around them.

'Some of them might have some difficult behaviours, but that's most often because of the backgrounds they've had – and they won't have contact with volunteers,' Kathy said. 'And it's one of the things I most admire about Battersea – that they take in any dog. No one turns their back on a dog in need.'

'I'm still not sure—'

'I have been around dogs a lot before, you know.'

'Yes, but that was with Dad. This just sounds like an awful lot to take on, especially at your age.' Alex took a sip of wine, his cheeks flushed.

And so there it was, thought Kathy. How society seemed to think she was past it – her own son included. But she had lots of good years left. What was she meant to do, just wait around and twiddle her thumbs and do nothing? But she had to admit her confidence had gone. Use it or lose it, she reflected, and she'd lost it. Wanting to be perfect, always knowing best – that was a way of hiding her insecurity that she didn't have a place in the world any more.

'It sounds really physical, and these are your years to relax,' added Jacqui.

If one more person told Kathy to relax, she would scream. She didn't want more relaxation! She wanted to be useful! And she was fit, fitter than most people her age. She thought of Ben huffing and puffing towards her – she'd wager she was older than him, and still in better nick. For some reason, the image of him, shoelaces undone, puffing, made her want to smile.

'I think I could manage it,' said Kathy. 'I'd be fine. And they train you, in all the things you need to know.'

Alex's frown deepened. 'Mum, really. Let's talk about it later. If you want to apply, fine, but they'll probably be looking for someone a bit younger and stronger.'

Kathy almost dropped her fork. What! Did Alex really think this, or was it his fear of losing her talking, his desire to protect her?

'He's just looking out for you, Kath,' chimed in Jacqui.

She always had to get a word in, didn't she! And what was with calling her Kath? Only John had done that.

'Let's talk about it later,' Alex repeated, pouring more wine.

This wasn't going as Kathy had planned. She felt tense and unhappy. Did Alex really see her as so incapable? Was there a truth to that? It had been a while since she'd retired, but surely she hadn't lost all the skills that had made her such a good, formidable headmistress. She'd done right by her pupils. She'd fought for them, set them rules and rewards, been firm but fair.

She thought about the colourful necklace she'd been given, put a hand to her neck to feel the comforting familiar shape of the beads. The pupil in question, Jessica, had been such a little star. Kathy had recognised her talent for music and had fought hard to get her a bursary for a violin so she could practice. Surely those skills for nurturing and organising hadn't got that rusty. But it had been a long time since she'd put them to use.

She hadn't had the time to get involved in much when John had been ill. People had tried to offer her support, but she'd found it hard to be the recipient of help, and preferred to keep her distance. After he'd died, people did try to get Kathy back involved in the community. Invites to coffees, gentle suggestions of how she might help with a fundraiser – but she'd turned them down. All of her focus had been on Alex. And then the invites had gradually stopped coming.

Fortunately, dessert was more harmonious. They all cooed over Kathy's Christmas pudding – even Becs – and she felt pleased she'd spent so much effort on it. This was more like the Christmas Day she'd imagined.

Washing-up soaking in the sink, they went into the living room to digest.

'Presents!' said Becs, smiling for the first time that day. 'Is it, you know . . . ?'

Jacqui shook her head. 'Becs, we've talked about this. I don't want to disappoint you, but we just can't.'

'What's this about?' said Kathy.

'I want a dog,' said Becs passionately. 'Any kind, I don't care.'

Jacqui groaned. 'We've explained this time and time again. We just can't. Not with the pub. They're a huge responsibility, they need a lot of looking after—'

'I'd look after it! All the walking, feeding . . .'

'Becs, the answer is no.'

Kathy suddenly felt sorry for the girl, who had turned away, her face dejected.

'Here, Becs, here's my gift for you,' Kathy said, handing her a parcel.

Becs tore open the wrapping paper eagerly and looked instantly disappointed. 'Oh. A book.'

'It's a classic,' said Kathy. She'd given Becs *Little Women*, hoping she hadn't read it. Clearly no risk of that. 'And there's another one, too.'

'*White Fang*,' Becs read out in a monotone. 'OK. Thanks.'

'That one has a dog in it,' said Kathy, but Becs just nodded and looked down.

Kathy's temper felt almost frayed to the limit. This girl needed a good talking to. Alex and Jacqui just did nothing; they let her get away with too much.

'Is this one for me?' said Jacqui, reaching for the carefully wrapped present.

'Yes,' Kathy nodded.

Jacqui tore open the paper. 'Oh! Well, it's . . . lovely.'

Kathy had bought her a classic navy blue scarf, a quality one. It was clear Jacqui didn't think much of it.

'You're not a fan?'

'No, I am, I am! I just normally go for things that are a bit more colourful, but this is so classic, thanks, Kathy.'

Jacqui wrapped it around her neck. It did look lovely, setting off her skin tone. Kathy felt bone weary. She suddenly wished the lot of them were gone.

'Here's yours,' said Jacqui, pushing a large present in her direction. 'From all of us.'

'You chose it, though,' said Alex, giving Jacqui a kiss.

Kathy took a deep breath and tore open the paper. A suitcase . . . Why? Did they want her to come and stay? That would be nice!

'Open it,' said Jacqui.

Kathy unzipped the case. Inside was a colourful travel book, entitled *100 Places to See Before You Die.*

Kathy choked out a sob. 'Before I . . . *die*?'

'Oh, Mum, it wasn't meant like that,' said Alex.

Jacqui laughed. 'Oh, God, I'm sorry. Obviously it wasn't meant to mean that! It's a good book. Loads of inspiration.'

They wanted rid of her. That's what this gift said. Bugger off, Kathy, and leave us to it. Use what little time you have left out of our sight.

'I don't see it that way,' said Kathy, choking back more tears. 'In fact, I'm rather offended.'

'Oh, God,' said Alex. 'Mum, please . . . I didn't see it . . . I wouldn't, we wouldn't—'

'I've tried so hard,' said Kathy. 'So bloody hard. I spent Christmas Day on my own, wrapping up leftovers. I set out all the food again today, spent ages with your gifts – which I can tell you don't appreciate – and I'm met with rudeness. From Becs, from Jacqui. And I'm patronised by you, Alex.'

'Well, hold on a second,' said Jacqui, her brows darkening. 'It's not exactly been a picnic for us, either. It would have been far easier if you'd come to us for Christmas, like we suggested, but instead all three of us have had to traipse all the way up here, when we're knackered after yesterday—'

'You were *meant* to be here yesterday!'

'And we're sorry, truly, but we're running a business. This is our livelihood! There was no other option. And then when we get here, you're breathing down our necks, shoes off, use this glass – we can't do anything right!'

'How dare you!' said Kathy. 'You are *so* ungrateful, you and your rude daughter.'

'Oh, do *not* call my daughter rude,' said Jacqui.

'If I'm in my own home when I am being treated so rudely, I will say so! And then you present me with this . . . this . . . *horrible* book! As if I'm already at death's door!' Kathy realised she was shouting.

'If that's how you see it, that's your problem and not mine!' yelled Jacqui.

Jacqui began gathering her things up. 'Becs, get your coat.'

Becs looked stricken. 'Mum, I—'

'Now.'

'Babe, there's no need to . . .' Alex began to intervene.

'No, there is,' said Kathy sharply. 'I think it's for the best if you leave.'

Her chest hurt, her heart was pounding. She forced herself upright and into the kitchen, where she began clattering the dishes into the dishwasher and violently scrubbing the surfaces.

She heard the front door close and breathed a sigh of relief as a car engine started.

'Mum.' It was Alex, coming into the kitchen, looking stricken. 'Mum, please, she didn't mean it like that.'

'It's so *thoughtless*,' said Kathy. 'And I'm surprised you're defending her.'

'I'm not – I'm just trying to get you to see it another way . . .'

'Alex, enough.' Kathy raised her hand. 'I've had enough.' Her tone was clipped and angry.

'OK,' said Alex, his voice now terse. 'I'll go.'

Kathy nodded. 'Bye, then.'

'Bye.'

She waited until the front door closed before she tiptoed back into the sitting room, the scene of such promise now ruined.

Kathy sat down, her head in her hands. She felt like she'd cried herself ragged yesterday. There were simply no more tears. She felt stunned. How had this happened? She looked again at the suitcase and kicked it, then poured herself a large sherry and downed it.

'Pull your socks up,' she said to herself.

She wasn't going to be pitied. She certainly wasn't ever going to put herself through a Christmas like this one again. She would have to fix it. Be self-sufficient. Expect nothing from other people – even her own son.

She looked at the cover of the ghastly book. Pine trees. A white beach, a crystal sea. Completely un-Christmassy. But she'd still rather be there than here, with the flashing lights of the tree mocking her. Right. Enough was enough. Kathy drew a deep, shuddering breath and poured herself another sherry. It was time to get fixing. She wouldn't spend another Christmas here like this. Nor did she fancy being on Jacqui's territory, in the unlikely event of an invite. And even worse, what if they spent next Christmas in Australia? She could rely on no one, she realised sadly. She looked again at the cover of the book and went to fetch her laptop, switching it on.

'Sunny Christmas escapes,' she typed into Google.

Thousands of images, just like the front of the book cover, popped up. Kathy gulped nervously. She clicked into one. Thailand. She and John had thought a lot about a big foreign trip before he'd got ill, and Thailand had been one of their choices. They both adored the food and it would be wonderful to visit such a different culture. Was she crazy to think about going alone?

She continued her research, typing in, 'Solo travel Thailand'. Hmm, lots of pictures of backpackers in hostels with enormous drinks – no thank you. But she kept researching until she found a travel company that offered advice for more . . . *grown-up* travellers.

She felt a flicker of excitement. Look at those temples, those amazing markets, those beautiful beaches! She looked up cookery courses and meditation retreats, mountain treks she thought she might be able to manage and spa resorts for after.

And then she looked up flights. From the fifteenth of December to the middle of January the following year. A whole month. That would get her away from the worst of the festive run-up next year and meant she could spend January in the sun. It appealed, even though she felt almost sick with nerves.

But she'd show them. She'd show them that she wasn't some old thing to be pitied. They clearly wanted shot of her anyway, so she'd just have to do it on her own terms. Hell, she'd even get herself a backpack and avoid that horrible fuddy-duddy suitcase!

Before she could talk herself out of it, she clicked confirm on the flights. And that was that. She was off to Thailand!

She felt almost breathless with nerves. But she had a whole year to get used to the idea. A whole year that would be about building herself up, regaining confidence and learning to make herself happy. She'd been frozen for the past few years, after John's death, and that was going to change.

She dangled her hand by the side of the sofa and imagined how lovely it would be to encounter Buddy's silken ears as he snoozed loyally by her side.

That reminded her of the Battersea Dogs & Cats Home and the volunteer vacancy. She'd loved being around a dog yesterday, even if only fleetingly. Before she knew it, her fingers were typing into Google and whoops!, there she was on the Battersea website. She read through the description of a kennel support volunteer. They were looking for someone physically fit, who was enthusiastic and self-motivated.

She found herself filling in the form. What was the harm? On the off-chance they did invite her to the assessment day, she could always drop out if she didn't feel like it. But somewhere burned the desire to show Alex, and Jacqui, that she wasn't past it. That she could still be useful.

She clicked 'send' before she could change her mind and went to bed. She surprised herself by falling straight to sleep, exhausted, where she dreamt of dogs on tropical beaches.

Chapter 3

Dear Kathy,

We would like to invite you to an assessment day in response to your application for Kennel Support Volunteer. Please come to Battersea Dogs & Cats Home on Saturday, 12 January at 10 a.m. and report to reception. The assessment will last approximately three hours.

Thank you very much for your interest in supporting Battersea.

Yours sincerely,

Freya Godwin

Kathy's heart jumped. It was a cold, rainy January day and she had been reading a magazine in front of the fire as the weather lashed down. It was the sort of thing that she used to find idyllic, but now she was aware of how easy it was for her to go a whole day without talking to anyone. Longer, even. She cleared her throat and read the email out loud.

'Well, well, well. Clearly, there's life in the old dog yet.' She wished someone else was there to hear the joke.

She was delighted to have been asked to the volunteer day, even though she was a bag of nerves as well. She wrote back before she could find an excuse to duck out of it, confirming her attendance and asking if there was anything she could do to prepare. Then she picked up her phone. She wanted to tell someone her news. But who?

Alex had rung her a few days after the Christmas argument. He'd wanted to give it a few days for them all to cool off, he'd said, in a text sent late on Boxing Day that she hadn't read until the following morning. He'd been upset that things had gone so badly.

'Will you come down here, Mum?' he'd said. 'I know Jacqui feels pretty terrible, as well. She didn't want that. I think it'd be easier if you came to see us.'

'All right, darling,' Kathy had said and they'd rung off on friendly terms, but she hadn't heard from him to fix up a date to visit and she wondered if it was a token gesture.

And she didn't want to tell him about the volunteering, not just yet. He'd probably just air his worries about her being able to cope in such a role again, sapping her of confidence. She sighed and put the phone aside, the happiness of being invited to the assessment day soured by her loneliness.

*

Kathy woke bright and early on the day of the assessment and got out of bed with a spring in her step. It felt good to have a purpose. She dressed in jeans and practical walking boots, taking care with her hair. The weather didn't look too bad come mid-morning, so she zipped up her waterproof jacket against the drizzle and stepped outside to walk to the centre.

As Kathy arrived at Battersea Cats & Dogs Home, the sun broke through the clouds, glancing off the modern glass building. She could see the entrance gates and saw a big banner featuring a photo of a lovely little white dog, head cocked to one side. 'Ready to be Loved' said the slogan and Kathy felt herself welling up. She was buzzed through into the main reception – naturally, she was early and was told by a smiling woman to wait just a little while. There were more posters here, stating 'Rescue is our Favourite Breed'. Kathy realised how much she wanted to play a part here, making sure the dogs were well cared for and loved until they made their way home.

The reception filled with the rest of the volunteer candidates, a real mixture of people, chatting happily to each other about Christmas and New Year. Kathy felt out of practice. She didn't want to talk about either Christmas or New Year – she'd cooked herself dinner and then gone to bed before midnight, rising early on New Year's Day and walking round the park in the early morning. She'd half hoped she might bump into Harry and Ben again but didn't see them. She'd spent the rest of the day planning her Thailand itinerary, imagining the confident, independent woman she'd be next New Year. She fiddled with her colourful necklace, which she'd worn for luck.

'OK, everybody!' came a woman's voice, friendly, calling above the hubbub. 'I'm Freya! If I could get everyone to walk after me, please.'

For the first two hours, they were told about the dogs' journey through Battersea and a typical volunteer day.

'So, you'll be doing lots of cleaning and feeding, as well as changing bedding,' Freya explained. 'You'll also spend time with suitable dogs in their kennels, getting them used to being around humans and helping them relax here.'

After three months, Freya went on, they'd be trained in dog walking and in-kennel enrichment sessions, where they'd use a variety of techniques to keep the dogs occupied and happy, and reinforce their training. Then after six months, they were trained in walking dogs in the park and a whole host of exciting workshops opened up, everything from dog yoga to brain games for dogs. Kathy's head was buzzing with all the information, but she felt excited, too – particularly at the thought of learning more and more. She wanted this!

After a brief break, they were put into groups for some assessment tasks. They were given pieces of equipment they would use in kennels, such as brooms, blankets and KONGs – the chewy rubber toys that could be filled with food. They had to explain what each object was and what it would be used for.

Kathy pulled her shoulders back and hoped she was speaking with confidence as she explained what a broom was while everyone nodded encouragingly. It was such a nice supportive atmosphere, she reflected. She'd been silly to get so worked up about it.

There was one woman in her group who looked vaguely familiar. Kathy had thought about asking if they knew each other but had felt too shy.

The woman leant over to her. 'We're neighbours,' she said. 'I moved in before Christmas.'

That was it. Kathy remembered seeing the removal vans. She really should have gone round – in the old days, she'd always brought new neighbours something to welcome them and offered her help.

'Oh, yes. I'm Kathy.'

The woman smiled. She was around fifty, with bright red hair escaping from a clip.

'Judith.'

Their next task was a scenario activity. They had to imagine they were in a kennel and a dog started jumping up at them, making them feel uncomfortable. What would they do?

Kathy began wracking her brains for possibilities. Should she use a treat? Try to distract the dog? Reinforce training?

'I'd probably leave the kennel and ask for some help,' said Judith.

Freya was nodding at her answer and Kathy inwardly groaned. Ask for help! Why hadn't she thought of that? Because you're terrible at asking for help, came John's voice, teasing her. It made perfect sense, though.

Each volunteer also had to wear a panic button, which they'd press in the event of feeling uncomfortable with a dog, at which point the canine behaviourists would come and help them immediately. They'd been clear that volunteers would only be allowed into the kennels of fully assessed dogs deemed suitable. Kathy wished that Alex could hear how well-thought-out the system was – she was feeling much more reassured, and surely he would, too.

The assessment day wound up and Kathy just hoped she hadn't embarrassed herself. She'd tried to speak up and encourage others to do the same, and she felt proud of herself for trying. It hadn't been as bad as she'd thought. She'd even met a new neighbour.

As Kathy left the assessment room, she saw a familiar figure running through the corridor.

'Hey!' said Ben as he neared her, slowing just a fraction. 'Can't stop! Late again! But you went for the volunteering? Fantastic, Kathy!'

He thundered past as she stuttered out a response. 'Yes . . . yes . . . OK, bye!'

'That man,' said Freya, chuckling. 'I don't know how he gets away with it.'

'I can't abide lateness,' said Kathy, although she'd been glad to see Ben's silhouette dashing towards her.

'Me neither,' said Freya, 'but Ben more than makes up for it.'

'How so?'

Freya shrugged. 'He's just got such a way with dogs and with people. He just sees to the heart of them, somehow. He's very special. He never gives up on a dog and we've had some tricky cases to rehome, but Ben always seems to find just the right person.'

Kathy remembered their encounter, how Ben had sounded so sincere. But she also remembered his carelessness with the dog's leash. No matter how charming people were, you simply still had to be organised.

'How do you know him?' asked Freya.

'Oh, we bumped into each other in the park at Christmas! Actually, I helped catch Harry after he'd run off.' After she'd said it, Kathy kicked herself for mentioning it – she didn't want to get Ben into trouble.

But Freya simply laughed and said, 'Oh, yes. He mentioned you. I was down here for a bit on Christmas Day and saw him. You were the hero of the hour, by all accounts.'

Kathy felt herself smiling. 'Well, I'm not so sure about that. How is Harry?'

'He's doing well. Do you want to say hello?'

'Oh, could I?' said Kathy eagerly.

She followed Freya through into the kennels and found Harry's pen. He barked excitedly to see them, and jumped up, tail wagging.

'I'll check with the kennel staff to see if we can go inside,' said Freya, and disappeared briefly. 'We can go in. We just need to make sure he's nice and calm before we do so. And don't fuss him if he jumps up; he needs to learn to keep all four paws on the ground.'

Once Harry had quietened down, Freya calmly opened the pen and they both slipped inside.

'Hello, boy. Hello, boy,' Kathy murmured, feeling her heart glow.

This was the magical thing about animals. How they healed you. It was so nice to be greeted by this happy dog, like she was the most important person in the world, especially after the Christmas drama that had left her emotionally bruised. She crouched down next to him and continued fussing him, Harry rolling onto his back for a tummy rub and making her laugh.

'You've got a lovely bond with him,' said Freya, smiling. 'Here, listen, I'm afraid I'll have to see you out. I need to get back to work.'

'I hope he finds a wonderful home,' said Kathy, even though she felt sad at the thought of not seeing him again.

Freya led her out via a different corridor and pointed out the exit.

'It's just that way.'

'Thank you. I'll see myself out. What's this?'

They'd paused by a wall that was full of pieces of paper with handwritten notes.

'Oh, that's our memory wall,' said Freya. 'Where people can post memories of loved ones, be they animal or human. They're all family, aren't they?'

'Mmm,' said Kathy, looking down at her feet.

Freya extended a hand. 'Thanks for coming.'

She turned and went back down the corridor, leaving Kathy alone. Kathy took a deep breath and turned to the wall.

She read some of the notes. The wall was crowded with them, layered over each other like fallen autumn leaves.

To our darling boy, Davey, who brightened up our days. We will love you forever.

To Casper, our naughty dog who made us laugh all day long. We miss you more than we can say.

For Riley, thank you for being my best friend.

My silly frog-face, thank you for changing my life and teaching me so much.

For beautiful Blossom, who lit up my days and made me feel I was never alone in the world. I will never forget you.

Memories. She didn't dare access her own for fear she'd be overwhelmed with what she'd lost. Some said memories brought them comfort; for her it was pain. To think that she'd never make another new memory with John – it broke her heart. Their time together had gone so fast. Sometimes she felt like she'd blinked and suddenly they were middle-aged. She'd never noticed time creeping up on them.

The sound of a door opening behind her made her jump. How long had she been standing there? Kathy realised her face was wet with tears and swiped them away.

'Hey! Still here?'

It was Ben, walking towards her. Kathy turned away from him, pulled out a handkerchief and blew her nose.

'Yes, just having a look round,' she said, managing to hold her voice steady. 'Actually, just on my way out.'

'You all right? Your eyes look a bit red.'

Bloody Ben! He had a way of paying attention, of making her feel like he saw everything about her, and she didn't like it. Those green eyes of his seemed to see right through to her bones.

'Yes, just a bit of a cold,' she said, forcing a smile. 'Well, I'll be off. See you later!'

And with that, she turned round and walked briskly away, taking deep breaths. It was silly to be so upset.

*

On Sunday, heading out to buy a paper, Kathy saw Judith again. Judith was trying to screw a knocker to her door frame, which kept slipping down before she'd had a chance to get the screw fully in. She should go and offer to help. She gathered up her confidence, reminding herself that they'd already met, and they'd have Battersea to talk about. Kathy often didn't know what to say to people about herself these days – that's why she overcompensated by telling them what to do.

'Want a hand?' said Kathy, stepping up the path. 'We met at Battersea yesterday. Kathy.'

'Hi! Great to see you again. And would you?' said Judith. 'That'd be great.'

Kathy held the knocker steady while Judith managed to screw it in firmly.

'Thank you so much,' said Judith, pushing back the tendrils of bright red hair that had escaped from her woolly hat.

'What are neighbours for? I should have dropped round earlier to introduce myself.'

'Can I tempt you in for a cup of tea? I'll throw in a home-made mince pie as extra thanks, unless you're sick of them already?'

Kathy smiled, feeling a warm glow at Judith's invitation. She nodded and unlaced her boots before stepping into Judith's house. There was a lot still to be unpacked, she noticed. The walls were bare, with occasional dashes of paint on them – Judith was clearly trying out swatches of colour.

'Come through to the kitchen; it's almost civilised in there,' said Judith, and Kathy followed her down the hallway.

The kitchen was a lot more homely, although the kitchen table was covered with boxes yet to be unpacked. Judith indicated a comfy, squashy chair draped with blankets.

'Sorry, bit limited on seating options. Make yourself cosy there. It's my favourite space for an afternoon read.'

'I can see why. And this lovely view of the garden as well. Ah, a bird feeder. Do you get much wildlife coming to it?'

Judith groaned. 'Yet another thing I've forgotten to do. Pick up any feed. Those poor birds, especially in winter.'

'I can drop you some over later,' said Kathy, 'if you like?'

'That would be so kind.'

She passed Kathy a chipped mug of steaming tea and a battered mince pie, and they chatted about the Battersea assessment day.

Then Judith leant forwards. 'Your necklace!'

Kathy smiled. 'It's one of my favourites. People always notice it. It was given to me by a former pupil and her mother.'

Judith grinned at her. 'You still don't recognise me, do you?'

Kathy stared at her. There *was* something very familiar about Judith.

'I'm Jessica Simmond's mum,' said Judith, putting Kathy out of her misery. 'And it was me – and Jessica – who gave you that necklace. I'm so glad you still wear it! We spent ages choosing it.'

'I knew there was something familiar about you!' said Kathy. 'Really! When I saw you at the volunteer day, I was trying to place you.'

She felt a mix of emotions at being recognised. If she was honest, her first instinct had been one of horror and to run away. She didn't want awkward questions about if she was still involved with this or that, or in touch with so and so.

But then, behind the panic was something else. That it might be nice to reconnect with who she'd been before and here was a way back.

'The red hair is new,' smiled Judith.

'It looks wonderful,' said Kathy. 'Tell me, how is Jessica? She was always such a star pupil.' Kathy could picture her, a chubby-cheeked little girl with blonde bunches.

'She's fine,' said Judith.

'What's she up to?' said Kathy, keen for more details. 'Did she keep up with the violin? She must be at university now?'

'Yes, that's right,' said Judith.

'Where did she go? Somewhere wonderful for music, I hope.'

'Mmm, she's abroad at the moment.'

Judith looked down and swallowed. Kathy wondered at her reticence. Was she missing her daughter? The horror she'd felt at imagining Alex moving abroad again was only too real and maybe Judith was struggling with the distance, too.

'That must be hard,' she said to Judith, who nodded and kept looking at the floor.

Kathy decided not to ask more questions. It was clearly emotional for Judith.

'They were happy days at the school,' said Judith.

'They were,' Kathy agreed, thinking of the hustle and bustle of the year.

They'd be back by now, back to the old building that smelt of poster paints and school dinners, and rang with the sound of children giggling and running around.

'How's life with you, Mrs Brentwood?'

Kathy rolled her eyes. 'Please. You're going to have to call me Kathy. I'm not the headmistress anymore. I retired several years ago.'

'Oh, really! I can't imagine you not being there. But are you enjoying it? Are you and your husband . . . I'm sorry, I can't remember his name . . .'

'John.' He'd often helped out at school events, selling raffle tickets, running the tombola, helping Kathy to arrange PTA evenings.

'Yes, such a lovely man.'

Kathy looked out at the frozen garden. 'I'm afraid John passed away a couple of years ago. Cancer. It was a tough few years we went through. It's why I took early retirement.' She took a gulp of tea to stop her lips from quivering.

'Oh, I am sorry,' Judith said, her eyes full of sympathy.

But Kathy wanted to halt any further talk of John. She cleared her throat. 'Might I have another mince pie?'

They were delicious, but she also wanted to be away from Judith's sympathetic gaze and change the subject, fast.

'And what about you, Judith? What brings you to our little street?'

Judith sighed. 'Well, it's not been a great time for me, either, Kathy. Me and Jessica's dad broke up shortly after she went to secondary school. And for a time we made a go of it in the south-west, but now it just seems the time to come back here. Where we have some roots. I still know a few of the mums from back in the day and I like the area.' She shrugged.

Kathy sensed she didn't really want to talk much about what had happened in the intervening years, either.

'Well, that makes sense,' said Kathy.

'I hope so,' said Judith, looking down. 'It can be bloody tough. I'm glad Christmas is over, to be honest.'

'Oh?'

'Spent it by myself, sat here, watching the garden, mostly.'

How silly, Kathy thought, that she had been so nearby and yet the two of them had sat there alone. She opened her mouth. She wanted to tell Judith that she, too, had spent Christmas alone and that Boxing Day had been memorable only for an argument with her family, but the words wouldn't come. Judith still saw her as capable Mrs Brentwood, full of life, always busy. Somehow, even though she knew she was being proud, she simply couldn't bear to tell her that she, too, had been alone at Christmas.

And then the moment had passed.

'Spent it with your . . . son, was it?' asked Judith.

And Kathy found herself nodding. 'Oh, yes. Alex.'

'That must have been so lovely. I really missed Jess on Christmas Day.'

Kathy smiled tightly. 'It was. We made quite the event of it.'

That wasn't lying, not really. It must be so hard for Judith, with her daughter abroad for Christmas. She should be grateful that Alex had turned up at all. Once again, she felt a deep sense of dread at the thought of him possibly heading off to Australia. She'd done the right thing in booking Thailand, avoiding the disappointment and the hurt.

She got up and brushed the crumbs of pastry from her. 'How about I nip back and get that bird feed, and then I could help you unpack a few boxes this afternoon?'

'Oh! That's too kind. I don't know if I can accept . . . Surely you're busy with other things?'

'Not so busy that I can't help out a new neighbour,' Kathy said, smiling.

In that moment, she realised how much she didn't want to spend the afternoon back at her house, alone.

'Well, that would be wonderful.'

Kathy returned home and scooped some bird feed into a Tupperware before heading back to Judith's.

'Shall we tackle the rest of the kitchen?' Kathy said, rolling up her sleeves and pinning her hair back a little more tightly.

Truth be told, she was itching to organise the drawers – she could see a mess of pans shoved into one that refused to close.

Judith agreed and before long, they had all the boxes open and were sorting the contents into various categories. The time flew by, with the radio on and Judith making endless cups of tea for them. They returned to the topic of Battersea and why they wanted to volunteer.

Judith worked from home and was keen to build up a sense of community. She also loved dogs but said she couldn't have her own at the moment. As the afternoon grew darker, Kathy relished the cosy feeling of being inside, chatting to someone else, the portable heater on and kicking out heat in a golden glow.

'I can't believe how much we've done,' said Judith, straightening up and looking around.

Kathy was impressed, too. The hours had flown by and she hadn't even realised.

'Well, many hands make light work and all that.'

'I think it's mostly your hands. I could never be this organised!'

Kathy laughed. 'Yes, I can't help myself, really.'

'I'm very grateful.'

There wasn't much left to be done, Kathy realised. She should probably get home and . . . do what, exactly?

Judith was looking at her. 'Look, Kathy, I know you've probably got something to rush off for, but if you don't, how about fish and chips? My shout. I can even offer you a plate, now they're unpacked.'

'That would be lovely.'

Judith went out to the chippy and Kathy busied herself setting out cutlery as best she could. Before she knew it, Judith was back with two steaming newspaper packages and a bottle of wine.

'I thought we deserved a house-warming drink,' she said. 'Might have to be in a mug. We can find the glasses another time.'

It was one of the best evenings Kathy had had in a long while. They ate fish and chips, salty and delicious, toasted Judith's new home and then crossed their fingers that they'd both got a volunteer role. They chatted about TV programmes they liked, gardening tips, New Year's resolutions. Kathy told Judith about her trip to Thailand – although not what had prompted it – and Judith's eyes widened.

'I wish I was more like you! Seizing life like that and heading off into the unknown. I've always wanted to travel.'

Kathy felt a flush of pride then guilt that she hadn't been entirely honest with Judith earlier. She just so wanted to be the woman Judith thought she was.

'Do you get to visit Jessica often?' she asked.

'Oh, once in a while. She's just so . . .' Judith waved her hand about.

'I'll bet she's busy. She was always like that in school, darting from one thing to another!'

Judith smiled. 'She was, you're right.'

Kathy felt herself beginning to yawn and realised she really had to go. She swapped numbers with Judith and promised to come round to help with the living room.

Back at home, she hung up her coat and took off her shoes, sighing as the door closed behind her and the silence enfolded her. She was conflicted about the house. It was her sanctuary. It was where she'd lived with John – and was

Alex's childhood home. She could never imagine leaving. Then again, it was so hard returning to it when it was silent and dark, when it echoed with memories of how things had once been. She couldn't bear to think of those days, the contrast was too painful. Kathy shivered, made herself a hot-water bottle and got straight into bed, falling asleep almost as soon as her head hit the pillow.

Chapter 4

Kathy almost leapt out of her skin when her phone rang.

'Hello?' she said.

'Hi, is that Kathy?'

'Yes, speaking.' Kathy held her breath.

This sounded like Freya from the rescue centre. A week had gone by since the assessment day and she'd decided that she hadn't got one of the positions. But it was kind of them to ring and let her know.

'It's Freya. I just wanted to say thank you for coming to the assessment day. And that we're delighted to offer you the volunteer role.'

Kathy leant back against the kitchen worktop. 'Wh-what?'

Freya laughed. 'The volunteer role, if you're still up for it? I'm sorry, we've been so busy after Christmas, it took a while to get back to you. We think you'd be a great fit with our team, and with the dogs, too.'

Kathy couldn't believe it. 'You mean, you don't want someone younger? Or fitter? Or—'

'Kathy,' Freya said, firmly but kindly. 'We want you.'

Delight flooded through Kathy like sunshine. 'Oh, gosh! Well, I'm so happy to hear that. Thank you! Thank you, Freya!'

They discussed the logistics and Kathy agreed that her regular volunteer day would be a Thursday. She hung up the phone and skipped around the kitchen. She was wanted!

She would finally be useful again! She prayed that Judith had got a role, as well.

Her phone buzzed again. Alex.

'Hello, darling,' she answered brightly.

'Hi, Mum, can't talk for long, got lunch service coming up.'

Kathy resisted the temptation to point out that he was the one who'd phoned her.

'Anyway,' he was saying, 'we both really want you to come down here. Make a weekend of it, do some bonding. Jacqui feels really bad about Christmas. Will you, Mum?'

'Yes,' she said, 'sure.'

He exhaled. 'OK, great. So, when can you do?'

'Well, what about the weekend after next?' She didn't want to appear too keen, like she had nothing else on.

'We've got a wedding party on here,' Alex said. 'Oh, and the one after that's no good, either. We're away for the night, hopefully. Then there's staff training as well . . .'

He sounded stressed, Kathy thought.

Eventually, they settled on a weekend that was in about six weeks' time, in early March, and Alex promised he'd be up from Lewes in the meantime to visit suppliers.

'Great!' Alex said in the tone of voice she was sure he must use when people made bookings. 'That's sorted! All good with you, Mum? Any news? Did you go for the screening?'

'Yes, and everything's fine.'

Alex exhaled in relief. 'That's great.'

Kathy cleared her throat. 'And, I got offered the volunteer role at Battersea – you know, the dogs' and cats' home? I just heard.' She felt so proud telling him.

'What? You went for that?'

'Yes, I did.'

A voice in the background, Alex whispering 'Hang on,' away from the phone and turning back to her, his voice dismayed.

'Mum, I told you I wasn't sure about this. I'd be worried about it, to be honest, you handling the dogs like that. Can we talk about it later? You've not said yes, have you?'

Kathy felt her happiness flood away from her. Why was he treating her like this? She'd hoped he'd be happy about it!

'Well, I wasn't asking your permission, dear,' she said, stalling for time.

He sighed. 'Look, Mum, I have to go, but let's discuss this later, all right? Bye, love you.' And he'd hung up before she'd even had a chance to reply.

Kathy sat down at the kitchen table and felt annoyed. She'd only had the chance to feel happy about getting the volunteer role for all of two minutes before Alex had called and taken the wind out of her sails. She was careful to let him get on with his life and she wished he'd support her a little in that way, too.

And Freya had been clear! They wanted Kathy. They thought she was perfectly capable – hadn't she already proved herself in catching Harry on Christmas morning? The more she thought about it, the more indignant she got. Her phone buzzed again with a notification and she felt like growling. If that was Alex with another message . . .

But it was Judith, asking, 'Did you hear anything?'

'I got it!' Kathy replied. 'And my fingers are crossed you did, as well?'

'Yes!' replied Judith. 'Want to come round and have a celebratory tea?'

Kathy headed over to Judith's with a Tupperware of biscuits she'd baked earlier that week.

Judith answered the door with a beaming face.

'Congratulations!' she said, hugging Kathy.

'We did it!' replied Kathy. 'I knew you'd get it! You were so good with that scenario question.'

'Well, I've never seen a broom presented quite as thoroughly as you did,' replied Judith, chortling.

Kathy felt herself smiling back. She had admittedly been quite overzealous with explaining everything she could think of about a broom.

'I'm just so glad we both got in.'

The two women smiled at one another, Judith ushering Kathy through to the kitchen, where a steaming pot of tea awaited.

'Your son will be so proud of you,' said Judith as she poured them each a mug.

Kathy got out the box of biscuits and handed them over. 'Couldn't arrive empty-handed. And I wish Alex was.' She rolled her eyes.

'What's up?'

Kathy sighed. 'Well, just after I got the call from Freya, he rang, so I told him, and he was saying how he wasn't sure I could cope with it and that he wanted to discuss it with me later.'

Judith snorted with laughter. 'He sounds like he wants to keep you back after class. Come on, you're joking, right?'

Kathy shook her head. 'No! He was deadly serious!'

And then Judith was laughing properly and Kathy felt herself joining in, indignation turning to humour.

'I know, I know, it's ridiculous,' she said. 'Him telling me off, but it did get to me a moment, I confess.'

'Oh, for goodness' sake,' Judith said, her voice warm. 'Honestly, Kathy, what's got into you? You're used to dealing with thirty screaming kids! A few lovely little doggies aren't going to faze you!'

'You're right,' Kathy said, feeling the tension dissipate. 'You're completely right. It's just been a while since I've been out of the workplace. And when Alex started querying it, it got to me, I confess.'

Judith shook her head, smiling. 'It's because he cares about you, Kathy. Deep down, that's where it comes from. Love. He's just being overprotective.'

Kathy hadn't seen it like that before.

'Thanks, Judith,' she said. It had been so nice to be listened to.

'Any time. What are friends for?'

Friend. The word made Kathy glow, her cheeks rosy, her heart glad.

Chapter 5

It was 7 a.m. and Kathy almost turned the alarm off. It was still dark outside, and she wanted to burrow down into the sheets and stay there. She'd had a hard time getting off to sleep the night before, bubbling with nerves about her first day volunteering. Judith had texted her to say good luck. They were going to be volunteering on different days, which was a shame as it would have been nice to have a friend there. Alex hadn't rung her since their previous call – a blessing, in its way. She'd just get on with it and prove him wrong.

'Come on, then,' she said to herself. 'Up and at 'em.'

As she showered and made herself tea and toast, a familiar excitement spread through her. She found herself looking forward to the challenges ahead. She'd had her induction training a week ago, where she'd had health and safety training, picked up her uniform and spent the rest of the day with the canine behaviour team. They'd provided lots of information on dog behaviour, followed by some hands-on practice in the kennels. Kathy had learnt how to enter and exit kennels safely and calmly, and how to make up the dogs' feed before carrying out a kennel session.

This was a vital part of the volunteer role. So often, the behaviourist had explained, when people were going in and out of the dogs' kennels, it was to do something with them. That might be training, a behaviour assessment, grooming or feeding. So it was really important to have other people go in there and just do nothing. It helped the dog to relax and start to bond with humans. And it sounded like heaven to Kathy, simply to sit and enjoy a dog's company, petting them if they wished, maybe reading aloud if that helped the dog to chill out.

At 7.30 a.m., she set off to walk to the dogs' home. It was still dark and chilly, her breath making clouds in the frozen air. She was there at exactly 8 a.m. and introduced herself to the receptionist.

'Welcome,' the woman smiled. 'First day?'

'It is,' Kathy replied.

'You'll soon get the hang of it.'

'Kathy?' A woman emerged from the kennel block Kathy was assigned to. 'I'm Gemma. Come on through.'

Gemma was the rehoming and welfare assistant she would report to. Kathy put her things in her locker and put on her panic alarm, ready for the day ahead.

'First up, cleaning time,' said Gemma with a grin, picking up two buckets and brooms. 'I hope you don't mind a bit of poop.'

'Absolutely not,' said Kathy, determined to muck in, even though the smell was making her wrinkle her nose.

Battersea had been clear from the start that cleaning was a big part of the role and she was keen to prove her worth.

They cleaned the first pen together, belonging to a sweet little mongrel called Juno. She was let out into the back run, so they could clean her pen without her in it.

Kathy soon had a sweat on as they scrubbed and sluiced the kennel down before removing the soiled bedding and replacing it with lots of fresh blankets. She glanced at Gemma, who was flying through the tasks. Kathy gulped and kept her head down.

'Although this part isn't the most glamorous,' Gemma explained, 'it's really important. We're the first ones to see the dogs in the morning, so if we notice anything like diarrhoea, we can let the nurses know. Plus, we have to keep a log of the dogs' bowel movements – it's a crucial way to check that we're keeping them healthy.'

Kathy nodded, hoping she would take it all in. Even though she'd been on the induction day, it was a lot to remember.

With one pen completed, they let Juno back in and moved on to the next pen in their section, occupied by a gorgeous Rottweiler puppy called Hugo. After they'd finished all their allocations, Kathy's cheeks were glowing and the muscles in her arms burned. This was tough work! But she had no intention of letting on to Gemma.

'And now, breakfast time,' smiled Gemma, and she took Kathy into a small room.

On the wall was a large whiteboard, on which was detailed information for each dog. On the opposite side of the room were big plastic bins full of dry feed and a cupboard full of tins, along with all different sizes of feeding bowl.

'This is where we prepare the dogs' food,' said Gemma. 'In this logbook here' – she pulled out a large ring binder – 'we've got all the details of the dogs' food. So, for Juno, she needs 150 grams of wet food, and then 100 grams of dry, in an enrichment feeder.'

'What's an enrichment feeder again?' said Kathy, hoping she didn't sound stupid.

'Oh, sorry,' said Gemma. 'Here they are.' She pointed to plastic trays of different shapes that looked a bit like puzzles. 'They're to make the dogs work for their food a little bit, keep their minds occupied. So look, if I put the dry food in here . . .' She shook out the pellets onto the feeder, where they dispersed around plastic cones of various shapes and sizes. 'Juno now has to snuffle around and work out how to get them, as opposed to just scoffing them all down.'

'Understood,' said Kathy.

'Then here's the whiteboard,' said Gemma, turning to a big board behind them covered in writing.

Kathy remembered this from her induction day, but there was so much information on there. How on earth was she going to make sense of all this?

'So here, we've got each dog's name with a note of everything about that dog, such as if they've had a kennel session that day, a walk, if they've got clinic, if they have a rehoming meeting. It's all here. And, very importantly, it says what dogs are suitable for you to spend time with in their kennels.'

Kathy stared at it and could just about make sense of at least some of it.

'Don't worry; you get used to it,' said Gemma as if sensing her discomfort. 'It's a lot to take in, I know. You can always ask if you're unsure about anything.'

'Oh, no, it's absolutely fine,' said Kathy briskly. She didn't want Gemma thinking she couldn't cope. 'Here, shall I help you measure out the feeds?'

She focused on measuring out the wet and the dry food with Gemma, writing each dog's name on the bowl with a wipeable marker. Soon, they had a row of bowls and dishes waiting to go. Gemma explained how with taller dogs, like greyhounds, they put their food on a little stand so they didn't have to strain their necks and Kathy realised how every little detail was taken care of to support the dogs. She felt proud to be playing her part.

'Think you could manage to get started on your own?' Gemma said. 'All these dogs are absolutely fine for you to go in with. I've just got to check a couple of things; I'll be back very quickly, though.'

'Oh, yes, absolutely,' Kathy said as Gemma left.

She looked at the bowls lined up and began stacking them in her arms. Surely she could fit them all into one run. She wanted to impress Gemma by having the feeding wrapped up by the time she came back. She stacked the last feeder on top of the pile in her arms and stood up very carefully. OK, so this was a little more precarious than she'd thought, but she'd done it now and she just had to ease her way out of the door. Kathy managed to get out of the room by opening the handle with her hip and began to manoeuvre her way towards a pen.

Bugger.

How was she meant to put the tower of bowls back down? She felt certain that if she tried, they'd just topple over. She hadn't thought this through at all and now she was stuck balancing the feeding bowls, unable to put them down, the dogs smelling food and barking around her, keen for their breakfast.

She felt herself begin to panic.

'Pull yourself together, Kath,' she muttered, and began to lower the stack of bowls to the floor when – *crash!* The top bowl wobbled off and bounced to the floor with an almighty clang, spilling food everywhere. The next one followed, a puzzle tray that sent biscuits flying everywhere.

Oh, *God.*

Her cheeks felt hot and tears welled up in her eyes.

'All OK?' A man's voice, familiar.

'Y-yes,' she managed to stammer out, placing the remaining stack of bowls on the floor, her heart beating fast.

Then Ben came around the corner. 'Well, if they weren't awake before, they are now!' He surveyed the mess. 'This is a right dog's dinner,' he added, chuckling at his own joke.

Was he just going to stand there and laugh at her?

'I just dropped a couple of feeding bowls,' Kathy said, straightening up and trying to look like she had everything under control. She stared up into his eyes, noticing again how green they were.

'And no wonder, since you seem to be carrying about twenty of them. This lot don't expect silver service, so just take your time, eh.'

Kathy bridled.

'Here, I'll give you a hand cleaning this lot up, then we can redo the spilled ones.'

Ben went and fetched a broom, and briskly swept up the biscuits, while Kathy took the bowls back to the feeding room. She sneaked a glance back at Ben sweeping up and groaned. Why did it have to be him? She did appreciate him helping her out, much as it pained her to admit it, and he'd calmed her down when she was in a fluster, but she supposed he'd tell Gemma what a mess she'd made of everything. And Kathy hated to have slipped up and, even more, she couldn't stand to be in someone's debt.

'All clear,' he said, poking his head into the feed room and then holding the door ajar so Kathy could see out into the corridor.

He'd done a great job tidying up. Just a shame he couldn't apply it to himself. A tuft of hair was sticking up over his forehead.

'Thank you,' she forced herself to say.

'No problem,' he said. 'I owe you one after Houdini's escape. But don't ever be afraid to ask for help, OK? We're a team here. No point trying to be superwoman.'

Kathy felt like she wanted to scream at him! He seemed to know exactly what to say to rile her, and maybe he had a point about her trying to carry the bowls, but she didn't need the lecture.

'OK, so it's Frankie and Dougie who need their food refilled, judging from the bowls?' he asked, turning to her.

'I can do it,' she said.

He smiled. 'I didn't say you couldn't. Just thought I'd give you a hand.'

Kathy realised they were standing shoulder to shoulder – well, in as much as that was possible, given how tall he was – looking at the logbook. She blushed and focused on turning the pages until they arrived at Frankie.

'Pass us a bowl,' Ben said, digging a scoop into the feed. 'And let's see how close I am to guessing this is 140 grams.'

He put the bowl on the scales and reset them, pouring in the feed.

'Bang on,' he said. 'Beginner's luck.'

Kathy couldn't help but smile.

'Let's see about Dougie,' she said, passing him another bowl.

'Take one each?' he suggested when they'd finished.

'That would seem sensible.' She smiled at him, and saw that ridiculous tuft of hair poking up again. She couldn't let him go through the day like that, not if he was going to be meeting people. 'Ben?'

He turned round, eyebrows raised.

'Your hair is sticking up. At the front. Sorry, I just wanted you to know, in case you had meetings or anything.'

Ben regarded her, his eyes sparkling suddenly. 'Oh, I know, Kathy. I just like it that way.' And he ran his spare hand up through his hair, making it stick up even more, before heading off to Frankie's pen.

She was lost for words. She didn't know what to make of him – he was chaotic and yet capable when it came to it, and he seemed to know exactly how to wind her up. She shook her head. Why was she bothered about working him out, anyway?

Kathy took the bowl to Dougie, a nine-year-old Staffie with the sweetest temperament. She concentrated on remembering her entry-and-exit training. It was vital that the dogs were kept calm and didn't start to become over-excited by people entering their kennel or upset by them leaving. She lifted her hand up, as they'd been trained, hoping the dog would take the cue to sit, or at least calm down if they were jumping up, with all four paws on the ground.

She was relieved when Dougie did sit and she dropped a treat on the floor as a reward. The dog snaffled it up eagerly. Kathy felt like it was OK for her to enter. He wasn't jumping up and was alert but calm, with all four paws on the ground. She'd felt worried about dogs escaping and running past her, but as she unfastened the pen and went in, she realised that Dougie was far more interested in her presence in the pen than in running off.

She put down the bowl of food, which Dougie ignored, preferring to come to Kathy for some attention. She was only too happy to give him some love. Staffies loved human company and kennels could be hard on them. After she'd given him a little bit of fussing, it was time to leave the pen and let him get on with breakfast. Exiting in the right manner was crucial. So she went to and from the door a few times, slowly, with Dougie remaining calm. Then she slipped out of the pen and stayed a while to interact more with him from the outside.

She remembered the behaviourist saying that it's really important the dog isn't immediately ignored when you leave the kennel, otherwise they'll try to stop you from leaving. The Battersea philosophy really chimed with her: that dogs were learning all the time and you had to set them up for success as much as possible.

So, when Dougie wandered over to his kennel door, she gave the sit gesture and rewarded him with a treat when he complied. After a few more interactions like this, he decided breakfast was more interesting and went to snuffle his food. Kathy felt relieved it had gone well, and felt far more confident delivering the bowls to the other dogs.

A short time later, she heard Gemma returning and greeting Ben.

'Done already?' Gemma said with a smile as Kathy walked up to her. 'That was fast!'

Kathy held her breath, waiting for Ben to comment about how she'd dropped all the bowls.

'She's flown round it,' said Ben, smiling. 'See, told you she'd be good.'

She let out a sigh of relief. So, he wasn't going to say anything?

'I never doubted it,' Gemma said. 'Kathy, do you want to take a quick break and get a cup of tea in the café? You've done a brilliant job.'

Kathy dared to peek at Ben.

'I'll see you later, Kathy. Enjoy the rest of your day,' he said, and winked at her before walking off.

*

By the time Kathy finished her day at 5 p.m., she was exhausted – but it was the happiest she'd felt in years. Once the feeding was finished, she discovered her favourite part of the day: spending time with the dogs in their kennels. Each and every one was different, and she'd loved adapting to their personalities. Some dogs had been particularly excitable and she'd had to wait a while before they were calm enough for her to enter. Others had stayed in their beds, thumping a tail in greeting. She'd played with some dogs and petted others, and with some she'd simply sat there quietly.

She'd loved each and every moment. She'd forgotten how much she adored being around dogs. They were such special beings – you wouldn't find a purer spirit than a dog, Kathy always thought. And it was funny: she'd thought that she would be the one helping them to settle down and feel at home, but she couldn't help but think it was ultimately the other way around.

The longer she spent around the dogs, the more relaxed and at home she felt. Kathy couldn't wait to go back. She'd also chatted with the other volunteers at lunch, where the conversation had flowed naturally as they shared stories of the animals. One of the volunteers ran a café that Kathy had visited frequently when she'd been working and in need of a coffee away from the hustle and bustle of the school. They had often hired it in the evening for events, as well.

'We missed you!' the woman, Asha, said. 'We wondered where you'd gone. You'll have to come back. First coffee is on me.'

Kathy had found herself nodding and agreeing to go.

Kathy made herself a bowl of soup as soon as she got in and managed to eat it without dropping off. Her muscles ached pleasantly.

Then her phone buzzed with a message. Judith, checking how her first day had gone. It was so kind of her to remember and Kathy once more felt the glow of a friendship kindling. She typed back that it had gone really well and wished Judith good luck with her first day, which was tomorrow.

'Don't be nervous,' she said. 'Everyone – including the dogs – makes you feel right at home!'

Exhausted, she went to bed early and fell into a deep, happy sleep.

Chapter 6

Suddenly, life seemed to pick up speed. The volunteering gave shape to Kathy's week, and she would also go in on other days if they were short-staffed. A month passed, then two. Kathy saw dogs come in and out of the centre. Some stayed only a short time, others would be there for longer. Every dog was different, but each one was treated with the same level of care and attention.

Kathy heard stories that broke her heart and others that made her cry with joy. She noticed muscles developing in her arms and the cleaning became easier each time she did it. The best bit, though, was bonding with the dogs, enjoying their companionship. She felt recharged with life after each and every day she was there. The days themselves were now getting longer, the first signs of spring peeking through, although it was still distinctly chilly.

Outside of Battersea, she saw Judith every week or two, to help with DIY, for a cup of tea, or to watch some television. Judith was easy company, friendly and funny and considerate. The only thing they didn't talk much about was family. Kathy was happy to steer clear, if she was honest, and Judith gave only brief details of what Jessica was up to. Had they fallen out? Kathy wondered. She observed that even though Judith had unpacked almost everything now, there were no recent photos of Jessica up on the walls – just a few old ones of the chubby little girl

Kathy remembered. Of course, she'd never ask about it. She was beginning to remember that, like dogs, you had to let people go at their own pace. Her own mantelpiece was still barren of photos and she would hate for anyone to query why.

Her own family was a source of dull pain. It wasn't the fresh hurt of Christmas, but she ached for things to be different. Kathy's weekend to go down and visit Alex in early March had been rearranged, twice, and now they were into April, with no date in sight. Alex had stayed over with her a few times in London, when he'd been up visiting suppliers. They'd had dinner together and watched some TV, but Alex had been exhausted after meetings and the conversation was stilted. Was this just how it was now? Kathy thought sadly. She was, of course, delighted to see Alex back in his stride, after how devastated he'd been over John's death. But was it inevitable to feel less close to her son as he built a life of his own?

*

One Friday in April, she was sitting down to a baked potato in the café, when Ben came in. She'd seen glimpses of him on her volunteer days, always busy, and they'd exchanged the odd word or two, but they'd not had a proper conversation for a good while. She'd seen him once in the park, over Easter weekend, and had gone over to speak to him. He'd been sitting on a bench, staring into the distance.

'Penny for your thoughts,' Kathy had said, and he'd jolted at the sound of her voice. She'd suddenly felt like she was interrupting him.

'Hi, Kathy,' he'd said before lapsing back into silence.

Kathy had glanced at the plaque on the bench.

'Lydia and Alfie,' she'd read out loud. 'I wonder who they were. Lovely spot.'

'Indeed,' Ben had said, glancing away. 'Indeed.'

She'd said farewell then and left him to it. Clearly, he wasn't in the mood for conversation.

At the time she'd been on her way to meet Judith and Asha for an Easter Sunday walk. Once again, Alex and Jacqui were tied up at the pub, leaving her at a loose end – or so she'd thought, until Judith had said she didn't have plans either and had suggested they do something together. She'd mentioned it to Asha and the three of them had decided to walk a section of the Thames Path together. And when she'd seen Ben, she'd had the mad idea of asking if he wanted to join them – but his demeanour had put her off.

But this time in the café was different. Ben smiled as soon as he saw her.

'Hello! Mind if I join you?'

Kathy had just taken a mouthful of hot potato, so she nodded and flapped her hands about, hoping he'd realise that that meant yes.

'How's it all going, then?' said Ben.

Kathy gulped down her potato. 'It's going well. I'm loving it, actually. I can't believe how much time has flown by. I'm doing the enrichment and walking training next week.' She couldn't wait to learn more about the enrichment sessions in particular, where she'd learn techniques to support the dogs and ensure they were as happy and well cared for as possible.

He smiled at her. 'I thought you'd take to it. You've got colour in your cheeks.'

'All that sweeping, no doubt.'

Ben reached for the salt and knocked his cutlery to the ground.

'Oh, damn!'

'I'd have passed it to you. You know, you only need to ask for my help,' Kathy replied, teasing him.

'I should heed my own advice more often,' Ben said.

Kathy laughed and realised it was so long since she'd teased anyone like that.

'Not tempted by a dog of your own?' said Ben.

'Only about four hundred times a day,' replied Kathy. 'But seriously, not at the moment. I don't want to be tied down. I've got travel plans coming up later this year.' She told him all about her trip to Thailand and his eyes widened.

'On your own?'

She nodded.

'Brilliant. You'll love it. I went myself a few years back, actually.'

'Oh! Did you like it?'

He nodded. 'It's a wonderful country. If you need any help with planning, let me know.'

'Thank you,' said Kathy. 'I will. And how about you? Not tempted to take home one of these dogs you're so good at rehoming?'

He laughed. 'I think about it a lot. You can't not when you love dogs so much. But I'm not considering it at the moment. I've done a bit of fostering every now and again, and I've loved that.'

Kathy knew that dogs went on foster for a variety of reasons. But she'd never actually considered how people *became* foster carers.

Ben chuckled. 'You've got that look in your eyes.'

'What look?'

'The one that you got when I mentioned the volunteering, even though you were saying you weren't going to do it.'

Kathy rolled her eyes. 'If this is another way of saying you were right all along . . .'

'Well I was, wasn't I?'

But Ben's eyes were twinkling and Kathy had to admit that this sparring between them made her feel lively. Kept her on her toes.

'So the fostering. Why might a dog need that?'

He shrugged. 'A lot of them get stressed here. You've seen it.'

Kathy had. As much as they did everything possible to keep the animals happy and calm, it was a tough environment for some.

'And some might need more medical attention round the clock than we can give them there.' He leaned into her and nudged her with his elbow. 'You're thinking about it, aren't you?'

'No, I am not!' But she couldn't help the smile that spread across her face. 'Well, maybe a bit. It would be nice to do something more.'

'You live nearby as well, don't you?'

Kathy nodded.

'Just to be clear,' said Ben, 'fostering isn't a way of road-testing adoption. The team need people to commit to being available long-term.'

'That's absolutely fine,' said Kathy. 'Suits me down to the ground. I wouldn't want to commit to a dog full-time, so this could be perfect. And I rather like the idea of helping as many dogs as possible.' She understood their position perfectly. Rules were rules.

Ben pulled out a piece of paper from his pocket and scrawled on it before passing it to her.

'Here. My number.'

Was he blushing? Kathy wondered, before realising her own cheeks were hot.

Ben cleared his throat. 'In case you've got any questions about it. Or if I can help.'

Kathy tucked the piece of paper in her pocket and, despite the rain that started lashing down outside, she felt like she was standing in sunshine.

When she got home to an empty house, she knew fostering was something she wanted to do. She loved being around the dogs at Battersea and knew she could offer more. She imagined how lovely it would be to have a dog curled up in the kitchen, how much a dog would enjoy zooming around in the garden. She liked the thought of helping a dog to improve in behaviour, of helping to guide the animal on his or her journey to their new home.

She retrieved Ben's number and looked at it. No, there was nothing in his gesture. He was simply being kind. She swallowed. Of course, the thought had crossed her mind as to whether or not she would be able to love anyone again, but it seemed overwhelming to contemplate. Where would you begin? She couldn't imagine going on a date. Still, she added Ben's number to her phone and saved his contact details as Battersea Ben.

*

'Well, here she is,' said Tom, one of the fostering coordinators. 'Meet Milly.'

Kathy's foster application had been processed and approved quickly. Her home had been visited, and she'd been interviewed about her exact circumstances and what she could offer a dog. The only slight issue was what would happen on Kathy's volunteer day, as dogs couldn't be left for longer than four hours, but the foster team felt they could work around it. Depending on the dog, he or she might be able to go into a spare kennel on Kathy's volunteer day or be kept in the office. Alternatively, Kathy could go home at lunchtime to spend some time with them. Judith had also said she'd work from Kathy's house if necessary, to keep the dog company.

And so here she was, meeting Milly in the paddocks at Battersea, with a view to taking her home. Milly was a sleek young greyhound who was finding kennel life very stressful. She lacked confidence, and was shy and cowed, despite their best efforts to reassure and bond with her. She'd been off her food, generally listless and worried, so the decision had been taken to put her into foster care. The canine behaviourists had explained everything about her and what she needed, and Kathy was given a foster care plan to stick to.

'I think we'll get along just fine,' she said to Tom. 'She seems a sweet dog, bless her.'

Tom nodded. 'She is. She just needs to gain some confidence.'

Kathy could relate to that one.

'I'm very happy to take her on foster. Can I take all the supplies now and come back for her later when my hands aren't full?'

Battersea provided everything the dog would need on foster, including food and bedding. Kathy took the supplies home, laid out a comfortable, squishy bed for Milly – as a greyhound, she needed plenty of padding for her skinny limbs – and then returned to get the dog.

'Any problems, just call,' said Tom as he handed over Milly's lead.

Kathy nodded. 'I'm sure we'll be fine,' she said, with a conviction she perhaps didn't feel. 'Come on, girl.'

The two of them walked towards the Battersea gates and then out into the street, turning towards Kathy's house.

Kathy let out a long exhale. It was just the two of them now. The poor dog looked so overwhelmed and frightened, pressing herself against Kathy's legs for reassurance.

'There's a good girl,' Kathy soothed her, trying to project an air of confidence that would rub off on Milly.

Kathy's heart went out to the dog as they made their way along the street, with Milly in her Battersea coat to keep her warm, nervously glancing up at Kathy every few paces.

'Everything's going to be all right. I'll put the fire on and you can just have a good snooze in front of that.'

They arrived at the front door and Kathy let them both inside, the dog waiting politely to follow her. She led Milly through to the back garden and unclipped her lead just in case she wanted to go to the loo. Once back inside, she allowed Milly to roam around as she pleased and settle in.

The dog hesitated a moment before setting off around the kitchen, sniffing everything. Then she darted off into the living room and began investigating there. Kathy knew this was normal as Milly settled in, and let her get on with it, heading into the living room after her to make a fire. She put some extra blankets and a small duvet that Milly had had at Battersea near the hearth, in case the dog wanted to lie down there, but she still seemed anxious, and was pacing back and forth. Was this normal?

She got out her phone and texted Tom, saved as Battersea Tom, just to be doubly sure. Then she saw Ben's number above Tom's. Before she could think too much, she typed, 'Hi, Ben, it's Kathy. Thought you should know you were right again. My first foster dog is just settling in,' and hit send.

Her phone buzzed instantly in reply. Ben!

'How are the two of you getting on?'

Should she confide in him that things were a bit more difficult? He'd told her to ask for help, hadn't he?

'We're OK, but she seems really anxious and won't settle. She's pacing around a lot.'

A pause and then her phone rang. Ben.

'There was no need to call, honestly,' Kathy said as soon as she picked up. 'We're fine. And I've asked Tom, the foster coordinator.'

'I'm sure you are fine,' said Ben, his tone amused. 'It's probably normal she's a bit restless, Kath. She's been anxious in kennels, too, remember. Just you stay calm and keep carrying on as usual, then she should settle in her own time. Start cooking your dinner. Honestly, every dog I've fostered has taken a while to settle down. So don't worry. I'm sure you're doing great.'

Kathy felt relief flood through her at Ben's reassuring tone. 'OK, thanks, Ben. Will do,' she said and put the phone down.

She'd had a message from Tom as well, saying pretty much the same thing.

She forced herself to stay in the kitchen, even though Milly was pacing to and fro, heading into the living room and back again, and switched the radio on to the comfortable chatter of Radio 4. That felt calmer already.

She got out her vegetables and began chopping, calmly, steadily, remembering Ben's words, the sound of his voice. And after a while, she became aware of another presence next to her. Milly, in the kitchen, still looking wary and uncertain, but no longer pacing back and forth.

Kathy went to put out some food for the dog.

'Dinner time, Mil,' she said, putting down the bowl.

A moment of hesitation, then Milly came slowly forwards and sniffed the food. Kathy petted her a little but sensed that the dog was tolerating rather than enjoying her touch. That was understandable. Like many greyhounds, Milly was under-socialised, used to a life of hard racing before being cast aside. It was so unfair. Greyhounds often made wonderful pets, given the chance. Milly sniffed at her dinner but didn't eat it. That was normal, too. She'd eat when she felt more settled.

Kathy took her dinner into the living room and sat on the sofa, switching on the TV and settling to a quiz show. She wondered how Milly was getting on in the kitchen and told herself not to go and check. She focused on the quiz show and before too long, a long snout poked its way around the living room door. Kathy giggled out loud and reached for her phone. This was too good not to take a photo of.

'I know you're there,' Kathy murmured softly.

The snout poked a little further into the room and then Milly's whole head came into view, her dark eyes locked on Kathy.

'You come in if you want to,' said Kathy, leaning back in the cosy armchair and focusing on the TV. Her heart leapt when, a few moments later, Milly did come in, her body language still wary, as if she didn't quite believe where she was. But the lure of the warm fire proved too much and the dog came quietly closer before lying down in front of the hearth, her long limbs stretched out. She exhaled a long sigh of relaxation and shut her eyes.

'That seemed a long time coming,' said Kathy. Then she reached for her phone and sent the picture of Milly's snout round the door, followed by another photo of Milly snoozing on the rug, to Ben.

'We're making progress,' she typed as the caption.

'Well done!' Ben replied.

Kathy took a moment to survey the room: the cosy fire, the comfy sofa, the dog snoozing on the rug. It felt very different compared with being in on your own. She sent the picture to the volunteer WhatsApp group and her phone instantly buzzed with notifications in response.

'What do you make of this lot, then?' said Kathy as the news came on.

Milly's ears twitched and she made a groan.

'I agree,' said Kathy. 'These politicians, eh.'

She took Milly outside again in case she needed the toilet. Greyhounds often weren't house-trained, and she gave Milly plenty of praise for doing her business outside, then settled her down in the kitchen. Kathy hoped she'd be able to rest in the peace and quiet, away from the hustle and bustle of kennels.

*

She was glad to see Milly still snoozing in her bed when she came down the next morning. The dog woke up, slowly, and Kathy opened the garden door to encourage her out for the loo again. Milly took a mouthful of food when she got back in, which pleased Kathy. She must be feeling calmer if she was eating.

She clipped on Milly's lead, as well as a muzzle, knowing Milly's chase instinct would still be strong towards any small furry creatures they might encounter, and they headed out to the park.

'Gorgeous greyhound you have there,' said a young woman, pausing from her run to stop and admire Milly.

She was as lean as a greyhound herself, Kathy thought.

'She is, isn't she?' said Kathy proudly.

Milly looked so sleek and smart in her Battersea coat.

'How long have you had her?'

'Oh, she's not mine,' said Kathy. 'She's actually a rescue at Battersea Dogs & Cats Home, awaiting adoption. I'm fostering her, as she found kennels a bit stressful.'

'Sounds like she's an introvert,' said the woman.

As if proving her words, Milly cautiously took a sniff in the woman's direction before retreating behind Kathy's legs again.

Kathy laughed. 'You could say that! She certainly appreciates being out of the bustle of the kennels.'

'And do they need a ton of exercise?'

Kathy shook her head. 'No, actually. That's one of the great things about greyhounds. They generally have a burst of energy and then are happy to snooze on the sofa all day.'

'Sounds like me,' said the woman with a smile. 'After this run, I'm done. Well, she's beautiful. I run here most mornings, so guess I'll see you again. Have a good day!'

That was one of several conversations Kathy had on their short walk. She was amazed at the difference a dog made. Before, her walks in the park had been solitary. She'd felt almost invisible, especially among all the couples and families. She'd always walked briskly, head down, making it clear that she was out for exercise. But now, with Milly in tow, she took a slower pace, allowing the dog to sniff and amble where she wanted. Milly would always be kept on a leash – this was one of the golden rules of fostering. Her sighthound tendencies meant she could be prone to chasing off after things and not coming back. It was her instinct, after all.

Milly showed little sign of hankering after the horizon, however. There was one funny moment where she'd pricked her ears up at the sight of a woman's furry bobble hat, but Kathy had distracted her with a treat.

'That was a smart move!' a thirty-something man in a suit had said to her with a grin. 'I've got a greyhound myself and he's a terror for anything fluffy.' They'd shared a laugh about it before he headed off.

Then there had been the old man out getting his morning walk, who was keen to say hello to Milly.

'I've seen you here before, but you've always looked in such a rush,' he said to Kathy. 'I think you taught my grandson, once upon a time.'

'I probably did,' said Kathy, and then the man was showing her a few photos of a young man she couldn't quite place in the memories of her pupils, but she wasn't about to admit that to him.

'I've put you on the spot,' said the man as if reading her mind. 'It must be so hard to keep track of all those little ones. But you gave him such a lot of confidence, we were all very grateful. I won't keep you and Milly any longer. I just wanted to say hello.'

'It's nice to slow down and talk,' Kathy said, before he wished her a good day and set off slowly on his way.

There had been countless 'hellos' from dog walkers, keen to know all about Milly and share tales of their own dogs. And there was only one sticky moment when Milly had whined and backed away from a boisterous dog, and Kathy had led her off to calm down, but overall, things had gone well.

Over the next few days, Milly became more and more at home, visibly relaxing. Kathy carefully noted down her behaviours so she could update the fostering team as accurately as possible. Using the Battersea training guide, she helped Milly with her 'sit' training and was delighted to see the dog responded. There were a few little accidents with toilet training, but on the whole, the dog was responding beautifully to being in a home.

On day three, Milly discovered the delights of sitting on the sofa. Greyhounds could be almost cat-like in finding the cosiest, comfiest place to call their own – and Milly had clearly been paying attention to Kathy's own favourite spot. But because poor Milly had never been in a home before, she didn't know how sofas worked, or how to get up on them.

Kathy watched, amused, as the dog tried to organise her long limbs to climb up on the cushions. It was like Bambi on the ice! But eventually, she made it, and flopped into a long sleep for the afternoon.

Milly also had trouble with stairs. As with many dogs who'd never lived in a home before, she'd never encountered stairs. Each time, she looked on forlornly as Kathy went up them and she couldn't follow. So Kathy began to encourage her near them, working up to putting a treat on a higher step to encourage Milly to put a paw up. She took the training slowly, with lots of praise and reassurance, as was the Battersea way. She then put Milly's harness on her, to hold her more securely, and hopefully give the dog confidence and stability. Soon, Milly managed to walk up the stairs beside Kathy, to the landing on the top floor.

'Well *done*!' said Kathy, absolutely delighted to see the dog's progress.

Milly leant against Kathy's legs as she petted her and gave her some treats. Kathy had forgotten just how satisfying it was to teach, to help another being learn something. Here she was, back in headmistress mode – and loving it.

But what goes up must come down and Milly looked apprehensive, peering down the stairs.

'We can do it,' said Kathy encouragingly.

She took a firm hold of the dog's harness. There was a risk that Milly might panic and try to jump down the stairs, which could be disastrous. Slowly, gently, she encouraged Milly to put her paws down one step at a time. It took a while, but eventually, they were back down in the hallway, all four paws on flat ground. Milly wagged her tail and looked up at Kathy.

'You clever, clever dog,' said Kathy, giving her lots of treats. 'Brave girl.'

Milly glanced towards the back door and Kathy wondered if she needed the loo. She took her out to the garden, where weak sunlight was filtering through the clouds. Milly peed on Kathy's favourite flower bed. Kathy raised her eyebrows.

'At least you have impeccable taste, eh, girl?'

The dog turned to look at Kathy.

'Coming back in?'

But Milly had other ideas. She lowered her front paws and kept her haunches high, looking up at Kathy. And was that . . . a tail wagging? Kathy realised that Milly was playing!

It was wonderful to see the dog let go. She'd been so focused on teaching Milly, on schooling her, that she'd forgotten to let the dog have a bit of fun.

'Come on, then!' said Kathy, and she brought out one of her squeaky toys and threw it gently onto the lawn.

Milly raced for it, picking it up and shaking it before tossing it in the air and zooming around the garden. Kathy felt her heart grow glad just watching Milly let her hair down and be a dog. Milly darted to and fro, prancing, bowing in play and then zipping from side to side, showing off her greyhound speed.

'Show me, show me!' Kathy called, picking up the toy and throwing it again for Milly as the dog darted all around her.

After peeking from side to side to check the neighbours weren't around, Kathy joined in with the merry dance, throwing her hands in the air and jumping from side to side to encourage Milly. Eventually, the dog came to a stop, panting beside Kathy, her tongue lolling out, her eyes bright.

She looked happy, thought Kathy, who was a bit out of puff herself, and she looked confident.

Milly came to her, her ears pricked up this time, and pushed her nose into Kathy's hand, as if saying thank you.

'Oh, you're welcome,' said Kathy, feeling almost tearful. 'And it's me who should be thanking you, Mil. In all that fuss to get it right, I almost forgot how to have fun.'

The dog leaned against Kathy's legs and pushed her head up against her hand. Kathy scratched the top of Milly's head and sensed the dog relaxing and enjoying the petting. The two of them made their way back into the kitchen and Milly lapped up some water before making her way straight to her favourite spot on the sofa, where she lay down with her legs stuck in the air. Kathy had to take a photo. Milly got into the most contorted positions to fall asleep and she loved sending Milly's latest poses to the volunteer WhatsApp group.

Chapter 7

The days flew by with Milly for company. Kathy took her for an early walk each morning and another one in the afternoon. She quickly began recognising people, waving hello and exchanging a few words, so that her day became filled with chatter. She often stopped off in Asha's café, where Asha insisted on piling up some blankets so that Milly could lie comfortably while Kathy sipped her latte. She also took Milly round to Judith's, where she was the model of decorum. She was definitely reserved when meeting new people and liked to be close to Kathy, but she was a lot more settled than she had been in kennels, and her new confidence was growing.

'You know, I feel like she's some member of the aristocracy, bestowing a visit on us,' said Judith as Milly lay down, her long paws crossed. 'She's so elegant! Do you know what I mean?'

Kathy laughed. 'I do! And that long nose – perfect for looking down at us if we misbehave.'

Milly thumped her tail gently as if joining in the joke.

'Has she met your family?' asked Judith.

Kathy shook her head. She still hadn't told Alex about the fostering. She'd been planning to, but then everything had happened so quickly.

Judith raised an eyebrow. 'Are you keeping her a secret?'

Kathy sighed. 'Not intentionally. I just haven't found the right moment. If Alex actually met her, he'd be fine. He adores dogs. I'm meant to be going down soon, so if she's still with me, she can come then.'

A date for the ever-rearranged visit was finally in the diary for the first weekend in May.

'Has she been assessed for rehoming yet?' asked Judith.

'Yes, she has. She's already up on the website, by all accounts.'

Kathy's heart twinged when she thought of giving Milly up. And the moment was to come only too soon.

At her next volunteering day, Ben came up to her. Milly had been in the office all day.

'You've worked wonders on that dog,' said Ben. 'She's completely changed. She's always going to be reserved, but she's so much more relaxed around people and her training is really coming on.'

'Thanks, Ben,' said Kathy, glowing with pride. 'It's been a pleasure having her.'

'And I've got some good news,' said Ben. 'I think I've found her a home. Someone rang a few days ago to ask about her, and came in today as they were passing by. I introduced them, seeing as Milly was here, and they really seemed to click.'

'Oh,' said Kathy, her heart plunging. She forced a smile. 'I mean. Oh, that's good news.'

Ben touched her arm. 'Are you OK? It's one of the tough parts of the job. We get really attached to these animals.'

'Oh, I'm absolutely fine,' Kathy said briskly. 'I'm certain I don't want a dog full-time. It's great to have seen Milly on her way.'

Then she was kicking herself. What he said had made a lot of sense, so why couldn't she nod and open up a bit? It was easier, somehow, to keep the superwoman mask on, even though her heart quailed at the thought of the house being empty again.

'So . . . when will she go?' Kathy said, careful to keep her voice steady.

Ben regarded her closely for a moment. 'We should hear tomorrow if Lorena – that's who's thinking of adopting her – wants to take her. Then . . . well, it'd be as soon as we can find a convenient time for you to bring her into the centre and for Lorena to pick her up.'

'It won't be a bother,' Kathy said, smoothing down her sweater. 'I'm glad. Milly deserves a wonderful forever home.'

Ben smiled. 'That she does. Here, you've almost finished your shift. Do you want to come and get her from the office?'

Kathy followed him to the shared office space, where Ben and the other rehomers worked. Milly got up to greet her, wagging her tail. Kathy had to bite her lip to stop herself from welling up.

'Off we go,' she said briskly. 'Ben, let me know as soon as you hear.'

'Will do,' said Ben. 'Enjoy your evening.'

As soon as they got in the door, Kathy sat on the sofa and let the tears come. She knew she was being ridiculous. She tried to control them for the sake of Milly. As with so many dogs, she just seemed to know that Kathy was upset and came to lay her head on Kathy's knee. Kathy rubbed Milly's ears and sniffed.

'I know I'm being silly, Mil,' she began. 'And I want you to have the most wonderful home. It's just . . . I'll miss you. And it's hard saying goodbye.' She choked up again. 'And it's hard thinking of the house being just me again.'

Milly let out a consolatory whimper and looked up at Kathy with her deep brown eyes.

'You're a dear dog,' said Kathy. 'I think we both got our confidence back a bit, didn't we?'

Her phone beeped. It was Ben.

'Hi, Kathy, just got word that Milly has a new owner, officially. I've spoken to Tom, as well. Would it be OK if Lorena picked her up tomorrow morning?'

Kathy didn't know it was possible to feel a leap of joy for Milly and such a plunge of despair for herself at the same time.

'You got the golden ticket, girl,' she murmured to Milly, who wagged her tail. 'You're going to make someone very happy indeed.'

Kathy texted Ben back, saying how happy she was to hear it and that she'd bring Milly to the rescue home the following morning. She suggested 10 a.m., as she couldn't bear a protracted waiting around for Milly to go. After they'd made the arrangement, Kathy swallowed a lump in her throat and resolved to make the most of their last evening together.

She cooked herself a tasty lasagne and fed Milly a little bit more chicken than was strictly necessary. Kathy felt a glow of pleasure when she reflected on just how far the dog had come in such a short time. She was much more confident with the stairs, was doing so well with her house training, and was even learning how to sit and stay. She knew she was sending her off to a new home with the best possible start.

After they'd both eaten in the kitchen, Kathy poured herself a glass of wine and went through to the living room with Milly.

'Here's to you, Milly,' she toasted her. 'To new beginnings.'

*

Kathy was at the rescue centre with Milly at 10 a.m. sharp, having taken the dog for a walk and groomed her so she'd look her absolute best for her new owner. Her black coat was sleek and shining and her ribs were covered with a little more flesh, which Kathy was delighted to see, as Milly had been a bit underweight when she'd started fostering her. And there was Ben, with a dark-haired woman, who Kathy guessed to be in her forties, beside him.

'Morning, Kathy,' said Ben. 'This is Lorena. Milly's new mum.'

'Delighted to meet you,' said Kathy.

Lorena had a ready smile and a calm, kind demeanour that made Kathy feel instantly better that this was the home Milly was going to.

'And you,' Lorena said. 'Ben's been singing your praises about everything you've done for Milly.'

'Oh, goodness,' Kathy said, flushing red and staring at her shoes. 'Well, I don't know about that.'

She risked a peek sideways and noticed that Ben was blushing as well. He smiled awkwardly at her, ruffling his hair up with his hand.

'Well, shall we do the honours?' Ben prompted.

They went into one of the meeting rooms, where Kathy let Milly off her lead. She trotted over to investigate Lorena and Kathy smiled to see how much more confident the dog was. Lorena had a quiet, warm energy to her that Kathy was sure would suit Milly.

She remembered what Freya had said – that Ben was a wizard when it came to matching dogs with their new owners.

'I've made up a bag with her things,' said Kathy, indicating a tote bag she'd filled with Milly's lead, her toys and a few favourite biscuits. 'She'll need to find the comfiest spot in the house to lie down in, somewhere well padded – think *The Princess and the Pea*! And she's been ever so good. Her training's come on a mile, especially with stairs, so you just need to be sure to . . .'

She was in headmistress mode, she realised, telling Lorena – a grown woman – what to do, but she didn't dare switch it off, for fear of being overcome with emotion. Lorena was nodding politely.

She felt a hand, warm and firm, on her shoulder. Ben.

'You've done a brilliant job, Kathy,' said Ben. 'And I know that Lorena is just the person to keep things going with Milly.'

'I promise I'll look after her,' said Lorena, and Kathy knew she would.

'Well, I should leave you to do the official business,' she said.

'Do you want to take a moment to say goodbye?' said Ben. 'While we get the paperwork?'

'Actually, that would be lovely.'

Ben and Lorena stepped out, and Kathy was alone with Milly again. She gave Milly a last cuddle, blinking back tears as she hid her face against the dog's smooth fur. Milly gave her a comforting lick. Then Ben and Lorena were back, and it was time Kathy left.

'I'll be in touch, of course, with Battersea, so you know how she's getting on,' said Lorena, and Kathy smiled and nodded.

'Enjoy her; she's a wonderful dog,' she said, before bidding them farewell and heading out.

Emotion was rising up within her, and the last thing she wanted was for it all to spill out in front of Ben and Lorena. How could she explain that saying goodbye to Milly brought back all those memories of the most excruciating goodbye of her life – the long farewell to John?

It was so hard walking through the gates without Milly. And once she was back inside, the house seemed empty and cold without Milly's presence. Kathy shivered as the memories became more vivid. Of holding John's hand in those last days as he slipped in and out of consciousness . . . She counted her blessings that he'd been at home then, able to look out on their garden from his bed downstairs. She'd stayed by him all night, determined not to fall asleep, to soak up every last moment of being with him.

When he was too weak to do anything else, he'd still run his thumb over her knuckles as she clung to his hand, still gave her hand a gentle squeeze. How well their hands fitted together, she'd thought. After all those years, it was like they'd been worn down like driftwood, to fit perfectly. And then that terrible day when he didn't squeeze her hand back any more.

Alex had only been back home for a few weeks. Kathy could hardly bear to think of when he'd arrived, how he'd dropped his rucksack and had run to John's bedside, gently cradling his father. John had somehow rallied for a few more days, then had gone downhill fast. He'd died just a few weeks later – faster than any of them had expected. Alex had been so brave in those last days, keeping it together in front of John but sobbing in Kathy's arms when John was asleep.

'I would have been here sooner,' he'd said to his father, voice trembling.

'I'm sorry, son. We should have told you.'

'You're here now,' Kathy had said. 'We're all together.'

Back in the present, Kathy realised her face was wet with tears. She swiped them away and went to put the kettle on.

If this was what fostering was doing to her, she didn't know if she could continue with it. She'd put so much effort into patching her life together after John had gone; the emotional pull of welcoming Milly into her home and then being devastated by saying goodbye, well, it was all threatening to pull her apart at the seams.

She made herself a tea, dunked two sugars into it, then busied herself with some tasks around the house. But the day lacked purpose without Milly to look after and she didn't feel much like human company. The sad feeling didn't go. It followed her on into the evening, when she sat down to watch TV. Now that she'd experienced joy again, it was almost worse when you had it taken away from you than when you'd forgotten it existed at all.

She glanced at her phone. A message from Alex, confirming their weekend was still on, but he hoped she'd understand if they had to work a bit. She rolled her eyes. She'd been looking forward to going there with Milly, showing them all how capable she was being, as well as having Milly's lovely companionship. And now, once again, she was getting shunted to the bottom of the pile.

The other message was from Ben.

'Thought you might like to see this.'

The message was accompanied by a picture of Milly, curled up in a squishy new bed at what must be Lorena's house. She looked happy and content.

'A lot of this is down to you,' Ben wrote.

And as Kathy looked at Milly, happy in her forever home, she understood that the emotional roller coaster had all been worth it. She just hoped she had the strength to do it all again, for another dog in need.

Chapter 8

It was only a week or so after Milly had left that Kathy got an email from Tom, asking her if she'd be up for another foster dog. She read the details. A Staffie with a chronic ear infection and skin irritation that wasn't healing in the kennels. She knew this could happen – when dogs were stressed, health conditions were exacerbated. She'd have to give him ear drops and apply creams, and take him into the rescue home every week for a veterinary check-up; it was an advantage she lived so close.

She took a deep breath and replied that yes, she was up for it. The next stage of the fostering process would be to meet the dog. Kathy knew she could halt the process at any point she felt a particular dog might be too much for her to take on. The fostering team were incredibly careful at matching dogs and homes. She arranged to go and meet the Staffie that afternoon.

'Here he is,' said Tom, just a few hours later.

Kathy peeked into the kennel and was instantly smitten. Baxter bounded forwards to greet them and stood on his hind legs, paws up against the pen, tail wagging furiously. He was such a handsome dog – stocky and powerful, and a beautiful blue colour, with a white bib. That is, where his skin wasn't exposed in painful pink patches.

'Why is he in such a state?' she said, putting her hand over her mouth in shock.

'We don't know,' said Tom. 'He was brought in by a couple who found him wandering around. It's clear he's been well-trained at some point, but who knows what's happened to him.'

'At least we know what happens next,' said Kathy, her mind made up. 'He comes with me, for as much TLC as he needs.'

Tom grinned. 'Kathy, that would be a load off my mind. Can I get you to chat to Fatima, the vet who's been looking after him? And then we'll get things in motion.'

'Absolutely.'

After Baxter had calmed down, they went inside the pen to meet him. Kathy put her hand out to the dog, who licked it furiously. He was so spirited! Kathy had grown to love Milly's stately demeanour, but she'd always have a soft spot for these . . . well, very *doggy* dogs.

Fatima briefed her on what care Baxter would need and showed her how to do it. It was mostly a case of bathing his poor skin and applying cream, and cleaning the ear and putting his ear drops in every day. Baxter clearly hated the process but sat still and good as gold, with a resigned expression on his face. Fatima warned Kathy that this would likely be a longer-term foster, as the ear infection could take weeks, if not months, to resolve. And so Kathy's second foster project began. And with it, her spirits lifted once more.

*

Baxter was a very different presence around the house than Milly. Whereas Milly had been shy and introverted, Baxter was nosy, boisterous and very sociable. The second he got in the door, he went and gave everything a good sniff, then came to cuddle up to Kathy. He was a lot cheekier than Milly. He didn't hesitate to push his nose into her hand when he wanted attention and would strain on the lead when they went for walks, enthusiastic to be out and about. He wanted to say hello to anyone and everyone – dog or human – they passed.

Kathy had to be quick off the mark if she dropped any food in the kitchen, as Baxter didn't hesitate to snaffle anything from the floor. He was also, she discovered, a bit of a chewer when the mood took him. He loved to pick a random object and hide it in his bed. Kathy was bemused by the things he chose, like a heavy wooden doorstop, but she couldn't help but laugh when she discovered them.

Baxter soon found his way into her heart, never more so than when he showed his courageous spirit as she attended to his ears and skin. She was sure it must be painful for the poor animal, but he sat patiently throughout and even wagged his tail gratefully.

'There's a good boy. I know it's not nice, but it's for your own good,' said Kathy as she carefully cleaned his ear.

He let out a tiny whimper that threatened to break Kathy's heart.

She was no stranger to nursing. She'd cared for John as much as she could, making him meals, helping him to wash. So many moments of tenderness, in among the horror of it, and John still making her laugh, still smiling at her, the love in his eyes as alive as it had always been, even as his body faded.

The pain of it all rose up, unbidden. She put down the cotton pad and put her cheek close to Baxter's head, where the fur grew smooth. She breathed in the comforting scent of the dog, felt his warmth on her face and the jolting feeling of his gentle pant. The pain subsided.

'Thanks, boy,' said Kathy quietly, pulling back and looking into Baxter's warm brown eyes.

Everything was so much easier with a dog beside you.

*

The next morning, she took Baxter out for his first walk of the day, heading to Clapham Common for a change. It was a lovely morning, the early light clean and pure. The dog was eager to be off, straining at the leash, and Kathy had to remind him of his manners more than once. He looked up at her each time with a cheeky expression and then dropped back to her heels, only to forget himself and surge forwards once more.

She took a route to a quieter part of the common, where they walked among the budding trees, Baxter eagerly tugging the lead in her hand. She loved drinking in the peace of the morning, the sound of the birds singing, the day just getting started.

And then, a shout:

'Oh! Please, keep him away!'

A young woman, not much more than a girl, was cowering back on the path. Baxter was keen to make friends and began woofing and trying to jump up. The woman squeaked in fear and flapped her arms, all of which made Baxter more excited to play. Kathy used all of her strength to pull back on his leash.

'Please, calm down,' said Kathy to the woman, trying to keep her voice steady and stop the panic.

'No! He's dangerous! Look at him, trying to get at me!'

Kathy bit her lip. Staffies suffered so much from this unfair reputation.

'Honestly, if you calm down, he'll calm down. Fold your arms and keep still.'

Somehow, the girl heeded her words and Baxter calmed down immediately. The girl glanced at Kathy before pulling her hoodie up around her face, which was half covered anyway by a thick, dark fringe. The young woman went to sit well away at the end of a bench, her knees hunched up to her chest. Her face was pale, with dark circles under her eyes.

Baxter looked up at Kathy, tongue lolling happily.

'Are you all right?' said Kathy.

The girl put her face against her knees and stayed quiet.

Kathy wasn't sure what to do.

'We'll be on our way, then.'

'Isn't that one of those dangerous dog breeds?' the girl said, her voice muffled against her knees.

Kathy hated the assertion of 'dangerous dogs'. So much of a dog's temperament was down to the way it was socialised and treated by humans. People were so quick to throw a damning label on an animal, instead of looking at the causes of why they behaved as they did.

But, she reminded herself, this young girl probably didn't know any better and she did look genuinely terrified. Here was a chance to change her perception.

'Well, Baxter here is a Staffie,' she said. 'A Staffordshire bull terrier. And actually, there's a bit of a misconception about them. People often think they're tough or dangerous, but they're generally really great with humans. They used to be called "the nanny dog", as they were so good with children. He just wanted to say hello to you and thought you were starting a game with him.'

The girl took a peek then.

'So I misjudged him, on appearance.'

Kathy noticed that the girl's face was smudged with tears.

'Do you . . . do you want a tissue?'

The girl nodded.

Kathy passed her a Kleenex and the girl blew her nose loudly.

'I'm fine. Just allergies making my eyes water.'

Kathy suspected otherwise but didn't want to pry. The girl's chin was jutted defiantly.

'What's his name?'

'Baxter.'

The dog turned round at the sound of his name and Kathy smiled.

'What's his story? Why's his skin like that?'

'He's had a rough time. He was a stray and Battersea took him in. I'm now fostering him, as he needs medical treatment for his skin. He's got a terrible ear infection as well, poor thing.'

'He must be brave,' said the girl, staring at Baxter. 'To be so positive even when there's so much wrong.'

'He is. Here, do you want to say hello? I promise you, he's a softie, really.'

The girl hesitated for a moment and Kathy sensed she was battling against herself.

'Go on, then.'

'So, if he gets excited, don't respond,' Kathy explained. 'He only gets attention when he's got four paws on the ground, not when he's jumping up.'

The girl nodded.

Kathy approached with Baxter. The girl remained still, hunched over, her arms painfully thin in her hoodie. Kathy hoped she wouldn't panic again. Baxter sniffed her shoes and looked up at her, wagging his tail.

The girl reached her hand down and let Baxter sniff it, before stroking him tentatively.

'Not so scary, after all,' said Kathy.

'No,' agreed the girl.

The girl seemed lost in her thoughts as she stroked the dog. Kathy sensed that Baxter wasn't the only one with a difficult past.

'Will you come here again?' muttered the girl.

She looked so young, Kathy thought. Barely twenty. Kathy wanted to ask her if she was all right, if she had somewhere to go, but was wary of frightening her.

'Yes, we have a walk every morning,' said Kathy. 'Either here or in Battersea Park.'

The girl nodded.

'And we can come this way tomorrow,' Kathy added. 'What's your name?'

The girl stared at the floor. 'Hope.'

'Well, I'm Kathy.'

'OK.'

Kathy got up to leave. 'Hope, it was lovely to meet you. And I hope we see you again soon.'

But the girl was just staring at the floor again and didn't react.

The next morning, Kathy walked the Clapham Common route again, but there was no sign of Hope. Kathy was disappointed. She'd thought about the girl a lot, how she seemed vulnerable, and had wanted to see her again. See if there was anything she could do to help. Maybe another day they'd bump into her.

She turned her attention to more pressing matters – the weekend ahead, with Alex and his family. She'd told Alex a few days ago that she would be bringing a foster dog. She and Alex had been discussing what time she'd arrive, when Baxter decided to start barking loudly at something in the garden.

'Is that . . . a *dog*?' Alex had said.

'Yes,' Kathy had replied, stalling for time. 'They do tend to make barking sounds.'

'A *dog*, in the *house*?'

Baxter chose that moment to come into the living room, jump on the sofa and start trying to slobber all over Kathy's face, trampling all over her lap. She could hardly tell him to get down quietly.

'Baxter, for goodness' sake,' she hissed.

'Baxter?' said Alex. 'Who's Baxter?'

And now she had to come clean. She'd been hoping to leave it till the day before she arrived, which she knew was cowardly in putting it off. She found Alex's disapproval hard to deal with. But the moment was here.

'He's a lovely Staffie,' she said brightly as Baxter plonked himself right on her lap, causing her to gasp. 'He's on foster from Battersea Dogs' Home. I'd like to bring him this, actually. Is that OK?'

There had been an ominous silence down the phone, then Alex exhaled sharply.

'Mum. A dog? Fostering? I was worried enough about the volunteering, but this is another step – and bringing him here? It's chaotic enough down here as it is.'

'I'm not asking you to look after him. From what you've said, you'll be busy with the pub, so it'll be nice to have company.'

'Fine, fine,' he'd acquiesced, but she could tell he wasn't pleased about it.

Well, never mind. He'd change his mind when he met Baxter, who seemed to win over everyone – even Hope.

Chapter 9

Kathy encouraged Baxter into a dog crate in the car with a treat, and he leapt in enthusiastically. She smiled. Having Baxter by her side soothed her nerves about the weekend. If nothing else, he could enjoy a few walks in the countryside. She'd driven him around her neighbourhood a few times to see if he was used to the car and he'd been absolutely fine. They had about an hour and a half drive ahead of them, all being well with the traffic.

She set off mid-morning and the roads were clear. Baxter seemed to be enjoying watching the countryside zoom past. She was glad one of them was, as she couldn't help but feel on edge. Please let it go well, she thought. She couldn't bear the thought of another row about Christmas, especially not in May.

They made good time, and were soon pulling up outside Jacqui's house. Jacqui *and* Alex's house, Kathy reminded herself. Alex had given up his own flat to move in with her and Becs. Maybe that's why Kathy hadn't felt at home there the other times she'd visited. Hopefully this time would be different.

She rang the doorbell, Baxter by her side with their various bags, and arranged her face into a smile.

Jacqui answered and Baxter immediately sprang forwards to greet her.

'Sorry!' said Kathy as she was jerked forwards, too. 'He's a bit over-friendly. Just ignore him when he's jumping up like that.' She'd soon have biceps like the Hulk, she thought.

'He's certainly got a lot of energy.'

Jacqui looked cautious and Kathy wondered if she was nervous around dogs.

'Did Alex mention him?'

'Yes, he did. I'll just wait till he's calmed down before I say hello. I'm sure he's lovely, though.'

Fortunately, Baxter remembered his manners before too long and Jacqui was able to greet him.

'There's a pot of tea on the go and sandwiches for lunch. Alex got called in to help with a supplier,' Jacqui said, grimacing, and Kathy's heart sank.

'Oh, that's a shame,' she said. 'But never mind. Where's Becs?'

Jacqui sighed. 'Upstairs, sulking.'

'Oh, dear.'

'I'll get her down in a minute. Wait a moment more before I poke the dragon. Come on through.'

Jacqui showed Kathy through to the living room. It was immaculate, a pale grey sofa lined with pink and forest-green cushions and a cosy white throw. The walls were decorated with tasteful black-and-white prints, including one of Jacqui and Alex together, holding hands.

'What a lovely picture,' said Kathy.

Jacqui glanced at it and smiled. 'Thanks. Friend's wedding, hence why we're scrubbed up so well.'

She'd laid the coffee table with a pretty teapot and cups, and a selection of sandwiches, cut neatly into triangles, and dainty cupcakes.

'You shouldn't have gone to the bother,' Kathy said before immediately thinking that it sounded wrong. 'I mean, it's wonderful of you. I just hope it wasn't too much fuss. I'm here to help, not create more work.'

'Oh, it was no bother at all,' said Jacqui breezily and, as she poured the tea, Kathy looked her over once again.

Her hair immaculate, her dark indigo jeans perfectly pressed, a bright pair of earrings dangling from her ears. She was so capable, Kathy thought. Keeping the house perfect like this, on top of making all these refreshments and running the pub.

On a desk at the back of the room, where it led to the kitchen, Kathy could see a series of ring binders, neatly labelled. One was open on the desk, full of colour-coordinated tabs and neat handwriting.

Were they going to mention Christmas? Kathy hoped not, but it also seemed like an elephant in the room. She'd given that horrible book to a charity shop. She'd gleaned a few good tips for Thailand from it, but she still couldn't look at the title without feeling upset. Maybe it was better it wasn't mentioned, after all, and that they just tried to build new, more positive memories.

As if he'd heard her, Baxter rolled over and looked at Jacqui appealingly.

She laughed. 'He's so sweet.'

He really was a terrible flirt, thought Kathy, but he'd already won Jacqui over with his charming nature and she was grateful.

Kathy took a sip of her tea and nibbled an egg mayonnaise sandwich.

'Delicious, thanks, Jacqui.'

'You're welcome.'

There was a stilted silence while they both looked at each other and Kathy tried to think of something else to say. She wished things felt easier and more like family. And why wasn't Alex here? Was it so much to expect him to ease things along a little bit? Were things really that desperate at the pub?

And then Baxter seized his moment and lunged up on the low table, snatching up a chicken sandwich and wolfing it down at lightning speed, looking very pleased with himself.

Jacqui burst out laughing.

'Oh, goodness, I'm so sorry,' said Kathy, 'He hasn't eaten all morning and—' But then as Jacqui waved her words away, still giggling, Kathy found herself joining in.

'It was his face,' said Jacqui, wiping her eyes once she'd stopped laughing. 'I'm sorry, but just his face – I saw it all, as if in slow motion! The gleam in the eyes, the lunge, the satisfied look that he'd outsmarted us both – it was too much!' She reached out her hand and fondled Baxter's head. 'I think this is the most excited anyone has ever been over my chicken sandwiches.'

Kathy laughed. 'And the way he just lay back down at your feet, like we wouldn't notice what he'd done!'

'Perfection,' agreed Jacqui. 'Maybe that's the way to style it out when you've made a mistake, just pretend it didn't happen.'

Kathy basked in their shared laughter. Finally, a genuine moment of warmth between the two of them.

Then the sound of keys in the door and Alex entered the room, looking weary, ruffling his hands through his hair.

'Hey, Mum,' he said distractedly, leaning over to give her a peck on the cheek before picking up two sandwiches and shovelling them in.

Was that the extent of her welcome? Kathy thought. At least Jacqui had made an effort.

'Is this the dog, then?'

'Yes, this is Baxter.'

He was up and excited again at Alex's arrival, panting loudly and pushing his nose against Alex's hand, even barking once or twice. Kathy shut her eyes momentarily. Baxter would learn to calm down in time, she just had to be patient. Not for the first time, she counted to ten.

'He's quite a handful,' said Alex, but he stroked Baxter nonetheless. 'Hello, boy.'

'Oh, he's nothing I can't manage,' said Kathy, praying that Baxter wouldn't choose that moment to launch himself onto the sofa and trample all over her, desperate for attention.

Alex was talking to Jacqui. 'We need to sort tables for tonight; someone's double-booked.'

'On it,' said Jacqui.

'Are you very busy, dear?' she asked her son.

Alex nodded. 'Yeah, but I'm sure we can still do the stuff we planned this weekend. Jacqui's had some great ideas.'

Jacqui turned her attention away from the desk and back to them.

'Yep. I thought we'd eat at the pub tonight, so you can experience the new menu, Kath. And we're dog friendly. Then tomorrow, we're going to Michelham Priory for a look around, the gardens are beautiful. Then in the evening, we thought we'd head off to a little food fete. One of our friends has organised it. We can wander around the stalls and sample everything, and there's some bands on, too.'

Kathy's mind was reeling. It sounded action-packed.

'Oh, um, great,' she said. 'Sounds wonderful. But really, don't worry about entertaining me. I'm happy just to fit in.'

'You're our guest,' said Jacqui firmly.

She wasn't sure she wanted to be thought of as a guest. She wanted to be family.

'Let me show you to your room.'

Jacqui picked up Kathy's travel bag – Kathy hoped she didn't notice she wasn't using the suitcase – and took it upstairs. She showed Kathy to a pretty guest room, made up in white and blue linens.

'Becs! Come out and say hello.'

A sigh, a thump, and a door on the landing opened to reveal Becs, scowling and looking at her feet.

'Hello,' she said, and prepared to shut the door again. Then she saw Baxter. 'A dog?' she said.

Kathy noticed how the girl's sulky face lit up.

'Yes,' said Jacqui. 'Baxter, Kathy's foster dog. And if you're good, and stop this ridiculous sulk, then maybe Kathy will let you play with him.'

Becs glared at her mother, her brows lowered once again. 'I'm not being ridiculous. And I don't want to play with the dog, anyway.' And she turned back into her room and shut the door.

Jacqui sighed. 'Sorry. She's in a sulk because she wants to go to some party tomorrow night and we've said no, she has to come with us. She's too young and her schoolwork's been slacking off.'

Kathy had felt a surprising pang of sympathy for the girl. She'd looked so unhappy in her own skin when she'd emerged. And when she'd seen Baxter, for a few brief moments, Kathy had had a glimpse of what Becs might be like in a different mood. It was a shame Jacqui had pounced on her, just when Becs was being drawn out of herself. But she should keep her opinions to herself, she decided. It hadn't gone well at Christmas when she'd attempted to intervene between mother and daughter.

'I might just take half an hour to settle in,' Kathy ventured.

'Of course! We'll just be downstairs.'

Jacqui bustled off downstairs, where Kathy could hear her talking to Alex about rosters and suchlike, and plans for the pub quiz the following week, plus they needed to talk about bookings for things like engagement parties, and they'd even had someone enquiring about wedding catering. Kathy's head buzzed. She remembered a time when she'd been that busy, when life had been PTA meetings, bake sales, staff meetings, assemblies – and it had flown by. And she had loved it.

Baxter gave a little groan as he settled down on the floor, finally tired out, as if reminding Kathy of what she was doing now. And he was right, she thought. Through Battersea, she did have a sense of her life having purpose once more. She felt herself growing in confidence as the months went by. Life wasn't quite like it had been before, but it was a start, wasn't it?

Kathy went for a walk in the afternoon, with Jacqui showing her around the town and Alex accompanying them, but he spent a lot of time on the phone, talking to suppliers.

Was it just her, Kathy wondered, or did things seem a bit strained between Jacqui and Alex? No wonder, given the pressure they were under, but before they'd left home, Alex had asked Jacqui if she'd sorted the table clash and she'd snapped, 'I'm waiting to hear back about the new time!' at him, and he'd raised his hands defensively.

As they reached the entrance to a pretty park, Baxter bursting with energy at the prospect of new people to meet, Jacqui's phone rang. She answered it, dropping back and motioning that they should go ahead.

Kathy was pleased to get a moment or two with Alex. It seemed so long since they'd spoken properly.

'So, how are things?' she ventured.

'Fine,' he said distractedly. 'Just very busy.'

'And all OK with Jacqui?'

'Yes, Mum. We're just under pressure.'

'I was just asking,' said Kathy. Was she that much of a busybody? She tried more neutral territory. 'It's so nice to come down here, after Christmas.'

'Mmm?' said Alex. 'Oh, yes. Spend some time together, that's right.'

'And it's nice you get to meet Baxter,' said Kathy. 'I know you were worried, but I'm loving fostering.'

'Sorry, Mum, I haven't asked you anything,' Alex said. 'I'm glad it's going well. He's a nice dog, that's for sure.'

Kathy bit her lip in frustration. She understood Alex's worry about her, but that didn't translate to being really interested in her life.

Then Jacqui was back, sighing. 'We're going to need to shift some tables, magic up some more room. They can make it a bit later, but not enough.'

Alex groaned.

'I did my best, Alex!' Jacqui said, her tone piqued. 'It's not my fault the booking was messed up!'

'Can I help?' said Kathy.

They both looked at her.

'Mum, it's shifting tables about,' said Alex. 'And you're meant to be relaxing.'

'I don't mind mucking in,' said Kathy. 'I'd rather help out the two of you than be lazing about.'

Alex blew out his cheeks. 'Well, if you don't mind, that would be great.'

But Jacqui didn't look pleased. 'If anyone is going to do it, it should be Becs. We've been on at her to help out more for her allowance.'

'Just leave her to it,' said Kathy firmly. Why couldn't Jacqui just accept her offer? 'Then we can all have a nice meal together tonight.'

Jacqui nodded but didn't smile.

They headed out of the park and walked towards the pub. Whatever the dynamic between the two of them, Kathy noticed how their eyes lit up as they showed her the results of their hard work.

The pub was lovely. It was an old building, made from

smart, sandy-coloured brick with square windows, the woodwork painted in bright white. A sign out front declared it as The Devonshire.

'It'll look really nice when the geraniums are out,' Jacqui said, glancing at Kathy, who'd spotted the neat window boxes.

'It looks wonderful now,' Kathy said, amazed at what her son and Jacqui had created.

They were a formidable team. She began to understand a little more about how much the business absorbed them, how much care and energy went into creating something like this.

Inside, the floor was lined with oak and the beer taps gleamed on a pristine bar. There were cushioned booths for people to sit in and a fireplace that would be incredibly cosy in winter. It was a perfect combination of being smart yet comfortable. Baxter glanced around and seemed right at home, tail wagging.

'What do you think, Mum?' said Alex nervously.

'It's absolutely beautiful,' Kathy replied.

'And you've not even seen the dining room – follow me.'

Kathy followed them to the back of the pub, to a dining room that had been opened out with a modern extension, lined in warm wood.

'And there's a room upstairs, as well,' said Jacqui, indicating with her arm. 'Which is normally what we'd let out for private dinners, but we can squish a few more tables in there tonight and rearrange.'

Kathy nodded and rolled up her sleeves. 'Just tell me what to do.'

'Boss, I need you in the kitchen.' A young woman, in chefs' whites, appeared by Alex's side, looking worried. 'Not sure we've got enough sea bass for the fish option tonight.'

'OK, I'll be in,' said Alex, snapping into professional mode. 'Don't worry, we'll sort it. Sorry to leave you to it, ladies, I'll join when I can.'

What followed was an hour or so of tough work as Kathy helped Jacqui to heave the heavy tables and chairs about, while Baxter did his best to get under their feet. Jacqui had an incredible amount of energy and Kathy was determined to keep up, though she gratefully accepted Jacqui's offer of a lemonade when they took a break.

'You're a real workhorse,' said Kathy, and Jacqui smiled.

'Not so bad yourself. And we really appreciate it. Could you help me with setting the tables, and then we can be off? Well, until we come back to eat!'

The tables set, they went home for a few hours and Kathy rested before freshening up for dinner. She put her colourful necklace on and reflected on how funny it was that Judith was back in her life. She wondered if she would get to see Jessica again and find out how she was getting on.

Whereas Judith could talk for England on almost any subject, she still seemed a bit reticent when it came to Jessica. And, come to think of it, she felt like Judith had been avoiding her these last few weeks. Maybe she was just being paranoid, but Judith hadn't answered her text messages with her usual speed and Kathy hadn't been over to hers, or vice versa, since she'd said goodbye to Milly, despite suggesting it once or twice.

Kathy picked up her phone and sent Judith a message, asking how her weekend was and saying they should walk another section of the Thames Path soon. Kathy hoped she hadn't done anything to offend her without realising.

They all returned to the pub for dinner with a silent Becs in tow. The meal was delicious – a generous serving of sea bass with fresh vegetables, followed by a sticky toffee pudding, and accompanied by several glasses of good wine. Alex did keep darting off to the kitchen, which made the conversation stilted, and Becs was monotone, replying only briefly to Kathy's questions, but Jacqui kept up her end of the conversation, with lots of details about plans for the pub and telling Kathy about her family back in Australia.

But Kathy couldn't help but feel it wasn't . . . *intimate.* It wasn't family, where conversation flowed and laughter was easy. It was an effort. Still, better than Christmas, she reminded herself, and touched Baxter's ears under the table for reassurance. At least she had him, she thought. Someone on her team.

The next day, they drove to the priory. The Tudor mansion was absolutely beautiful, as were the gardens and winding moat, teeming with life. Baxter grunted his approval, and was very excited to see a dragonfly.

'Would you like to take him for a bit?' Kathy asked Alex, praying he'd say yes. Baxter was so strong.

'Sure.' Alex took the lead from her. 'Dad used to love stuff like this, didn't he, Mum?' added Alex, glancing over at her.

'Yes, he did,' Kathy said.

She wanted to say more. She'd been thinking the same thing, remembering how John had often bundled them into the car and driven them to all sorts of places. He was a real history buff.

'I just love imagining all the people who have walked here,' he'd say to them, eyes shining, and she and Alex had been caught up in his enthusiasm.

She remembered one funny incident, when Alex had been young, where they'd encountered a man dressed up as a Roman soldier, leading a tour group. Alex had seen him and had run back to them, shouting, 'There's a time traveller!'

She wanted to see if her son remembered, but when she opened her mouth, the words wouldn't come.

'Ice cream season looks to have started,' she said instead, gesticulating to a small girl licking a vanilla cone as she walked past them.

And then she was off, another memory rising up. She remembered that whenever she said that, John would insist it was never too cold for an ice cream. She'd fed him spoonfuls of sweet vanilla in those last days, watching him savour every tiny morsel. She felt tears form in her eyes. All these memories, even the happy ones, were tinged with pain. Would she ever be able to feel otherwise?

'I'm not sure about an ice cream, but I could do with a coffee,' Jacqui said. 'Shall we head to the café?'

'Good plan,' Kathy said briskly, and set off at a pace.

When they got back in the car afterwards, Alex's phone rang.

He groaned as he looked at it and answered with a curt, 'Hello?'

Kathy had a sinking feeling, and she was right. After he got off the phone, he looked around at them all.

'I'm so sorry. Jacqui, we're going to have to go in tonight. Sasha's off sick and they're still a server down. I'm really sorry. It means we can't go to the fete.'

'Oh, what a shame,' Kathy said.

But it was Becs who groaned in frustration and kicked the seat.

'I never get to do *anything*! At least some of my friends who weren't going to the party might have been at that.'

'Maybe Kathy would still take you?' said Jacqui.

Kathy wasn't sure about that. It would have been one thing going with Alex and Jacqui, but it was quite another going and being in charge of Becs, who hadn't said more than two words to her.

'No,' said Becs. 'It wouldn't be any fun. So, it'll just be *another* Saturday night in by myself.' She pulled up her hood and turned to look out of the car window, scowling.

Kathy raised her eyebrows and counted to ten. She reminded herself that Becs was at a contradictory, difficult age.

'Well, we could do something,' ventured Kathy. 'Even if we stay in. Watch a film?'

But Becs just shrugged and turned even further towards the window.

The mood in the car had soured. Jacqui and Alex were now focused on discussing the staff, if they should look for someone else who could help out in these kind of circumstances, and if they could afford it. Becs' frustration and unhappiness radiated out. Only Baxter, dear Baxter, was still smiling.

*

Kathy was glad to get some space of her own. Becs had stomped up to her bedroom as soon as they'd got in, and Alex and Jacqui had headed off immediately, apologising over and over again.

'Don't worry,' Kathy had said, and she meant it. But there was a nagging feeling that she didn't fit here, that she didn't have a space.

She fed Baxter and settled down to watch some TV with him. Still no message back from Judith. She fixed herself a light supper of leftovers from the fridge, wondering if she should have called up to Becs to see if she wanted any food. As she assembled her plate, she became aware of a particular kind of silence – a suspicious silence. Every dog owner seemed to develop a sixth sense around this silence and she was no different. Baxter was up to something.

She went into the hallway, where, sure enough, Baxter was delightedly chewing Becs' trainers. She'd left them untidily in the hallway as soon as they'd got in. Kathy groaned. She should have thought to tell Becs to put them away. There was absolutely no point scolding him. She offered him another toy instead, saying, 'Drop it', then praised him when he came away from the trainers.

They were absolutely ruined. Those powerful Staffie jaws had well and truly mashed them. And no doubt Becs would be furious and then Jacqui would be angry at Becs for not putting her trainers away – or worse, angry at Kathy for not keeping an eye on Baxter. She'd have to confess to Becs what Baxter had done.

Swallowing her nerves, Kathy climbed the stairs to Becs' room and knocked on the door.

'What is it?' came Becs' voice from within.

'Can I talk to you for a moment?'

There was the sound of Becs getting off the bed with a sigh and then the door opened.

'Yes?'

'I'm really sorry. But Baxter has chewed your trainers.'

Becs' face was a picture of disbelief. 'Really? Are they ruined?'

Kathy nodded grimly. 'Yes, I'm so sorry. I'll buy you some new ones, of course, and—' She broke off as Becs' face split into a wide grin.

'This is fantastic! I *hate* those trainers! Well done, Baxter! Where is he? Can I see . . . ?' And she was out of her room and zipping down the stairs.

Kathy followed her. She'd put the trainers on the kitchen table and found Becs laughing in delight over them.

'Oh my God! He's done a good job. Where is he? Baxter!'

Baxter didn't need to be asked twice. He came straight over at the sound of his name and Becs fussed him adoringly.

Kathy let her – it wasn't like Baxter would associate the attention with having chewed her shoes ten minutes ago.

'You're the best dog in the world,' cooed Becs.

'So . . . you're not angry?'

'No, he's done me a favour, getting rid of those. They were so old, anyway.'

Well, Kathy would take a win where she could get it. This was the most animated she'd ever seen Becs.

'Won't your mum be angry?'

'She can hardly be cross with poor old Baxter, can she? She adores him. So, what's the deal with his skin? And his ears?'

Kathy explained it all to her. 'Actually,' she said, glancing at her watch, 'I should probably give him his treatments now.'

'Can I help?'

Kathy was pleasantly surprised by the girl's eagerness. 'Yes, of course you can.'

She began setting out everything they needed, including the ear drops, clean water, cotton pads and his skin cream. Baxter's face fell when he saw what she was doing.

'Poor boy. He hates this part,' said Kathy.

Becs nodded. 'Does it hurt him?'

'A little bit, I think,' Kathy confessed. 'And I hate hurting him.'

'But his ears would hurt him anyway,' said Becs, making eye contact with Kathy for the first time. 'So, you're doing the right thing.'

Kathy appreciated her words. 'That's a nice way of looking at it.'

Kathy showed her what she was doing and Becs watched closely. She kept her hands on the dog, soothing him as Kathy worked.

'I'd say you've got a friend for life there,' said Kathy.

'I wish,' said Becs, smiling. 'He's brilliant.'

'Do you want to apply a bit of cream?'

Becs nodded and Kathy handed her the ointment then watched as she gently applied it.

'That's it. Well done! That's him all patched up for tonight.'

'How long will it take for it all to go?'

'His skin's making progress already.' This was true – she'd taken Baxter for his weekly check-up with Fatima and she'd been pleased at the signs of improvement. Visibly, it was all much better. 'But his ears will take longer. The infection is very deeply rooted, unfortunately.'

Becs shook her head angrily. 'I can't believe people let him get like this.'

'I know,' said Kathy. 'It makes me so furious. But on the bright side, he's getting the best possible treatment through Battersea now.'

Becs cleared up the bowl of water and the used cotton pads. Baxter visibly relaxed now that he knew the treatment was over. He went over to Becs again and pressed himself against her legs, his tail thumping on her calves. Kathy saw how genuinely she smiled as she bent down to fuss him. She had a lovely gap between her front teeth and there was a lot of Jacqui in the shape of her jawline. It was heart-warming to see a different side of her emerge, all thanks to Baxter. Animals could reach people in a way humans sometimes couldn't reach each other.

'It must be boring for you, stuck in on a Saturday night,' Kathy ventured.

Becs straightened up and sighed, pausing before responding.

'It's just . . . it's just . . . *lonely*,' she said to Kathy, making eye contact briefly before turning her gaze back to Baxter.

'It's always the pub. And they're a team. And I'm left feeling like a nuisance who needs to be looked after.'

Kathy wanted to rush in, to say, 'Oh, don't be silly, they love you!' but she forced herself to be quiet.

'That sounds tough,' she said after a pause.

Becs nodded. 'It can be. And my friends, they live a bus-ride away, where the school is. So they're always able to meet up and do things. And if I can't get a lift from Mum or Alex, I just have to stay put.'

Suddenly, Kathy was seeing things Becs' way. It must be difficult for her, spending so much time by herself, without brothers or sisters or friends nearby.

'Do you know,' Becs continued, stooping down again to pet Baxter, 'I always dreamed of having a dog.'

Kathy remembered the girl's excitement at Christmas, when she'd thought that might be the moment her wish came true.

'Just someone to look after, and to look after you. To be with you.'

Kathy smiled. 'I know exactly what you mean.'

Becs looked at her. 'Do you?'

'I do. I'm also alone a lot of the time. And it's hard to admit to being lonely, isn't it?'

'That's it,' said Becs. 'Even with my friends. It's not cool to say you had a boring weekend waiting for your mum to finish work. They seem to be off doing stuff all the time. And if I had a dog, I could take him for walks. We could hang out all the time. It wouldn't be so bad.'

'Well, when you're older . . .' Kathy began before realising she was stepping right back into a cliché. 'Sorry. You must hear that all the time.'

'I do,' said Becs, but her tone was light. 'And yeah, I can't wait until I can have a dog all of my own.'

'Well,' said Kathy. 'We can share this one, for as long as I've got him.'

Becs beamed. 'Really?'

'Yes. You could even come up to London and see him.'

'I'd really like that.'

'So, if you're practising being a dog owner, do you want to come with me for his evening walk? He just needs a few minutes round the block to stretch his legs.'

Becs looked thrilled.

'Yeah!'

She went and pulled on her parka and boots, while Kathy went to get Baxter's lead, fastening it to his collar.

'Here, you hold him.'

Kathy passed Becs the lead and they headed out of the house. It was dusk, the light fading from the sky. Becs' posture and demeanour were so different, Kathy noticed. Shoulders back, head up as she spoke to Baxter with a bright voice.

'And you'll need these,' Kathy said with a smirk as she handed over the poo bags.

'Oh, gross! Do I have to pick it up?'

'Yep,' said Kathy. 'It's a very important part of being a dog owner.'

She was expecting some theatrics, but Becs simply got on with cleaning up after Baxter and they continued their walk.

'Will you take a photo of us?' said Becs, passing Kathy her phone.

'Sure.'

Taking a photo was quite the operation, Kathy found out. Becs came back to check what she'd done and advise on the camera angle, insisting she took more shots, but eventually they had one she was happy with.

'And now a selfie with you,' Becs said. 'If we crouch down, I can get us all in. Smile!'

'Oh, God, take another!' said Kathy, examining her chins. When had *they* appeared?

Becs obliged, offering Kathy still more advice about how to pose, and they ended up with a photo they all loved. Baxter, naturally, looked good in every one.

Back at home, they slumped in front of the TV.

'There's all sorts of terrible television on, you can choose,' said Kathy, passing Becs the remote. 'Baxter doesn't mind. Hopefully, he'll fall asleep – and to be honest, I might, as well.'

Becs chose some terrible reality TV dating show that Kathy could barely follow. But she was surprised to find that they ended up chatting most of the way through it. Becs was keen to hear all about Battersea and what they did there. And she replied fully when Kathy asked about her life, about school, about her favourite subjects and teachers. With Baxter snoozing by the hearth, and the background chatter of the telly, the living room was cosy and intimate. Kathy realised that she now felt at home here.

'Look, I want to say something,' said Becs. 'Those books you got me for Christmas. They were really good. Especially *White Fang*. So, thanks. And sorry. About how I was. Friends?'

'Well, likewise,' said Kathy. 'I think I could have taken a different tone. So I'm sorry, too, and we're absolutely friends. And I'm glad you liked the books. They're two of my favourites.'

Baxter's legs began twitching as he lay asleep.

'He's dreaming!' said Kathy, and they both watched, amused at the flickers that animated the dog's face.

'I wonder what about,' said Becs.

'His forever home, probably,' said Kathy. 'Or your trainers.'

'Don't you want to keep him?' said Becs. 'How will you cope when he goes?'

Kathy sighed. 'A very good question. And one I'd rather not think about. I just know that he has to go to a home that can give him everything he needs.'

Becs shook her head knowingly. 'I reckon that's your dog. Our dog. You just need to realise it for yourself. You'll see.'

And Kathy wondered if she might just be right.

Chapter 10

Kathy and Becs had turned in before Alex and Jacqui got home. On Sunday morning, though, Jacqui was still first up, bustling in the kitchen with the kettle boiling.

'I can do that,' said Kathy, coming downstairs to let Baxter into the small back garden.

'Oh, it's no bother,' said Jacqui, smiling brightly.

She looked tired, thought Kathy. There were dark circles under her eyes.

'What time did you get in?'

'About 2 a.m. By the time we'd finished clearing everything.'

'You must be exhausted. Look, I have to confess something. Baxter made mincemeat of Becs' trainers. I am sorry. He can be a bit of a chewer and I just didn't notice what he was up to. I'll pay for a new pair, of course.' Kathy felt nervous about how she'd respond and was glad to see Baxter head towards Jacqui with his most appealing expression.

Jacqui sighed. 'Oh, well, it's done now. You can't be cross with this face for long. And I should imagine Becs will be very happy to have a new pair.' She rolled her eyes at Kathy, who suddenly felt defensive of the girl.

'She's a wonderful girl. We actually had a very nice time together last night, chatting about Battersea and—'

'Great,' interrupted Jacqui. 'I'm glad. So, what's this about Battersea? I'm going to look it all up as well.'

She was like a laser beam, thought Kathy. Sweeping round everything, keen to miss nothing. Why had she jumped in, when Kathy would have gone on to tell her more about Battersea anyway if she hadn't interrupted? She supposed it was interest, but it felt like Jacqui wanting to be in control.

'There's tea in the pot. I'll just take Alex a cuppa and then I'll be back down.'

'Don't worry, Jacqui. I confess, I was about to take myself a cup of tea and drink it in bed, wake up slowly as it's Sunday.'

Jacqui looked relieved. 'If you're sure?'

'Absolutely sure. And you should do the same. There's no point us all being up if Becs is having a lie-in, and I'm not even hungry yet.'

'Well, there's always things to be done,' said Jacqui, but Kathy could tell her heart wasn't in it.

Jacqui poured two mugs of tea and went back upstairs, Kathy following shortly after, having retrieved Baxter from the garden.

She checked her phone.

A reply, from Judith.

'Hi, Kathy, sorry to be a bit AWOL. Is this the weekend you're with the family? How is it?'

'Lovely, thanks,' Kathy typed back.

She half wanted to explain the truth of it – that Alex had been distracted, that even though Jacqui was making an effort, it all felt a bit strained – but she somehow couldn't bring herself to shatter the perfect idea that Judith had of Kathy's family. And there had been good parts. Spending the evening with Becs had been lovely.

She sent the selfie of the three of them. 'Baxter went down a treat! You'll have to come round and meet him. How are things with you?'

'I certainly will!' said Judith. 'Glad you're having a good time.'

And that was it. No mention of how things were with her. Kathy felt sure there was something up. She resolved to drop in on Judith for a coffee and see what was going on.

Kathy ventured downstairs again at about 9 a.m., her stomach rumbling. She'd heard movement from Becs' bedroom and hoped she was getting up, too. In the kitchen, there were eggs laid out. Kathy thought she'd make herself useful and scramble them, so she cracked them into a bowl and began whisking them.

'Oh,' said Jacqui, coming into the kitchen behind her. 'I was going to do poached.'

'Sorry,' said Kathy, feeling in the way again. 'I didn't think.'

'I like scrambled, anyway,' said Becs, entering the kitchen and giving Baxter a big kiss on his head.

She looked up at Kathy and winked. Kathy smiled back, glad that at least someone seemed pleased she was there.

'I hear the two of you had a good night in?' said Jacqui to her daughter.

'Yeah. I've been looking at the Battersea website this morning!'

Becs pulled out her phone and showed her mum. 'See, how amazing does that look? And look, all these dogs, in need of a new home.'

'Don't start,' said Jacqui sharply.

Becs scowled. 'I wasn't. I was just showing you. What Kathy does. Anyway, we're sharing Baxter now, aren't we?'

Kathy nodded, unsure of how to navigate this territory. She didn't want to annoy Jacqui, but she wished that she'd let Becs speak.

Jacqui sighed. 'Let's have a look, then.'

Becs handed her the phone and Jacqui scrolled through the photos.

'What are you looking at?' said Alex, coming through into the kitchen, yawning, stopping to pet Baxter, who was in seventh heaven with all the fuss.

'Good morning, darling,' said Kathy, delighted to see her son. 'Come and sit here. I'll pour you some tea.'

'Already done,' said Jacqui, placing a fresh cup in front of Alex.

'We're looking at the Battersea website,' said Becs.

Alex peered at the phone screen over Jacqui's shoulder and tapped the screen once or twice.

'Tugs on the heartstrings, all right,' he said. 'Mum, was Buddy from there?'

'Who's Buddy?' asked Becs.

'He was our family dog when Alex was growing up. And no, he wasn't – we took him from a friend of your dad's, who couldn't cope with a puppy. We always wanted another dog, a rescue, of course, but then life got . . . complicated.'

'Have you got a picture?' Becs wanted to know.

Kathy shook her head. 'But I tell you what, I'll have a look when I get home and send you one in a message, all right?'

Becs nodded happily.

'Hey, look at this,' Jacqui said, holding up the phone. 'The Muddy Dog Challenge! It sounds fun! It's an obstacle course race, to raise money for Battersea. You can do either 2.5 kilometres or 5, with or without a dog. And they're in some beautiful places. We could all go?'

'Yes!' said Becs, eyes shining. 'And Baxter, too! He deserves a big day out.'

'I'm not sure I could cope with an obstacle course,' Kathy began, feeling nervous. Sweeping up was one thing, but picking your way through mud was quite another. 'And I'd have to check with the foster team to see if they thought Baxter would be all right.'

'We could pick one that's a few months away. Get some training in,' Jacqui continued, flicking through the options. 'Oh, look – there's this one, in Windsor! That looks beautiful! How about it?'

Kathy's heart plunged. Windsor had been one of her and John's favourite places.

'Mum? What do you think?' said Alex. 'Or would it be too much for you to handle?'

Now Kathy was torn! Alex thinking it was too much for her to handle would be a convenient way out of the situation, but she hated that he saw her as so frail.

'Oh, well, I'm—' Kathy began.

'Honestly, Alex, I'm sure she'll be fine,' said Jacqui. 'It says here on the website that it's for all levels of ability.'

Kathy had to fight hard not to roll her eyes.

'Didn't we used to go there with Dad when I was little?' asked Alex.

Kathy nodded, not trusting herself to speak without tears welling up.

'Well, surely that settles it?' Jacqui said. 'Look, I can just click on the registration now . . .'

She was such a bulldozer, Kathy thought. But then she caught sight of Becs' face, looking at her, eyes hopeful.

'Please, Kathy?' said Becs. 'Please? And with Baxter?'

'There's no guarantee I'll still be fostering him then,' began Kathy, but Becs was smiling.

'No, because you'll have adopted him properly by then,' Becs said, and Kathy didn't have the heart to correct her that fostering was meant to be temporary.

'I think the race would be fun, Mum,' said Alex. 'And it would be nice to do something as a family again.'

How could she say no? Wasn't this what she'd wanted? She'd just have to grit her teeth and get on with it, try to ignore the painful memories of John. With any luck, Alex and Jacqui would have to pull out of it, given how busy they were with the pub. She felt devious thinking like that, but she could make it up to Becs some other way. Take her and Baxter for a long walk elsewhere.

'Absolutely,' Kathy said with a conviction she didn't feel. 'I'll have to check with the foster team first.'

'You do that and I'll handle registrations,' said Jacqui with a smile. 'Now, let's eat.'

*

Kathy left mid-morning after breakfast, having taken Baxter for a walk with Becs. Alex and Jacqui were putting their heads together about changes to the menu and had stayed at home.

'It never stops, does it?' said Kathy to Becs, who shook her head ruefully.

'Thanks for coming,' said Becs. 'It was really nice.'

'Oh, I'm glad you enjoyed meeting Baxter!'

'Not just Baxter,' Becs said, looking up shyly at Kathy. 'You, too. It was nice to have someone to talk to.'

'I'm always here if you want someone to talk to,' said Kathy. 'Really.'

And then Becs gave her a hug. Kathy was taken aback at first, but then her arms found her way around the teenager's small frame and she squeezed Becs back.

'And I really am sorry,' said Becs, 'for being such a nightmare at Christmas.'

Kathy laughed. 'We all have our moments. Me included.'

'Do you think you'll come to our house for Christmas this year?'

'Oh,' said Kathy. 'Oh, well, I'm not sure . . .'

Kathy was stalling for time. She hadn't yet told Alex about the Thailand plan. If he'd been dubious about her volunteering at the rescue home, he wasn't exactly going to be thrilled about her heading off to the other side of the world for four weeks. She had to get cracking on arrangements, as well, do some proper planning. She'd feel more confident when things were in place.

'Well, I hope you do,' said Becs. 'You and Baxter. His first Christmas at home! How good would that be!'

Kathy smiled at her. 'Come on, best be getting back. I've the drive back to London to tackle.'

*

When she got back in the early afternoon, it was a relief to open the front door and be home. Baxter scampered in ahead of her, his claws clicking on the tiles in the kitchen, then he stretched and shook himself vigorously.

'Pleased to be home, eh, boy?' said Kathy.

Baxter turned and looked at her, his smiling mouth wide, tongue lolling.

'I tell you what,' said Kathy. 'Why don't we freshen up and go and pay our neighbour, Judith, a little visit?'

She was still sure that something wasn't quite right with Judith. She had a quick shower and a change of clothes, then headed over.

She knocked on the door a couple of times and was about to give up, when Judith eventually answered, bleary-eyed.

'Oh, Kathy! It's you. I was just snoozing on the sofa.'

'I'm sorry,' said Kathy, 'I should have checked beforehand. I just wanted to see if you fancied a quick walk with me and Baxter; he was keen to meet you.'

Judith looked down at him and smiled.

'I think I feel quite "in", but why don't you come in for a cup of tea?'

Kathy wondered if she'd done the right thing, turning up unannounced, but Judith seemed happy to see her. She went through to the kitchen and sat down while Judith boiled the kettle.

'So, how's your weekend been?' Kathy asked.

'Fine!' said Judith brightly. 'Actually, Jessica was here this weekend. A flying visit, she's so busy.'

'Oh, I wish I'd known!' said Kathy. 'When did she go?'

'Just this morning.'

'Have you got any photos? I'd love to see her all grown up.'

Judith shook her head. 'No, we didn't take any. Too busy catching up. Biscuit?' She passed Kathy the box.

'Do tell her hello from me,' said Kathy. 'Where is it she's living, remind me?'

'Paris,' said Judith. 'She's doing her masters there, in music.'

'And I bet she's loving it!' said Kathy. 'What a wonderful city to live in. She must be an adventurous young woman.'

'She is,' said Judith. 'She's really enjoying life out there, all the restaurants, seeing the sights.'

'And what will she do afterwards?'

'The plan is to join a professional orchestra, but it's a competitive world, so she's considering teaching as a back-up.'

Kathy wondered why she'd thought there was something wrong with Judith. She'd been mistaken, clearly. She seemed happy, enjoying talking about her daughter; although it did seem a bit strange that Judith hadn't wanted to show her any photos.

'And will you go and visit her?'

'Oh, yes. Perhaps at Christmas.'

'That'll be lovely! The two of us, off on our travels.'

'What does Alex think about you heading off?'

Kathy glanced at Judith and sighed. 'He doesn't know. I need to find the right moment to tell him. I don't want him to worry about me. That'll make me worried about going. I need to get planning, actually.'

'It's just because he's protective over you. He'll come round. Look, I've always dreamed of going to Asia. Could I help you a bit with the planning?'

'Oh, wonderful!' said Kathy. 'I've got a few ideas of my own, but it would be great to have two heads on it.'

'Let's do it one night this week,' said Judith. 'Whenever you like. Just let me know. I can come round to yours, or you could bring him over again.' She reached out to Baxter and patted him.

'I'll leave you to your Sunday,' Kathy said, draining her tea and getting up.

She said goodbye to Judith and it was only as the door shut behind her that she realised she'd left Baxter's ball in there. Drat! She turned back, ready to knock again, when she heard a small muffled sound coming from inside the door. A sob. There was no mistaking it.

She wasn't sure what to do. She felt like she'd intruded enough on Judith. And if she wasn't ready to talk, Kathy could hardly make her. She turned back and walked quietly down the path, wondering what on earth was going on.

Chapter 11

There was no sign of sadness from Judith when Kathy went round later in the week. They spent a pleasant evening together, swapping tales of their volunteer days and scribbling down plans for the Thailand trip in a notebook, hooting with laughter at some of the possibilities the trip posed.

'I'm not keen on this backpacker malarkey,' said Kathy, peering at a photo of the Khao San Road.

They were checking out accommodation options. Although Kathy knew the done thing was to go with the flow and find accommodation as you went, the organiser in her quailed at that kind of approach. She didn't fancy these backpacker hostels that much; they looked full of twenty-somethings getting very drunk.

'Can you picture their faces if I walked in?' said Kathy. 'I can't imagine a bigger buzzkill than me turning up!'

'Maybe there'd be some former students among them,' suggested Judith.

'I'd send them to the naughty corner if any of them were carrying on like that lot are!'

After a lot of looking, they found a pleasant, affordable hotel in Bangkok, out of the way of the main tourist area, but still nice and central.

It was becoming more real, Kathy thought. She gulped back nerves. It would be the trip of a lifetime. And yes, Alex and Jacqui might invite her down for Christmas, but who's to say it would go any better than before? Would Alex and Jacqui have to go to the pub last minute? Or worse, what if they all went to Australia? Jacqui had looked so wistful when she'd described it to Kathy. No, the Thailand plan was the best. And she should stick to it.

*

The following week, after his check-up, Kathy went to Asha's cafe with Baxter, to continue her planning. She kept getting interrupted by people keen to know about the dog, and it was always a pleasure to talk about him. He was such a brilliant ambassador for the Staffie breed. She was finally getting engrossed in the *Lonely Planet* travel guide, when a voice made her jump.

'Diving in Koh Tao,' Ben said, holding a takeaway coffee. 'Planning for your trip?'

'Yes,' she replied. It was a while since they'd spoken and she was surprised to find she was flustered.

'Well, let me know if I can be of any help.'

'Actually, that would be handy. Any tips you've got would be great.'

'I've got to dash, but would you fancy grabbing a bite to eat and I can tell you then? I know a great Thai restaurant we could go to.'

'Oh, well, yes, yes,' said Kathy, stuttering, knowing she was blushing to the roots of her hair. 'Sure! That would be lovely.'

'Great,' said Ben, smiling. 'I'll message you about it. See you later!'

Her heart was pounding. He couldn't have meant a date, could he? No. He meant it as friends.

Asha came over, one eyebrow arched. 'You know, the way he looks at you . . .' she began.

'I don't know what you mean,' said Kathy primly. 'There's not much to look at, anyway.'

Asha rolled her eyes. 'For goodness' sake, Kathy! He's a bit dishy, isn't he?'

Kathy didn't know how to answer and settled for 'Mmm.' Couldn't Baxter choose this moment to knock something over?

'Bit of a man of mystery, though,' continued Asha. 'I'm clearly a much bigger gossip than you are! No one at Battersea is quite sure of his personal life, keeps himself to himself. Who knows, maybe he has some glamorous celebrity wife in tow.'

Kathy knew that Asha was only joking around, but she felt uncomfortable. Did Ben have something to hide?

'I think he's just being friendly,' she said firmly, draining her coffee.

'Take no notice of me,' said Asha. 'I'm sure you're right. I should stop watching so many soap operas.'

*

That said, Kathy found herself picking out her outfit carefully the following Tuesday night. She settled on a black polo neck, flattering jeans and her colourful necklace from Jessica and Judith. She kissed a snoozing Baxter goodbye and set off to the restaurant, feeling nervous.

Ben was already there waiting for her, which was a surprise given his punctuality record.

'Kathy!' he said, standing to greet her, and somehow knocking his knife to the floor. 'Oh, whoops!' he chuckled and stooped to retrieve it, seemingly not noticing the other diners glancing round at the clatter.

Kathy felt self-conscious. 'Hi, Ben,' she said stiffly.

'Sit down, sit down. I've ordered us some prawn crackers to nibble on. What do you fancy to drink?' He motioned the waiter over, who beamed and came immediately to their table. 'This here is Kasem, working here while he saves up for uni.'

How did Ben already know that? wondered Kathy.

'I'll have a glass of white wine, please,' she said.

'Just a sparkling water for me,' added Ben. 'Thanks very much.' And then, when the waiter had gone, 'I'm a bit of a regular here. Once you've tried their pad thai, you'll find yourself craving it with alarming frequency.'

'Well, I'll need to warm up for Thailand itself,' said Kathy. 'I can't wait for the food.'

'You'll love it,' said Ben. 'I came back several pounds heavier. Here, take a look at the menu. And whatever you fancy – it's on me.'

'Oh, no, I couldn't,' said Kathy, blushing again, but Ben held up his hand to still her.

'Please. Consider it a thank you for all the brilliant work you're doing with Baxter. His skin is looking so much better. I get updates from the foster team and we're hopeful that we can start looking for his forever home before too long, though he'll probably be with you a while longer. With dogs that have these chronic conditions, it's important to find them an owner who truly understands. I wonder if the poor lad was turfed out when they realised just how much care he'd need with his ears.'

'It makes you sick,' Kathy said. 'You don't just turn your back on someone because they need looking after.'

Ben tilted his head to the side, listening intently. 'No, you absolutely don't.' He seemed to hesitate, looking at her as if he was about to say something, then changed his mind. 'So, what do you fancy?'

They decided to share a pad thai, a red curry and a spicy Thai salad.

'This was one of my biggest surprises when I was there,' said Ben, grimacing. 'I thought I'd get something plain, a green salad, as I'd been a bit unwell, and these strips of green papaya turned up and almost blew my head off with the heat. So be warned.'

Kathy laughed.

'But you acquire a taste for it,' said Ben. 'Honestly, I envy you! What an amazing time you're going to have.'

'So, where did you go?' said Kathy, sipping her wine.

'I flew into Bangkok and then I went down to one of the islands, Koh Samui.'

Kathy pulled out her notebook and began scribbling.

Ben grinned. 'Let me guess. You were a teacher?'

'How did you know?'

'Look at how neat your handwriting is. And oh my goodness, are those colour-coded stickers?'

'They might be,' said Kathy.

She was unsure of how she felt. She knew that Ben was just teasing her, but she felt self-conscious. Planning was how she coped with life.

He held up his hands. 'Sorry. I didn't mean to annoy you. I wish I could be more organised, sometimes.'

Kathy found herself looking at his ring finger. No ring there, but was the skin paler? She told herself to stop it; Asha had just been gossiping.

'So, then, where did you go?' asked Kathy.

'I think . . . Now you're testing me. So, from there I went to a few of the other islands, including Koh Tao, and did a dive there.'

'Really?' said Kathy. 'And how was that? I'm thinking of it, but I don't know.'

'It's magical,' said Ben. 'Seeing the coral, this whole living system – and all those colourful fish. I'll never forget it.'

She wanted to ask if it had been a load of young students on the diving course – that was her fear, being seen as old and past it, but she could hardly say that to him.

'It's on the list,' she said instead with a smile.

'What else is on the list?'

'Cooking school, a trek in the jungle, a massage course, perhaps learning some Thai,' she counted on her fingers.

Ben smiled. 'Just leave some free time, is all I'd say. I didn't plan anything before I went. Instead, I just ended up chatting to people and hanging out with them for a while. Sometimes I spent a long time in one place and other times, just a night in somewhere everyone else loved but I thought wasn't me.'

'You didn't plan *at all*?' said Kathy, appalled. 'But how did you get anything done?'

He laughed. 'I think I was happy with what I did, just going by instinct.'

Their main courses arrived.

'How do you want to divide them?' asked Kathy. 'Shall I do half and half?'

Ben looked bemused. 'Or, we could just pick from each plate?'

'OK,' said Kathy uncertainly.

Her mind was buzzing, thinking it would be simpler to divide them in half, exactly, and fairer, but she'd try Ben's tactic. His approach to travel, however, made her quail.

'But what about accommodation?' she said. 'Did you book in advance?'

'No, not really,' he said. 'The first night or two I had a hotel that I'd found online. But after that, I just took my chances.'

'And that . . . worked out?'

'Overall, yes. There were a few duff experiences, including one with some cockroaches that was very unpleasant, but there were also some great ones. A Thai family I met on an overnight train let me stay with them and I wouldn't have missed that for the world. We still email, in fact.'

'But, Ben' – Kathy couldn't contain herself any longer – 'don't you see how dangerous that is? And yes, it worked out, but it may well not have done! You have to be careful!'

Ben looked down and chewed his pad thai for longer than was necessary. She'd irritated him, she knew it.

'Sorry,' she muttered.

The atmosphere between them had changed. Any thoughts of this being a date went out of the window. She found herself thinking longingly of John and the easy team they'd been. Yes, he, too, had teased her for her planning, but they'd been together for so long, the way he balanced her out felt completely natural.

He cleared his throat. 'Anyway. I'd say to check out the islands in the south and then definitely Chiang Mai city in the north. That's where you'll find your good cooking schools. I'll dig out an email I think I still have that has some recommendations from my Thai friends.' He looked down at his plate and deftly pincered some noodles with his chopsticks.

'How do you do that?' she said. 'With the chopsticks. I don't want to make a fool of myself when I'm over there.'

He smiled. 'You hold one still like this, against your forefinger.' He showed her. 'And then you kind of use the other one like a pincer, with your thumb.'

Kathy studied his hand carefully and tried to do the same. But the pincer chopstick simply slipped away. She sighed in frustration.

'Here,' said Ben. 'Like this.'

Gently, he rearranged her fingers and positioned the chopsticks in her hand. Kathy felt shivers all the way up her arm. Did Ben feel them, too?

'Try now,' he said, and she picked up a grain of rice. 'There you go.'

It was a good job she only had to chew and swallow a tiny piece of food, as her stomach was tight with butterflies.

'Although,' said Ben, his voice light, 'they actually don't use chopsticks in Thailand very often, and only for noodle dishes. It's more normal to use a spoon and a fork.'

'You could have told me that when I was struggling with the rice!' Kathy said, but she was laughing, and Ben grinned back at her.

'What, and miss out on being able to teach you something? I don't think so.'

Kathy shook her head at him, trying to be disapproving, but she couldn't keep a smile from her face.

'How long . . . How long have you worked at Battersea?' she asked. Asha's comment was circling in her head about him being a 'man of mystery'.

'About seven years,' said Ben.

'And what did you do before that?'

'I was a corporate lawyer.'

Kathy almost choked on her food. Ben, a lawyer? In some huge law firm, with big glass windows and tidy desks and everyone looking deadly serious?

'Struggling to imagine me in a suit, with my hair tidy?' He raised his eyebrows.

'Well, yes, to be honest,' Kathy said, blushing. He could read her mind.

Ben laughed. 'Good. I'm glad I've changed so much.'

The atmosphere felt much warmer between them now.

'And believe me when I say, the most challenging dogs at Battersea have nothing on my former colleagues.' He grinned at Kathy, who smiled back.

'So why the change?' she asked.

Ben exhaled. 'It's complicated.'

And like that, by his tone, Kathy knew the subject was closed. Funny, for someone so warm and open in some ways, he was actually very good at keeping his distance. Asha had been right. It only piqued her curiosity more.

'Do you miss teaching?' he asked.

'Yes, I do,' she admitted. 'I love organising, as you've probably noticed. And it was lovely being around so much life and laughter all the time. But it's funny, actually, how life works. I'm not sure if you know her, but Judith, one of the other volunteers turned out to be one of the mums from the school! Her daughter was there; she left for big school a few years before I retired. God, why am I still calling it "big school" – some habits refuse to die!'

'How wonderful that you still keep up these connections,' Ben said. 'That's what life's all about.' He looked down for a moment, his expression wistful.

'Not in touch with any of your old work colleagues?'

Ben shook his head. 'Not a chance.'

He was so adept at dodging her questions!

'So, what are you up to this weekend?' she asked.

'I'll be painting.'

'Decorating?'

'No, although I probably should get round to that.' He hesitated, before continuing, 'I . . . I love to paint landscapes. People occasionally, if I can persuade anyone to sit still for long enough.'

'Can I see some?'

Again, the hesitation. Ben looked up at the ceiling.

'Honestly, if it's private, don't worry,' added Kathy.

Ben shook his head. 'Sorry. I hardly ever show people what I do.' He pulled out his phone. 'These are just little snaps of them.'

Kathy took a look and almost gasped. The pictures were beautiful. They were mostly seascapes, swirling greys and blues, flecked with white and gold. They were wild, tender, full of emotion. Some were gentle and calm, the sea sparkling on a summer's day. Others were storm-filled, so that Kathy almost shivered from imagining the sting of water and salt on her face. She thought of the painting John had bought her, its sunshine languishing under the stairs.

'Ben, these are . . .' she said. 'I mean, you're so talented.'

'Oh, thanks, but they're just me messing around.' He looked pleased, though.

'Enough of your false modesty, mister,' said Kathy. 'You know they're good.'

He laughed. 'I'm just glad you like them.'

'Do you exhibit them?'

He shook his head. 'They tend to be more just for me. And certain privileged members of the public. You could come round and see the originals some time. If you like.'

Kathy felt her heart pounding again. 'Oh, yes, definitely.'

'I'll send you my address,' said Ben. 'Just pop over whenever suits you. Let me know first, in case I'm out.'

She didn't know how to read him. This all sounded very casual and not remotely date-like. Not that she was thinking of going on a date with him, was she? Kathy's head was spinning. Fortunately, they were soon back to chatting about Battersea.

'Have you ever rehomed a dog to anyone famous?' asked Kathy.

'I couldn't possibly tell you.'

Kathy proffered the last spring roll.

'I am very subject to bribery,' Ben said, halving it with a knife. 'We'll split it.'

Technically, it was his anyway, but Kathy appreciated the gesture.

'But yes, I have,' he said. 'Naming no names, I once matched a very famous rock star with a three-legged poodle.'

'You did not!'

'I did! They were the perfect match. Yes, he'd said he wanted something that went with his rock and roll image – I think he'd imagined a Rottweiler with a studded collar, silly bloke – but I just knew he'd be better off with little Nellie. And it was love at first sight. They got on famously.'

Kathy could just about believe it, although she was dying to know who the rock star was. She knew Battersea had matched dogs with the likes of Geri Halliwell, Jemima Khan, Robbie Williams and Kenneth Branagh, so it wasn't much of a stretch to imagine the likes of Mick Jagger heading in. The thought made her smile.

The rest of their dinner passed quickly, and after coffees, Ben paid the bill.

'I'll walk you back,' Ben said as they left the restaurant.

Kathy was about to launch into her usual routine of saying he needn't fuss, it was hardly late at all, there was no bother on these streets, when she realised how nice it would be to have Ben accompany her on the walk home.

'That would be lovely,' she said.

They walked together through the quiet streets in a comfortable silence, each alone with their thoughts.

'This is me,' said Kathy as they arrived at her gate. 'Do you want to say hello to Baxter?'

'I'd love to. If I'm not intruding?'

'Not at all.'

Kathy fumbled with her keys. She wasn't usually this clumsy, but she was aware of Ben standing behind her. Finally, she got the door open and they both stepped through into the hallway.

'Here he is.'

Baxter dashed towards them, tail wagging, tongue lolling, pressing himself against Ben's legs.

'Who's enjoying their luxury break, then,' said Ben, kneeling down to the dog, who was giving little whimpers of excitement and joy. 'He seems so much more relaxed. And look at how his skin is healing.'

'Oh, I hope so,' said Kathy. 'I love having him here. But I know you'll find him the best forever home.'

'Will it be hard for you when he goes?'

'Oh, no,' Kathy said. She wanted Ben to see her as capable, remembered how exposed she'd felt when Milly had left. 'I knew when I signed up for fostering that it would be like this and I've had a bit of practice with seeing them off, after Milly.'

Ben straightened up and she was struck again by how tall he was. They were standing near each other, as the hallway was narrow. Their eyes met and they each looked down and away from the other's gaze, then back again.

'So,' said Ben, and the word seemed to hang in the air.

The moment went on forever. Kathy opened her mouth to say something and then couldn't think of anything, only how green Ben's eyes were and how her fingers still tingled from where he'd helped her with the chopsticks. Would he hear her heart racing?

And then, 'Woof!' and Baxter dropped an enormous log on Ben's foot.

'Jesus!' said Ben, looking down. 'That hurt!'

Baxter looked very pleased with himself.

'He takes them from near the fireplace,' Kathy said. 'God knows how he manages to carry them.'

Time had started again. The moment between them had passed.

'I should be going,' said Ben. 'But thanks. For a lovely dinner.'

He stooped to kiss her on the cheek, his hand briefly resting on her shoulder, and then he was opening the door and off down the path, raising a hand in farewell to her and Baxter.

When he'd gone, Kathy pressed her hand to her shoulder, where she imagined the warmth of his touch still lingered. She exhaled. Did she have feelings for Ben?

Chapter 12

'Here you are!' said Kathy.

The girl on the bench turned to her and tugged her hoodie over her face. It was early in the morning on Clapham Common and Kathy had wondered if they'd see Hope.

Baxter had woofed happily when he'd seen Hope's hunched figure, straining at his lead to go over to her.

'He remembered you,' said Kathy. 'He gave his special woof when he saw you.'

'Really?' said Hope from under her hoodie. She regarded the dog again. 'Can I . . .' And slowly, she extended her pale, thin fingers towards Baxter.

He remained still, as if sensing her nervousness, and wagged his tail even harder when she made contact with his head and gave a little scratch.

'Not scary, after all,' said Hope. She shuffled closer to him. 'His skin looks way better than the time before.'

'It's really improving.'

The girl kept scratching Baxter's ears, silent, lost in her own thoughts.

Kathy sat down at the other end of the bench and stared off into the distance. She loved these dreamy early mornings, the air still tinged with the blue of night. It was a few days since her dinner with Ben and she hadn't slept much after he'd left. She kept thinking of that moment in the hallway. He'd messaged her the following day, sending his address and telling her to pop round whenever, but the tone was casual, making her think she'd imagined the spark between them.

She wanted to know him more, she realised suddenly in that early light. But that would mean him knowing her better, wouldn't it? Him asking her those difficult questions about John. And what about the guilt of even thinking of another man? John had been her world.

'Penny for your thoughts?' said the girl, making her start.

'Oh, gosh, I don't even know where to begin,' said Kathy. 'I suppose . . . I was thinking about new beginnings.'

The girl turned her gaze away towards the trees. 'Deep stuff. Do you think it's possible? To make new beginnings?'

'Ye-es. But maybe you have to take something of the old with you. Find a balance.'

'And how do you think you make a new beginning?'

This was a very intense conversation for so early in the morning, thought Kathy. She considered the question.

'I think you have to do things that scare you a bit, I suppose. Get out of your comfort zone.'

'Like what?'

She wasn't going to go into the ins and outs of her thoughts about Ben.

'Well, I'm signed up to do a charity race, with this one,' she said, gesturing to Baxter. 'And I haven't told anyone else, but I'm quite scared about doing it.'

'Why?'

'I suppose because it's an obstacle course and I'm worried about being unfit, or falling over in front of everyone, or getting tangled in Baxter's lead.'

That would have to do. She wouldn't tell this stranger that she was terrified of going back to the place that was so significant to her and John, of the pain of memories.

There was a silence between them. Kathy got the impression that Hope wanted to say something, so she kept quiet and looked ahead.

'So, when is it?'

'In September, so a bit of time away.' This week marked the beginning of July.

Another silence.

'Well, maybe I could . . . help. I mean, if you think I could be any use. But I like running, so . . .' Hope picked at her nails.

'I'd love your help,' said Kathy, the words unfamiliar in her mouth. She told herself it was mostly to help Hope.

'Cool! I'll look up a training programme and then we can make the obstacles here!'

Kathy heard the enthusiasm in Hope's voice and knew she'd made the right decision.

'The way I see it, you *have* to do it,' Hope continued. 'Not just for you, but also for this one. Everyone deserves their moment in the spotlight, don't they?'

Kathy laughed. She'd often said that to the kids at school, to encourage them if they were nervous before plays or show-and-tell assemblies. 'Give other people a chance to see you and appreciate you,' she'd said. Wise words. If only they weren't quite so hard to follow now.

'Well, that would be very kind,' said Kathy.

'Once a week, this spot? I don't know if I can come more. My life's a bit . . . complicated,' and she made a wobbling gesture with her hand.

Was there anyone whose life wasn't? Kathy wondered. Once again, she thought of people holding back. The sense that Judith wasn't being honest with her, that Ben, too, had secrets.

'It's a deal,' said Kathy, shaking Hope's hand.

*

And just like that, the summer weeks gathered pace. Kathy's birthday fell at the end of July and she combined her celebration with the volunteer summer party, which fell on the same day and would be held at Asha's café. She'd been shy about telling people that it was her birthday, but Judith had encouraged her.

'People want to celebrate you!' she'd said, and then Kathy saw that she'd sent a message to the volunteer WhatsApp group: 'It's also Kathy's birthday, so extra celebrations are in order!'

The morning of her birthday, she was touched to find her phone full of notifications wishing her a great day and looking forward to seeing her later. She was even more touched when Becs rang, singing 'Happy birthday' down the phone to her, before Alex and Jacqui came on, wishing her many happy returns and suggesting she come down to see them soon. Alex said he'd be up in London soon, as well, and would take her for a birthday dinner then.

'Do you have plans for later?' he asked.

'Yes, actually.' And she told them about the Battersea summer party.

She was looking forward to it, she realised. She didn't feel nervous about going – instead, she was excited about a drink or two with Judith and Asha, as well as mingling with volunteers she didn't yet know.

The café was bustling when she arrived and it was a warm summer evening, thankfully, so the party had spilled out onto the pavement.

'Here's the birthday girl!' yelled Asha as soon as Kathy arrived.

Kathy initially felt mortified at the attention, then made herself look around and saw everyone's smiling faces.

'Over here!' called Judith, waving her over and introducing her to some of the volunteers on her shift.

Kathy found the conversation flowed easily as they swapped stories. Then she heard the first tones of 'Happy birthday' strike up and more people joined in, their voices raised and raucous, and Asha was coming towards her with a cake, lit with candles.

'Oh, for goodness' sake,' Kathy said, beaming.

She blew out her candles and everyone clapped. It felt wonderful.

'You all have to help me eat it.'

'And Asha and I got you these,' said Judith once people were munching on cake. She handed Kathy a little box.

'Really, you shouldn't have,' Kathy began. Then, 'Oh! They're beautiful.'

They were the matching earrings to the necklace Judith and Jessica had bought her all those years ago. Kathy was stunned. It was such a thoughtful, generous gift.

Judith beamed. 'Put them on!'

Kathy was only too happy to oblige.

'Oh, they look lovely,' said Asha. 'And, just so you know, Ben chipped in as well.' She raised an eyebrow. 'I should check things are OK in the kitchen. Happy birthday, Kathy. It's so good to have you back on the scene.'

Then, out of the corner of her eye, Kathy saw Ben, standing quietly at the back of the room. When had he arrived?

'I should thank him,' she muttered to Judith, screwing up her courage.

She picked up a bottle of wine and a slice of cake, then made her way through the crowd.

'Hi,' he said. 'And happy birthday. I got here just in time to see you blow out the candles.'

'I'm grateful I managed it in one go. Would you like some wine? I can find you a glass, I'm sure.'

He shook his head. 'No, thanks, Kathy, I don't drink. I wouldn't say no to a bit of cake, though, if there's any left.'

'This slice is for you,' she said, handing him the plate. 'Thank you so much for my earrings.'

Ben craned his neck slightly to look at them. 'Beautiful.'

Kathy couldn't bring herself to make eye contact with him.

'So, how are your paintings?' she mumbled, staring at the top of his ear instead.

'Fine, fine. How's Thailand?'

'Plans are picking up pace. Thank you for your advice.'

'Pleasure. Listen, I'm going to get a lemonade or something, can I get the birthday girl a drink?'

She took a deep breath and pulled herself together. Too much wine, that was it. 'I'll come with you. I could do with a glass of water myself.'

They stood side by side, waiting to be served. Kathy gulped gratefully at her water when it arrived; it was warm in the café.

Ben pulled out his wallet and opened it, searching for the right change. Kathy caught a glimpse of a faded passport photo. A woman . . . She looked to be in her early forties, but it was barely a glimpse, and she was worried Ben had sensed her interest, as he closed the wallet tightly. They talked for a little longer, then Freya, the volunteer coordinator, came over to wish her a happy birthday and she was soon being introduced to lots of other people. Then, somehow, it was time to go home – she couldn't remember the last time she'd been out so late or had so much fun. There was no sign of Ben. When she checked her phone, there was a message from him:

'Sorry I left without saying goodbye. You were surrounded by your adoring fans! I'm glad you like the earrings.'

*

Every Tuesday morning, Kathy would meet Hope at 7 a.m. on the common to work out. Hope had taken things seriously. She'd printed out a training plan and had Kathy warming up by the bench, doing her stretches, and then walking and jogging up and down for a set number of minutes.

'Look how much better you are than the week before!' she'd call out encouragingly, and Kathy had to admit, she was getting fitter and fitter.

She was barely tired after her volunteer days at Battersea at all any more and had completed her six-month training, so she was allowed to take dogs out in the park. She felt confident with them, even some of the bigger ones, and her physical fitness helped.

Then Hope started building in obstacles, encouraging Kathy to drop and crawl – which caused them much hilarity, Baxter barking around them – and hop from side to side, which she found exhausting.

'We should be training Baxter as well,' Hope said, her eyes bright.

There were to be obstacles in the race for the dogs as well, such as slalom poles and hurdles.

'We should,' Kathy agreed. 'We don't want you letting the side down, eh, boy?'

And so, with advice from her friends at the rescue centre, Kathy set about training Baxter for the event. He loved the training. He was so smart and alert that it suited him to have his energy focused – and he had so much energy, so she was grateful for any ways in which she could burn it off.

She messaged Becs and suggested she come up for a night, so she could be part of it. In the end, they'd decided that Alex wouldn't sign up for the race too in case he was needed at the pub, but he was still caught up in Becs's enthusiasm and gladly brought her up to London for training. They set up a miniature slalom course in the garden, with a makeshift tunnel, and encouraged a delighted Baxter around it with treats. They laughed until their sides hurt, watching his antics – he was so excited and keen to please them that he kept looking up at them at key moments and bashing into a slalom pole.

'It reminds me of when we used to play with Buddy in the garden,' said Alex, smiling at Kathy. 'They were good times, Mum.' He slung his arm around her shoulder and squeezed her close.

When had her baby got so tall? she wondered, yet again.

'They were.'

'Do you have the photos anywhere?'

She knew exactly where they were, in the cupboard under the stairs, but she didn't want the pain to surface on such a lovely evening.

'Oh, they're somewhere. I'll have to dig them out for you.'

'I'd love that.'

And then Becs was squealing at them to watch what Baxter was doing. She'd finally got him to hop over a jump instead of scampering round it, and the girl and the dog were chasing around the lawn like mad things. Kathy's heart soared to see it.

Later, as they collapsed in the living room with pizza as a belated birthday treat, still laughing about Baxter's antics, Kathy felt a contentment and a happiness she hadn't felt in years.

'This is nice, isn't it?' she said to Alex, who raised his head sleepily from the arm of the sofa.

'It is, Mum. And I have to say, I was completely wrong about you volunteering at Battersea. It's been great for you. And it's brought us all together as well now, hasn't it?'

It was Baxter, thought Kathy, gazing at the dog, passed out in front of the fire, his ribs rising and falling as he snored. It was Baxter who'd brought all this out in her.

He was a magical dog, she thought. Each time she woke up, fearful about the Muddy Dog Challenge, the thought of Baxter doing it by her side was the only thing that soothed her. He brought out the very best in people. Look at how Becs had come alive around him, how transformed she was when it was all about Baxter. Today, there'd been none of the sulky girl who'd appeared last Christmas. Becs couldn't do enough to help, from tidying up the obstacle course, to clearing up the plates and making the tea. And now the girl was taking after Baxter and nodding off.

'Becs,' Kathy whispered, waking her gently. 'Time for bed, I think.'

Becs had nodded, rubbing her eyes and getting up before hugging Kathy tightly.

She'd waved them both off with a lump in her throat the following morning. She was sad to see them go but happy at how close she felt to them. Things were undoubtedly improving on the family front.

*

Judith seemed much brighter, as well, and Kathy felt they were firm friends now. Once every two weeks or so, Kathy would head round to help her with whatever still needed doing in her house. They'd painted the living room now and assembled some bookcases from IKEA, with only a moderate amount of wine.

'It just seems easier to work out these instructions once you've had a tipple,' Judith had said, and Kathy agreed, screwdriver in hand.

Taking advantage of summer evenings, they'd turned their attention to Judith's garden, mowing the lawn, pulling out the weeds and tidying up the hedges.

'Next up, a table and chairs for out here,' Kathy had said.

'Oh, great idea!'

In return, Judith would help Kathy with her Thailand planning. They had most of her itinerary put together now, and it took in temples, jungles, islands and cities. Despite what Ben had said, Kathy knew she'd always be a planner. The more planned out it was, the more relaxed about the whole thing she felt. They'd filled a ring binder with everything printed out and lists of what still needed to be sorted.

'You do realise I'm so jealous,' said Judith, looking wistfully at the photos in *Lonely Planet* of luscious palm trees and endless beaches. 'You're going to have to send me constant updates.'

'Well,' said Kathy, 'you could always come with me?'

Judith's desire to travel was so apparent that Kathy felt guilty about having nerves.

But Judith shook her head. 'I'd love to, Kathy, but it's a bit beyond my budget. And I need to be around for Jess.'

Why Judith needed to be around for her daughter when she lived overseas and seemed to rarely visit, Kathy didn't know, but she stayed quiet.

'I'll be sure to bring you back something lovely,' she said. 'I can't thank you enough for all your planning.'

*

And then there was Ben. She found herself thinking of him more often than she would have liked to admit, especially after seeing him on the night of her birthday. He hadn't asked her to do anything again, but he had given her the email address of his Thai friends. They'd said they'd be delighted to help her in any way possible and she should come to their apartment for dinner when she was in Chiang Mai, which had made her feel better – that she'd have friends to visit all the way over there.

She'd also seen Ben one day when she brought Baxter in for his check-up and he was delighted to hear about his excellent progress. She knew she should text him, and arrange to go round and see his paintings, but she didn't have the courage. She wasn't sure what she wanted, or certain of her own feelings towards him.

If she imagined kissing him, it was overwhelming – she felt almost nauseous with it. It had been decades since she'd kissed anyone but John and the thought seemed wrong. But she could imagine walking side by side with Ben, through the park, the comforting bulk of his arm brushing hers. She sighed and pushed the thoughts away. Silly. He was being friendly and professional towards her, that was all.

*

As summer moved through August, it seemed that life was in full bloom. Kathy walked across the common for her last training session with Hope before the big race, the grass scorched from the summer heat. She reflected on how she now jogged all the way to meet Hope at their usual spot, with Baxter trotting by her side. His coat was gleaming now and she was so proud of how he'd come on.

Hope was there, ready and waiting, clutching a form and a pen.

'Do you think . . . do you think you could help me with this?' she said. 'It's for a job.'

'Of course,' said Kathy, taking the paper from her.

'It's this personal statement thing. It's for a job at a café, but I want it to be good. First thing I've gone for in a while.' She chewed on her nails.

'Well, I think it's excellent,' said Kathy. 'And look, I'd be more confident about your skills! Think how much you've helped me. You've made me a training programme and stuck to it. You've turned up every week here, rain or shine . . . So, I think we should put in a sentence or two about your organisational skills and your motivation – can I write on this?'

Hope nodded and peered round to see what Kathy was writing, petting Baxter's head.

'But apart from that and a couple of tiny things, I think it's great,' Kathy finished.

Hope took the sheet of paper back from her. 'And I . . . I was wondering . . . could I put you as a reference?' She was so nervous asking Kathy that she was almost shaking.

'Yes, of course you can,' said Kathy, reaching out and giving Hope's shoulder a squeeze. 'I'll give you a glowing reference!'

'Oh, thanks!' said Hope, exhaling in a sigh of relief. 'Thank you so much! You don't know what it means. It's just hard when . . . when . . .Well, thanks, Kathy.'

'You'll have to let me know how it goes,' said Kathy. 'After the Muddy Dog. I'll still be walking round here every morning . . . well, for as long as I've got Baxter.'

Hope looked at her. 'You're sure you don't want to keep him?'

No, Kathy thought. Not sure at all. But she'd put her plan in place for Thailand and who knew what she'd do after that. She'd made a promise at New Year to push herself, explore new horizons, and she should stick to that.

'He's been a wonderful guest,' Kathy replied, 'and whoever gets to have him forever is so lucky. I just count my stars that I got to play a role in his life. But I've got plans of my own, so I couldn't keep him, even if I wanted to.'

'I'll miss him,' Hope said suddenly. 'I'll really miss seeing him every week.'

'Oh, Hope.' Kathy didn't know what to say.

She knew that Becs was going to be devastated, as well. They kept in regular contact over Baxter, with pictures and questions flying back and forth between them.

'Come on, let's have a good last training session before the big day.'

Chapter 13

Kathy looked over everything she'd laid out on her bed. It was the Friday afternoon before the Muddy Dog Challenge the next day and she had everything prepared. Trainers, her old comfy ones. Leggings to run in, a warm hoodie, too – and a mac in case it rained. Not that she'd notice if it rained during the event; she and Baxter would be covered in mud.

She was amazed at the sponsorship she'd collected. Friends from her volunteer day, dog walkers she chatted to in the park, Alex and Jacqui, Judith, Asha – and Ben, too. From everything she'd heard, it was a friendly, welcoming day, where everyone could go at their own pace, and there was always help on hand.

'So, there's really no need for us to be nervous, eh, boy?' said Kathy, glancing down at the dog's brown eyes and fighting the butterflies in her stomach. 'We'll have each other, all the way round.'

Baxter thumped his tail in agreement.

'And who knows, maybe your forever home will see you from the crowd,' Kathy continued, though her heart hurt at the thought of Baxter going.

With his ear and skin recovered, he'd been assessed by the rehoming team. His profile had gone up last week, so the search for his home could begin. Kathy couldn't bear to look at the webpage. It made it all too real.

She went downstairs and heard her phone buzzing on the kitchen worktop. She didn't reach it in time, but when she picked it up, it was a missed call from Alex. Along with five other missed calls and a message saying could she call him urgently.

Panic rose in her. What on earth could have happened? She rang him back immediately.

'Mum,' he said, his voice tight with anxiety.

'Darling, what's wrong? What's happened?'

'It's Becs. She's gone missing. Is she with you?'

'No, she isn't. When did you last see her?'

Alex exhaled. 'This morning, before work. I left before Jacqui. I don't know why she'd do this; we're really worried. She's been so excited about Muddy Dog, really happy.'

'Do you think she's run off?'

'We're just not sure. We've tried her phone and no answer, to either messages or calls.'

'And what about the police?'

'Jacqui's calling them now.'

Kathy felt as if an icy hand were gripping her throat.

'What can I do? Shall I come to you?'

Baxter whined and pressed himself against her legs. She reached down to him for comfort, worried she might faint.

Alex exhaled. 'Nothing for now. Or try calling her . . . I don't know, in case she's cross with us or something and will answer to you.'

'I'll do that now,' Kathy said. 'Call me as soon as anything changes.'

They said goodbye and Kathy immediately called Becs' phone. It went straight to voicemail. She left a message, saying no one was angry with her and please call her straightaway. Then she sent her a WhatsApp message: 'Becs. Please call me as soon as you get this and let us know you're all right. We all love you.'

But the message didn't even deliver.

Kathy couldn't do anything bar pace up and down the hallway, checking her phone every ten seconds. Baxter followed her, sensing her agitation.

'What could have happened to her?' Kathy whispered to the dog. 'Oh, please, please let nothing bad have happened.'

An hour inched past, agonisingly slowly. It was early evening now. Kathy couldn't bear the thought of a whole night where they didn't know where Becs was. Awful images popped into her head, of Becs lost and alone and scared in the dark.

Then her phone rang, making her leap into the air. Ben. He must want to talk about Baxter, or something to do with the Muddy Dog Challenge.

'Ben, I'm sorry, I can't speak now,' she began.

'Kathy,' he cut across her. 'I've got Becs here. Here, here she is.'

Kathy felt like her legs were going to give way with sheer relief.

'Becs! Hello, darling,' she said, trying to keep her voice calm.

'I'm sorry,' Becs said, her voice breaking, gulping back sobs. 'I'm sorry. I just wanted to come and find you, and I couldn't remember, and then my phone died and I, I . . .' She dissolved into tears.

Kathy could hear Ben soothing her.

'Do you want to come down to the dogs' home?' Ben said to Kathy. 'We'll just wait here, the two of us, and have a cup of tea.'

His voice was so calm, he seemed completely unfazed by the situation.

'Yes, I'll be right down,' Kathy said. 'I'll call Alex and Jacqui on the way.'

'Just be careful,' said Ben. 'No rushing. You've had a shock.'

She dialled Alex's number.

'Alex, she's here. She's in London,' said Kathy as soon as he picked up.

'Oh, thank God,' said Alex. 'Jacqui, it's Mum. She's got her. She's in London.'

Kathy heard Jacqui burst into tears. Her heart ached for her. What a nightmare to go through all these hours.

Jacqui came on the line. 'Kathy? She's with you? Oh my God, I just can't—'

'She turned up at Battersea, the dogs' home,' explained Kathy. 'My colleague just rang and I'm on my way there to get her. Then I'll come back here with her, don't worry.'

Jacqui took some deep breaths through her tears and Kathy could hear the effort it took her to calm down.

'I can't thank you enough. And I'll set off for London just as soon as I've calmed down. Alex will hold the fort here. I'll be there as soon as I can, though.'

'Leave it a little while,' said Kathy. 'You've had an awful shock and you'll only get caught up in the rush hour. Eat something first. Listen, I'm just heading out the door and I'll call you as soon as I'm with her, OK?'

With Baxter by her side, Kathy ran to the rescue centre as quickly as she could.

She was let in by the receptionist and through to the rehoming office. There was Ben, with Becs at his side, showing her the profiles of all the dogs online. Becs looked pale and tired, but perfectly safe.

Kathy went straight over to her and hugged her as tightly as she could, her heart thudding against her ribs.

'We love you, Becs,' she said quietly into the girl's ear, stifling a tear. 'You're not in trouble. We all love you so much.'

'I'm sorry, I'm so sorry,' said Becs, pulling back briefly from Kathy's embrace and looking at her with tear-filled eyes. 'I had to come and see you, so I got the train after school and then my phone ran out of battery. I'd not brought my charger . . . I didn't think to bring anything, and then it was too late – I was in London Victoria and didn't know where you lived. The only place I could remember was Battersea Dogs' Home and it was just so busy, people everywhere. I was too scared to ask for help.'

Kathy could only imagine how disorientating London Victoria at rush hour would be to a young girl who wasn't used to it.

'Then I saw a train that went to Battersea, so I just got on that and then I found my way here,' said Becs. She knelt down and hugged Baxter to her. 'Hello, boy.'

Baxter snuffled at her reassuringly.

'You did really well to do that,' said Kathy. 'Smart girl.'

'And then I asked for you at reception and they said you weren't here. Then Ben came out and overheard me asking,' finished Becs, looking at him gratefully.

'And that's when we worked things out and I rang you.' Ben took over. 'And in the meantime, she's been giving me a hand sorting out my filing.' He winked at Kathy.

'Chance would be a fine thing,' she smiled back at him.

'I'm sorry for all the worry I've caused,' said Becs, eyes wide. 'Do you think Alex and Mum . . . are they really angry?'

'No,' said Kathy. 'We're all just relieved you're all right. Here, why don't you give them a quick call from my mobile and then we'll walk back to my house?'

She dialled Alex and put Becs on. It would do them good to hear her voice. Becs turned away from them as she spoke.

Kathy blew out her cheeks. 'My God, Ben. I was so worried,' she said softly.

He remained silent. Then he reached out his hands and took hers in his. She glanced up and saw his gaze on her, his eyes calm. The warmth of his hands, the gentleness of his touch, was more soothing than any words could have been.

'It must have been awful,' he said, his voice sympathetic. 'She's here now. Everything's all right.'

Kathy nodded, not trusting herself not to burst into tears. Ben squeezed her hands.

'Your hands are freezing. Take my jacket.'

Kathy was going to refuse politely, but she was too tired to. It was so nice to be looked after.

Becs hung up the phone and crossed back over to them.

'Can we go home?' she asked, putting her hand over her mouth as she coughed.

'Absolutely, darling,' Kathy said.

'I'll see you home,' said Ben.

The four of them left Battersea's gates in silence, Baxter's lead in Becs' hands. Kathy wanted to be close to Ben, to his calming presence. She was warm and cosy in his jacket, and she grew calmer again as the adrenaline started to fade.

'Go and start running yourself a bath,' said Kathy, as soon as they were in the door.

Becs had been sneezing on the way home and Kathy was worried she was coming down with a chill. Becs nodded and walked upstairs.

Kathy leant back against the wall. Finally, she could relax. Becs was under her roof. She wanted to talk to the girl, find out what on earth had made her run away like that. She took off Ben's jacket and held it out to him.

'Here. Thank you. For looking after me. And Becs.'

He took it from her. 'It was nothing.'

As he stepped away from her, he hesitated for a moment, and she felt like he wanted to say something.

But then he shook his head and simply said, 'See you tomorrow,' before heading out into the night.

The Muddy Dog Challenge! Kathy groaned. She felt so exhausted by the events of the afternoon that she could barely contemplate getting up so early and completing the obstacle course.

She called up to Becs, who was already in the bath. 'Do you want some pizza?'

'Yes, please!'

She dug out two frozen pizzas and started to heat the oven. Once Becs was downstairs, dressed in some spare pyjamas and her hair wrapped in a towel, she put them in the oven.

Ten minutes later, they were eating in the living room, plates on their knees. Becs had colour back in her cheeks and Kathy was glad to see it, although a tickly cough persisted. She felt energy flooding back into her, as well. She'd let the girl eat and settle in before she asked her any questions.

Baxter had shuffled over towards Becs and lay down by her feet. Kathy noticed how Becs stroked his head for reassurance as she ate. When they'd both finished chomping on the last crust, Kathy took a deep breath and turned to Becs.

'So, Becs. What happened? What made you come here? You're not in trouble. I just need to understand.'

Becs made eye contact with her before staring down at her fingers and twisting them around.

'I . . . I . . .'

Kathy forced herself to wait patiently. Baxter looked up and licked Becs' fingers.

'It's Mum and Alex,' she said, the words tumbling out. 'They're going to have a baby.'

'Jacqui's pregnant?' Kathy gasped.

Becs nodded.

A flood of emotions poured through Kathy. Alex was going to be a dad! And she a grandmother . . . A new life! Then she caught herself and looked again at Becs' face, which had fallen.

'See, you can't help it,' said Becs quietly. 'I can see how excited you are. It's only natural. You'll have a real grandchild. And as for me . . .' She trailed off.

'What are you scared of?' said Kathy softly.

Becs sighed. 'I'm scared that I won't have a place in the family. It's hard enough feeling like I do anyway, what with how much I'm on my own. How left out I feel. Not just with Mum and Alex and the pub, but with my friends, as well.'

Kathy remembered what Becs had said on their walk – how hard it was to be alone, a town away from her friends.

'And then there'll be this cute little new baby,' continued Becs. 'Alex's proper daughter. A new baby for Mum. Not like me, being difficult and moody. You'll have a granddaughter. And so, I thought I'd run away, up here. Come and get Baxter and . . .' She shrugged. 'To be honest, I didn't really think much further than that. Just getting to you and him.'

Kathy got up and went to sit beside Becs on the sofa.

'Come here,' she said.

And Becs sat up, slowly at first, and cautiously leant into Kathy, who put her arms around her and squeezed her tightly.

'You know, I really admire you,' said Kathy.

'Me?' said Becs, pulling back to stare at Kathy.

She nodded. 'Yes. Because you're a lot younger than me and you're able to talk about what you're afraid of. Here's the thing. I do know how you feel, I think. When Alex moved in with Jacqui and you, I was worried I didn't have a place. I felt left out. And I'm still scared, to be honest. That I'm some lonely old thing there isn't a space for.'

Becs looked stricken. 'You're not! You're our family!'

Kathy smiled. 'And so are you. I'm not going to pretend to you that it might not be . . . complicated, having a baby around. But you're going to be a big sister! You're going to have someone to hang out with and show things to. And this little baby is going to be so lucky having a big sister like you.'

Becs smiled. 'I hadn't thought of it like that.'

'And if you ever do feel lonely, or left out – and it might happen, I know it does to me – we can just pick up the phone to each other and commiserate. I know I should have done that a lot more often these past few years.'

'After John died?'

Kathy was surprised that Becs knew his name. 'Yes.'

'Alex talks about him to us. He tells us all these funny stories about what he was like.'

'Does he?' Kathy felt a pang of pain slice through her heart.

Becs nodded and coughed. 'Yeah, he told this one about Buddy crashing into the middle of a romantic picnic, and John chasing after him and falling right into this woman's lap!'

Kathy laughed. 'I'd completely forgotten about that!' John had had her in stitches with that one.

'I hope he wasn't about to propose,' he'd said. 'Because Buddy probably would have eaten the ring.'

She smiled at the thought of it, then got up and went to the cupboard under the stairs. She took out the framed photo and showed it to Becs.

'Here we all are.'

It was her favourite photo – her, John and a young Alex, gap-toothed and grinning madly, his arms around Buddy's neck. A lump formed in her throat as she passed it to Becs.

'You all look so happy,' Becs said. 'John looks so nice. I wish I could have met him.'

Kathy pressed her lips together and nodded. 'Me too. And, yes, he was very nice.'

Becs looked at her closely. 'Why don't you have the picture out?'

If Becs could be so honest about her fears, Kathy had to do the same. She took a deep breath.

'I'm . . . I'm scared to remember. It was so hard when he died. And it's hard not thinking of that. And if I think about the happy memories, it makes me so sad that he's not here any more.' She realised her face was wet with tears.

'Oh, Nan,' said Becs. 'It's OK to miss him. Really, it is.'

She reached over and hugged Kathy tightly. Kathy took a deep, shuddering breath and tried to pull herself together.

'You called me nan,' she said, realising what Becs had said.

'Yeah,' said Becs. 'Is that all right? I've never really had a grandparent. I mean, obviously Mum's, but they're in Australia. And it's best not talk about anything to do with my dad.'

'I'm honoured,' said Kathy, wiping tears from her face. 'Goodness me, it's meant to be me comforting you! Not the other way round!'

'Well, we're a team now,' said Becs forcefully.

'Would the team like a hot chocolate?'

'Yeah!'

Kathy smiled through her tears as she went into the kitchen and began preparing a comforting drink. When she went back through, she saw that Becs had put the framed photo on the mantelpiece, right in the middle. It looked good.

*

A few hours later, with Becs fast asleep upstairs, Baxter on the floor by her side, and Kathy not far from dropping off on the sofa, there was a soft knock at the door.

Kathy sat upright and rubbed her eyes before heading to open the front door.

There, on the doorstep, looking exhausted, her hair pulled back and greasy, was Jacqui.

'I'm so sorry,' she began. 'The traffic, it was awful. Is she here? Can I see her?'

'Come in, come in,' said Kathy. 'She's absolutely fast asleep. Here, come with me.'

They tiptoed up the stairs and Kathy carefully pulled open the door of the spare room. She'd left a soft lamp lit and they could see Becs fast asleep in bed, her hair over her face, one arm outstretched over the side to rest as near to the sleeping Baxter as possible.

Kathy heard Jacqui gulp and felt her shoulders shake. She turned her head to see Jacqui's eyes brimming with tears.

'She's OK,' Kathy said softly. 'She's right there. It's all right. She's absolutely fine, bar a bit of a cough. You can go in and see her.'

Jacqui shook her head. 'I don't want to wake her; she must be exhausted.'

'And so must you.'

For once, Jacqui didn't say otherwise. She just nodded.

'Come downstairs,' whispered Kathy, as they moved away from the bedroom door. 'Have you even eaten anything this evening?'

'No,' Jacqui replied. 'Just a banana before I drove here. The stress of it . . . the worry . . .' She shook her head. 'God, Kathy. I thought . . . I thought something terrible must have happened to her. I can't even . . .'

And then she was crying again, covering her face with her hands.

Kathy hugged her. She didn't think she'd ever hugged Jacqui before. Just polite kisses on the cheek hello and goodbye. This was different. Jacqui rested her head on her shoulder and took a few deep breaths.

Kathy made her a herbal tea and some toast with butter, and Jacqui wolfed it down as she stood in the kitchen, suddenly starving. Kathy put on another round for her.

'Jesus, why did she do it?' said Jacqui suddenly. 'I don't know if I should be angry at her for what she put us through. She has to realise that she can't do things like this! I don't know if it's attention-seeking or what, but she can't just run off like that!'

Kathy considered what she was about to say carefully. She didn't want to tell Jacqui how to parent her own daughter. And she wasn't sure if she should let Jacqui tell her about the pregnancy in her own time.

'You know,' Kathy began carefully, 'Alex once ran off. We were out shopping and he was bored, so he ducked away from me and wandered off in the department store. I was absolutely terrified. We found him within half an hour, but it was awful. And I felt so powerless. So utterly powerless. When I was used to being in control and having all the answers.'

'That's exactly it. I just don't know.' Jacqui took a slurp of tea, lip quivering. 'Sometimes I just feel such a mess. With keeping the pub going, with being a good mum to Becs and now . . . well, there's a baby on the way.' She gave an uncertain smile through her tears.

She looked so young, thought Kathy suddenly. She went and pulled up a chair opposite Jacqui and took her hands.

'That's wonderful news,' Kathy said. 'I'm overjoyed for you all.'

'I'm happy, too,' said Jacqui, faltering. 'Of course I am. And for Alex, he'll be the best dad. But, God, Kathy, I'm scared. Of doing it all again. It was so hard with Becs, after her dad left. And of course this time it'll be different, but I'm still scared about being able to manage everything – give enough to Becs, the business, Alex.

'My own mum is on the other side of the world and I really miss her. I feel like half the time I'm just flailing around and it's so hard, when I know what a superwoman you are. When Alex is always talking about you and how incredible you are, how you coped with John's illness, how you put him back together afterwards, how there's nothing you can't handle . . . And now it looks like my own daughter prefers you to me! You can certainly get through to her in a way that I can't. It's hard not to feel like a failure.'

Kathy was reeling. Jacqui felt like this? Jacqui, who was always one step ahead of the game, who was always so perfect?

'Jacqui, I don't know what to say. Apart from the fact that it's me who's often thought you were superwoman. The way you run the pub, how immaculate your house is, how much of a team you and Alex are together. And, God, believe me when I say I'm not superwoman. Far from it.'

Jacqui shook her head, smiling. 'And so the two of us have been thinking exactly the same about the other. I was so scared of not living up to your expectations. So keen to be as perfect as you.'

'And there was I, keen to prove what a perfect life I lead,' said Kathy sadly.

Jacqui tilted her head to one side. 'What's the truth? Are you OK?'

It was time for honesty, Kathy decided. She took a deep breath.

'I think the truth is somewhere in the middle. Yes, I am OK. But sometimes I'm not. Sometimes I miss John so much that . . . that I just can't think about it. And so I block the memories away and try to organise everything so I don't have to think.

'But sometimes I'm so lonely, here on my own. And I've felt so lost these past few years. It's why I've been doing the volunteering, really. And having the dogs with me. That's really helped.'

'God, Kathy, I had no idea,' said Jacqui. 'We thought that you were just always so happy and busy in your own life. It's not my place to say, but I know Alex would love to talk about his father more. He's felt . . . he's felt . . . that you don't want to, like at the castle when you came down.'

'He's right,' said Kathy. 'I'm just afraid that if I start missing him, I'll never stop. And I don't want Alex to be worried that I'm not coping. I'm not sure if he told you about . . . how he found out about John.'

Jacqui nodded. 'He did. And to be honest, I think it would be good for Alex to see you a bit differently, as well. That you're neither superwoman nor someone he has to put in cotton wool and worry about. But don't hide away your good memories. You and John spent all those years making them. You can still enjoy them, even though he's gone.'

She squeezed Kathy's hand.

'And you're family, Kathy. I know we've not always seen eye to eye, but now I'm thinking that's because we weren't really seeing each other properly at all.'

'Agreed,' said Kathy. 'And I'm here to support you, especially with the new baby. I know your family is far away, and that must be so tough. But I'll do anything you need – and I promise you can tell me if I'm being interfering.'

Jacqui laughed. 'You already do so much. Becs adores you. Look, did she tell you anything about why she ran away? I want to understand. She seemed a bit off after we told her about the baby.'

And Kathy found herself explaining what Becs had said to Jacqui. She hoped she wasn't breaking the girl's trust.

'I appreciate you telling me this so much,' said Jacqui. 'I had no idea she felt like that. She seemed fine when I told her. I wish she could have been honest with me.'

'She's a wonderful girl,' said Kathy. 'She really is. She's kind and brave and honest. And a lot of that is thanks to the way you raised her.'

Jacqui beamed. 'You have no idea how much that means to me, to hear you say that.'

She glanced at her watch. 'Oh, goodness, it's almost 1 a.m. And it's the race tomorrow. I hate to say it, but I don't think I can run it, what with the pregnancy and everything that's happened today. But we're not going to spoil your big day. We'll make sure you're up and get there in time.'

Kathy felt exhausted at the prospect. 'I'm not sure—'

Jacqui touched her arm. 'Get to bed now and have a good sleep. We'll see how you are in the morning. I know how hard you've trained. I'd feel terrible if this drama stopped you from competing.'

On the landing, the two women hugged goodnight.

Kathy fell asleep, exhausted by the day's events but somehow happy. Things had changed with Jacqui and Becs. They felt like family.

Chapter 14

Kathy woke blearily to a knocking on her bedroom door followed by coughing. What on earth . . . ? Then the events of yesterday rushed back into her mind. The door opened a crack and Baxter scampered in, full of energy as usual.

Then followed Becs, up and dressed, carefully carrying a tray stacked with a hearty breakfast of toast, eggs and tomatoes. Behind her was Jacqui, holding a steaming mug of tea.

'Breakfast in bed for our champion!' said Jacqui.

Kathy smiled and shifted herself upright, yawning.

'I am so, so sorry about yesterday,' said Becs, her eyes wide, her voice croaky.

'You sound terrible,' said Kathy. 'I think you've picked up a bug.'

Becs nodded, her face downcast. 'Mum says I can't do the race.'

'I think she's right, to be honest.'

'But you're going to do it, aren't you? Please? I haven't ruined it for you?'

The truth was that Kathy felt exhausted. Bone-weary from the adrenaline of yesterday.

'I honestly think . . .' she began.

'Give her a moment, Becs,' said Jacqui, placing the mug on the bedside table and ruffling her daughter's hair affectionately.

They must have been up at the crack of dawn, Kathy thought, to surprise her like this. She felt a new energy rush through her at the thought of their gesture. She reached over and took a welcome sip of hot tea.

'Kathy, if you're too tired for it, we completely understand,' said Jacqui. 'But we wanted to say, we'll do everything to get you there. Breakfast, and then I'll drive so you can sleep in the car.

'And we'll cheer you and Baxter on all the way. And then afterwards, we'll bring you back here and have a family dinner, all together. Alex says he can either meet us at Windsor or come here. It's up to you. We'll give you a moment to have your tea.'

Baxter stayed with her, head cocked to one side, eyes bright. At least one of them was raring to go, thought Kathy. She checked her phone. A message from Ben.

'Hi, Kathy, how are you all after last night? I was thinking – I'm volunteering at the Muddy Dog and I could change your start time, to give you a bit of extra rest before you have to be here. Let me know. Hate for you to miss out.'

Her heart flooded with relief. That would be brilliant! The more she woke up, the more she wanted to take part in the race. She thought of all the training Hope had done with her, of the money people had sponsored. She thought of how wonderful it would feel to finish the race with her family cheering her on. And she thought of John. How he'd tell her to seize the opportunity, enjoy the day, and sleep in the next morning. Well, this was life, wasn't it? You didn't always get the perfect night's sleep before the big day. Things got messy and complicated. And you kept on at it. And for the first time in a long time, she had a team around her.

She glanced down at Baxter.

'Are we going to do it then, boy?'

He barked.

That was it settled. A resounding yes.

*

A few hours later, they arrived at the Windsor start line, registration complete. Kathy had managed to go back to sleep for another half an hour and, judging by their refreshed faces, so had Becs and Jacqui. They'd met up with Alex in the car park, where he'd embraced Kathy tightly.

'I can't thank you enough, Mum,' he'd muttered in her ear. 'And you know the news?'

Kathy had pulled back from him, looking at her baby boy. She couldn't believe he was grown-up enough to be expecting a child of his own.

'I do,' she said, beaming at him. 'And you're going to be a brilliant father.'

'I just hope I can live up to Dad,' he said, looking at her nervously.

Kathy remembered Jacqui saying that Alex would like to talk about his father more.

She smiled at him. 'He would be so, so proud of you, Alex. He already was – and he'd be even more so to see the wonderful life you're building. I don't think you need have any fears in that department.'

Alex had tears in his eyes and swallowed hard. 'Thanks, Mum. You know, I was thinking as I drove up here that he used to love Windsor Park so much. All those memories we have of us here.'

For the first time, Kathy let her emotions well up. Sadness, joy, hope, fear, all intermingled.

'He did love it,' she said. 'It's one of the reasons I'm nervous about coming back here. All the emotion. All the memories.'

'We're right here with you,' Alex said. 'You're not on your own, Mum, with anything.'

They hugged tightly once again, and then it was time to complete her registration and head to the start line, marked by Muddy Dog banners. Kathy had on her turquoise Muddy Dog T-shirt and Baxter was looking smart in a matching neckerchief. He was absolutely delighted to be there, wagging his tail and looking around, taking it all in, trying to charge off and greet anyone and everyone.

Kathy's nerves calmed as she looked about. Everyone looked so friendly and welcoming. She smiled at a few familiar faces from the dogs' home, who waved over at her. There were Freya and Tom. No sign of Ben, though.

'There's all sorts of people here, hey, boy?' she murmured, patting Baxter.

And it was true. All sorts of shapes and sizes, and ages and levels of fitness. She'd been so silly to worry about if she was up to the challenge. It wasn't a timed event – the focus was on enjoying yourself, celebrating the bond between dogs and people, and there were plenty of willing hands to help at every obstacle. Nonetheless, she was glad of Hope's help. It would be nice to enjoy it without being out of puff.

She lined up along with the rest of her group.

'Kathy!'

She looked up. It was Ben, waving to her from the side of the start line. Her heart flooded with gladness to see him. She waved back.

'I'll keep an eye out for you going round!' he called, and she grinned and gave a thumbs up before he jogged off.

Then Alex, Jacqui and Becs appeared, clutching coffees.

'Go, Nan!' called Becs, jumping up and down.

Kathy chuckled to herself. At least she had a bit of time to adjust to being a nan before the new baby arrived.

'Lovely your family have come along to support you,' a blonde woman said next to her, a little Yorkie shivering in her arms.

Kathy glowed. They *were* her family.

And then the countdown began and they were off!

'Get in there! No giving up!' shouted Jacqui, and Kathy had to laugh at her competitive spirit.

She and Baxter trotted off eagerly, and even though they were hardly Olympic sprinters and a lot of the competitors were walking, Kathy couldn't help but get caught up in the excitement of it all.

'Come on then, boy,' she said, and surprised herself by breaking into a little run across the grass, delighted by the sight of Baxter's strong little shoulders moving under his harness.

His coat was looking beautiful, she noted proudly. Just in time to get completely wrecked by the mud!

The first obstacle was a tunnel. Baxter was completely unfazed and ran into it boldly. Kathy bowed her head and scuttled through it, receiving a round of applause from the volunteers watching. One down!

They ran over to the next obstacle – a crawl net, suspended over muddy ground. Kathy shuddered. Well, this was it. She'd come to get muddy, hadn't she . . .?

She slowed as they approached, feeling uncertain about how to handle it.

'Are you OK?' said a friendly voice – a boy, one of the volunteers. 'Here, I'll hold the net up a bit and that'll help you get started.'

Well, she could hardly refuse now. She nodded gratefully and got down on her hands and knees, ready to crawl. Baxter spurred her on, looking round at her, keen to be on their way. Oh my goodness! The mud was cold and wet. She shuddered as it soaked through her knees.

'Come on, Nan!'

She looked up to see Becs, stood with a few other spectators, her cheeks rosy from having run to keep up.

'You can do it!' she shouted.

And so Kathy gritted her teeth and got on with it, the mud splashing around her. When she got to the other side and stood up, she was completely soaked and covered in it!

'Well, at least that's over with,' she said to Baxter and they set off jogging again.

Kathy was keen to keep warm now that she was covered in mud. Although the air was warm, it was cloudy overhead and she suspected she'd chill quickly if she stopped moving.

The next obstacle was an inflatable ball pit, filled with colourful balls and water. As they approached, Baxter looked nervous. He wasn't keen to jump in, Kathy could tell.

'Come on, boy,' she encouraged.

He looked round at her doubtfully.

'How about he follows my dog?' said the blonde woman from the start. 'He might feel more confident if he can see another dog get in there first. And funnily enough, Missy absolutely loves water.'

'Let's give it a go,' said Kathy.

She stood aside to let the woman pass. Baxter pricked his ears up when he saw the little terrier happily splashing through. She was so tiny that she almost disappeared among the balls. What a little cutie, thought Kathy.

And then Baxter decided to give it a go, launching himself awkwardly into the water with an enormous splash that well and truly drenched any remaining dry spots on Kathy's T-shirt.

Oh, what the hell! She thought and launched herself in as well, giggling as she splashed through. And just like that, when she emerged dripping with water and mud, Baxter shaking himself vigorously, a thin ray of sunshine appeared in the cloudy sky.

The grass was slippery and sloped downhill to the next obstacle, so she took it at a brisk walk, chatting a little with the Yorkie's owner, who introduced herself as Sue. Kathy marvelled at how pristine she still looked, hair up, make-up applied. How had she managed to avoid getting as messy as Kathy had?

'You first, this time,' said Sue, frowning a little as they contemplated a set of tyres steeped in mud. 'I'm convinced I'll trip up.'

'Well, I'll help you right back up if you do,' said Kathy. 'I'll go first.'

She tried to remember the tips Hope had given her. Focus on the next step, don't think about the whole picture.

She hopped into the first tyre, landing with a squelch. Mud shot up and spattered her face. Baxter barked happily. No time to think! She hopped into the next tyre and the next, and before she knew it, she was at the other end, several fresh layers of mud applied, cheeks glowing.

'You can do it!' she called to Sue, who was still looking doubtful. 'Here, I can take Missy, if you like?'

She doubled back round to take hold of the dog's lead, leaving Sue with both of her arms free.

'Think more side to side than going forwards,' Kathy suggested, and Sue set off slowly, soon gaining confidence.

Then, just as all seemed to be going well, Sue tripped on the edge of one of the tyres. As if in slow motion, Kathy watched as Sue stumbled forwards, landing with a splat in the mud. Kathy held her breath as Sue looked up at her with a shocked expression.

'Oh my God, Sue, are you all right?'

And then Sue's face cracked open into an enormous grin. She crawled up onto her knees then dug her fingers back into the mud and smeared it across her cheeks.

'Might as well go the whole hog with this new look,' she said, laughing.

'It suits you!' Kathy said, enjoying their banter.

She'd never have had the confidence to do this before, she thought. She'd have been so concerned with getting it all right, she would have forgotten to enjoy it. But now she was used to socialising, used to meeting new people again – and it was wonderful to remember this side of her personality.

She passed Missy's leash back to Sue.

'I'm going to walk and catch my breath,' said Sue. 'I think you're a bit fitter than me, so don't let me hold you back.'

Kathy did feel energy surging through her body.

'Well, I'm sure you'll catch me up at the next obstacle,' she said. 'And thanks for your help earlier.'

She waved goodbye as she set off at a gentle jog again, her heart beating fast. She heard whooping, and turned to see Alex and Jacqui clapping her on.

'We've got photo evidence, Mum!' called Alex, brandishing his camera.

Oh, Lord. She must look a right state.

'Get Baxter's best angle!' she called back, making them laugh.

The two of them splashed through another muddy pool, taking it in their stride, cheered on by volunteers and spectators. Baxter attempted a couple of agility jumps with medium levels of success, but Kathy was so proud of his big heart for having a go.

'He's a gorgeous dog, yours,' said a young man, who ran past her with a Border collie in tow, and she barely had time to smile and agree before he was off into the distance.

She was halfway round, then suddenly there was only half a kilometre to go. And Kathy could see where this part of the route went. Right past a spot where she and John had sat on one of their last outings together. It was as if winter had fallen. She slowed almost to a halt and walked slowly, her head down.

Baxter sensed something was wrong and looked up at her with a small whine, tugging on the leash, keen to be off again.

'I don't know if I can . . . I don't know if I can . . .'

She felt tears prick behind her eyelids, and she felt cold for the first time and began to shiver. She was aware of other runners near her and could see some up ahead, but it felt like she was all alone. The clouds were lower, a sprinkling of drizzle moving through the air, and it looked like there was more rain up ahead.

The memory crowded in. It had been one of the last days out they'd had before he was housebound. She'd taken him in his wheelchair, helping him out of the car and wheeling him around the grounds. It had been spring, the leaves budding on the branches and the grass bright green. They'd stopped to rest on a bench, enjoying the feeling of the sun on their faces.

'I could look at you forever,' John had said.

She'd opened her eyes and met his gaze, full of love. She'd squeezed his hand. Normally she'd shoo him away when he was romantic, while secretly loving it, but that time she remained quiet.

'I love this time of year,' John had continued. 'Everything coming back to life after the winter.'

'It's beautiful,' Kathy had agreed.

'Kath.' His voice was serious, tender. 'We both know . . . this might be it for me. And it breaks my heart not to grow older together, to be by your side and do all those things we'd planned. But I want you to know, when I'm gone, keep living your life, like those green shoots coming through the ground. Don't stop just because I'm not here.'

'John, don't be silly,' said Kathy firmly. 'There has to be another treatment, in the States, maybe, there has—'

'Shh, Kathy,' John interrupted her gently. 'We both know. And God knows, I'm so grateful for the life I've had. Full of love, with you and Alex. Hey, don't cry, love.'

He'd reached to wipe the tears from her face, and Kathy had clasped his hand in hers.

'I will miss you so much,' she sobbed.

'You'd better,' he'd said with a cheeky smile, looking exactly the same as when they'd met, aged twenty-two. 'And I have to say this. If you meet someone else, someone special enough for you, go for it, with my blessing.'

'John! I could *never*! How could you even think that?'

He met her gaze once again, pushed her hair back behind her ear. 'I wouldn't mind someone else seeing your eyes sparkle, Kath. Keep on living. Promise me.'

'I promise,' she'd said, choked up.

He'd sat back then, content, eyes shut in the sun. And they'd stayed there for a long time, just the two of them, Kathy vowing to remember every moment of how it felt to be by his side.

Kathy gasped as the memory hit her, as vivid as if it were yesterday. She'd forgotten their conversation; she'd blocked it out for years. She looked down at Baxter, at his trusting brown eyes. She thought of how he deserved to run over the finish line – 'Every dog has his day,' wasn't that how the saying went? She thought of her son waiting for her, with Jacqui and Becs. She thought of the new life that was just beginning. She would run towards that, even if it meant facing the pain of loss. She would keep her promise.

And then a sudden stronger beam of sunlight appeared through an opening in the cloud. It formed a faint rainbow, visible just for a moment, but it was all Kathy needed. It was if John were giving her a sign to keep going.

She set off running again, her muscles feeling tired now, glad of Baxter's encouragement as he ran ahead on the leash. As she got closer to the finish line, there were more and more spectators. She spotted Alex kissing Jacqui tenderly on the forehead, his arm around her. She saw that Becs was craning her neck, no doubt trying to spy her. Kathy pulled her shoulders back and lifted her chin, then ran more strongly towards them.

Towards her family.

And then in that moment, she realised that Baxter was part of her family. She couldn't give him up. He'd brought them together. He'd healed them. She'd tell Ben she would adopt him permanently. The resolve gave her a last burst of energy.

Her trainers thudded on the grass as she picked up speed. Alex spotted her and pointed her out. Jacqui and Becs pressed forwards against the spectator barrier, encouraging her on with shouts, Becs' voice hoarse.

And then, his deep voice joining theirs, she saw Ben.

His hands were raised over his head, clapping, and he was calling, 'Go for it, Kathy! Go for it!'

And just like that, she realised she was running towards him, too.

Maybe there could be something between them, if she just let her guard down a bit. She passed the bench where she and John had sat, that last agonising time. She felt the pain, the grief, rise up as she passed it – and then she felt a blessed relief. The sorrow replaced by the cheers and laughter of the crowd, the barking of excited dogs, the feeling of blood rushing in her veins . . . She was completely overwhelmed.

Kathy burst into tears as she ran over the finish line.

'Kathy, you did it! You did it!'

It was Ben, up ahead of her, his green eyes sparkling with delight.

Kathy surprised herself even more by running straight into his arms and sobbing against his chest as he hugged her.

They were mad, confused moments that could have gone on for seconds or forever, she wasn't sure. But then she breathed in deeply and pulled back from the warmth of Ben's embrace, to see she'd absolutely covered him in mud.

'Oh my goodness! I'm so sorry,' she gasped.

Ben smiled at her. 'Don't worry, at all. Here, I wanted to be the one to give you this. I don't think anyone here deserves it more.' Carefully, he placed a Muddy Dog medal around her neck. 'And a rosette for this boy here.' Ben crouched down and fixed a turquoise rosette to Baxter's harness.

'Ben, I've been thinking,' Kathy gabbled. 'I'll keep him, I'll adopt him permanently! I just realised, during the race, that . . .'

As she kept talking, she realised that Ben's face had fallen. His easy smile was gone.

'Kathy, we'll have to see. I mean—'

But his words were cut off by the arrival of Alex, Jacqui and Becs, who crowded around Kathy with words of congratulations.

'Watch your nice coat!' Kathy warned Jacqui, who replied that she couldn't care less about the coat and gave Kathy an enormous hug.

'I'm so, so proud of you, Mum,' said Alex. 'When you were running that final leg – I was choked up! You looked so alive. You looked like . . . like you used to be.'

'I felt alive,' she said. 'And I felt that somehow, your dad was cheering me on, too.'

Alex's eyes flushed with tears. 'Oh, Mum. I'm sure he is.'

'Here, we've brought you a tea, to warm up. And we can put this blanket over you. There's hoses so we can rinse you both off, or we can just bundle you into the car and get home.'

Jacqui was fussing around Kathy, but this time, it felt loving. How could they have misread each other so badly?

Becs was crouched down, making a fuss of Baxter.

'He's a hero, too! I saw him do the water, when he was scared and that little terrier helped him!'

They moved away to the side, to let other racers finish, chatting happily about the race. What a difference a day makes, thought Kathy. Yesterday they'd been in crisis mode and today, all seemed well. The future seemed full of possibility.

She looked around for Ben, but he was already off, welcoming other finishers, and she didn't want to bother him. She felt embarrassed at how she'd flung herself into his arms, but it had felt so right. She'd message him later and repeat the fact that she wanted to adopt Baxter, permanently. And maybe, just maybe, she'd pluck up the courage to ask him for a coffee.

*

Back at her house, Alex cooked them a simple supper of pasta while Kathy went for a hot shower. She insisted that Jacqui take a bath herself to relax, and was glad when she accepted with a grateful smile. Becs took on the task of uploading the photos from the day to Alex's laptop so they could see them clearly.

'Glass of wine?' Alex offered, as Kathy came into the kitchen carrying a battered cardboard box.

'Please,' she said.

He poured her a generous glass of red and she took a welcome sip. She could feel the tiredness setting in, but she didn't want this day to end.

'Who was the chap at the finishing line?' Alex asked.

Kathy could tell he was trying to be casual. She blushed.

'Oh, a friend. He works at the dogs' home. He's the one who put me on to the volunteering scheme in the first place. Then the fostering.' She took a sip of wine.

Alex nodded. 'Sounds like we've got a lot to thank him for.'

Kathy smiled. 'We do. Love, I'm thinking I'll adopt Baxter permanently. What do you think?'

'I think that's the best decision you've made in a long time,' said Alex, smiling. 'He's part of the family already.'

'And talking of family . . .' Kathy hesitated still. She placed the box on the kitchen worktop and lifted a packet of photos out of it. 'Here's those photos you were asking about. Of us.'

She'd retrieved the box from under the stairs. It was time she allowed her memories to remind her of what she'd been lucky enough to have, not just what she'd lost.

'Oh, Mum.' Alex stopped stirring the sauce and carefully wiped his hands before he turned to the photos. 'These are beautiful. I can't thank you enough.'

'I was thinking, maybe you'd help me sort through them. There are loads of packets of photos in there, most of them probably rubbish, and it would be nice to get them in order. Maybe put a few in frames and in albums.'

'I saw you'd put that one back on the mantelpiece. Made me glad.'

'That was our Becs' influence.'

Alex pulled a photo out and smiled at it. 'Look, Mum. Christmas with all of us. We're going to have some good ones coming up. I promise you.'

She looked at the photo. It was a beauty. John and Alex tearing into their presents, both delighted – Alex the very image of his father, even at that young age.

'Oh, but, Alex . . .' She'd have to come clean about Thailand. And think what to do with Baxter. Hopefully, he could go and stay with them. 'I wanted to tell you, I booked a trip, over Christmastime.'

A few months ago, she'd dreamed about this moment of telling them. Of how good it would feel to show her independence, that she didn't need them at all. But now, her heart sank at Alex's crestfallen face.

'Really, Mum? Are you sure that's . . .'

She saw the panic flash across his face and saw the effort he made to stop himself from falling into old fears.

'Sorry. I need to be better at supporting you leading your own life. Where are you going?'

He was putting a brave face on it; she could tell by his voice.

'Thailand.'

He looked surprised. 'That's so far.'

'Your dad and I always talked about going there,' she explained. 'And after last Christmas . . . I was . . . I don't know, I was afraid I wouldn't have a place with you all. So I took matters into my own hands and thought I'd do something positive.'

Alex stirred the sauce, silent for a moment. 'Gosh, Mum. I wish we'd all handled this differently. I had my head in the sand, too. I knew it had gone badly. And then I got caught up in work and time went by . . . And me and Jacqui were trying for a baby and it was putting us under a lot of stress.

'So I just told myself that you were all right, that you were superwoman, that you weren't that bothered. I didn't acknowledge how hurt you must have been. And I'm sorry.'

Until he'd said those words, Kathy hadn't realised she needed an apology.

'I'm sorry, too,' she said. 'For putting us all under so much pressure. I was determined everything would be perfect.'

'But Thailand is going to be great,' Alex said. 'It'll be the adventure of a lifetime! We can look after Baxter; Becs will love that. And the following Christmas, the baby will have arrived and we can have that one together.'

'Yes,' said Kathy. 'That'll be just right.'

But suddenly, the trip had started to feel like a weight on her shoulders, not an escape.

Chapter 15

Kathy turned up for her volunteer day the following Thursday still feeling like a champion. Her family had even hung around for most of the day on Sunday and they'd gone for a walk together on the common, reminiscing about the Muddy Dog Challenge – they'd be signing up again next year, for sure. Kathy had kept an eye out for Hope, but there was no sign of her all week. Funny. Maybe she'd already started the new job, but Kathy hoped she'd see her again and be able to tell her how much her training had helped, plus the good news that she'd decided to adopt Baxter.

At the centre, plenty of the Battersea staff and volunteers had attended the Windsor Muddy Dog or were planning on organising future events. There was lots of chatter about different obstacles, as well as comparing notes on the aches and pains they'd suffered the next day.

Kathy went about her work with great contentment. She couldn't believe how much she'd changed since starting the volunteering earlier that year. How close she felt to her family, how comfortable she was in the Battersea team. Now, she didn't hesitate to ask for help or join in with a chat.

She brought Baxter in with her as he had a vet check-up and could be looked after in the office while she went about her shift. Kathy resolved she'd catch up with Ben at lunchtime about the formalities of taking him home, for good. But Ben was nowhere to be seen. Odd. She asked if he was working today and the other staff said yes. Maybe he was doing a home visit.

It was only towards the end of the day that she saw him, striding across the central courtyard of the centre, an anxious expression on his face.

'Ben!' she called out to him.

He turned to look at her. 'Ah, Kathy.' His face looked grave.

'Ben, I've been looking for you. Can we get the official papers sorted for Baxter? Like I said at the Muddy Dog?'

Ben looked down at the ground and didn't speak for a few seconds.

'Kathy. I'm so sorry. But Baxter . . . he has another home, all arranged.'

Kathy reeled at his words. He couldn't be serious.

'What . . . what do you mean? Ben, stop it, you're joking.'

He looked agonised. He couldn't make eye contact with her.

'Kathy, I'm sorry, it was already in motion. You knew he was on the website. You knew people would be able to come and meet him on the days you were both here . . .'

'And so you just went behind my back?' Kathy knew her voice was high-pitched, trembling, and she could barely hold back the tears. 'Do you know how much this dog means to me and my family?'

'I'm sorry. Truly. But all along, you said you couldn't adopt permanently – and we always make it clear to foster carers that it isn't a way to test adoption. You always said that you couldn't, that you had travel plans, and other plans, too.'

Ben's voice was steady, and that incensed her even more.

Kathy shook her head, tears running down her cheeks. 'I *trusted* you.'

She remembered how good it felt to be in Ben's arms after the race. How stupid she'd been to ever think there could be anything between them.

Ben looked upset at her words, at last pushing his hands through his hair. 'Jesus, Kathy, I'm sorry – but I had to make a choice. And I made what I thought was the best choice, for Baxter, too. Knowing what I knew then.'

Kathy forced herself to stop crying. 'So, when are they coming, his new owners?' she said, her voice hard.

'It might be over the weekend, or even tomorrow,' said Ben. 'I can pick Baxter up and bring him to the centre, if that makes it easier?'

'They won't even come to my house, so I can see who's taking him?'

'Kathy, it's confidential. I mean, I can see, but . . . it might be easier this way.'

Kathy's heart felt like it was breaking all over again. The pain was indescribable. Baxter had brought her back to life, had brought the family back together – and now all that was swept away. She should never have done this. She should never have risked her heart again. Because this is what happened – you lost it all and you were left with nothing but a broken heart and the memories of what you had.

'God, Kathy,' said Ben, his voice trembling. 'I didn't know . . . But please trust me when I say I thought I did the right thing.'

'Text me before you collect him,' said Kathy, her voice cold.

How dare he talk about trust! She turned on her heel to go and gather her stuff from the office. She wouldn't come back here. She wouldn't risk her heart again.

On her way out, Baxter at her heels, she passed the memory wall once more.

'For John and Buddy,' she wrote on a piece of paper. 'Always and forever.'

*

That night was awful. Instead of the happy glow of knowing Baxter was home forever, she had to pack up his things and tell Becs the awful news. The only glimmer of consolation was feeling close enough to her family to be able to pick up the phone to them.

'God, I'm so sorry,' Jacqui said. 'I know how much you gave to that dog. You must be gutted.'

Jacqui passed the phone over to Becs, who burst into tears at the news that Baxter was leaving.

'But . . . but why not us?' she wailed.

'I don't know, darling,' said Kathy, her heart heavy.

Becs texted her later on.

'The only way I can think about this is if someone needs him more than us. We've got each other, after all.'

Once again, Kathy was startled by her wisdom and generosity. Her heart hurt too much to be so altruistic. Outside, rain poured down, lashed against the window by a strong wind. Summer was truly over.

She sat beside Baxter until she was practically asleep, soaking up the comforting warmth of his fur and wondering what on earth she was going to do without him, tears running down her face. She gazed up at the photo of John and Buddy on the mantelpiece and felt her loss all over again. This is what she was afraid of. That you built things up, you loved, and it could all be swept away – yet again.

She stumbled blearily up to bed in the small hours, having dozed off downstairs, and slept fitfully.

At first light, she got up and took Baxter for a walk, keeping her head down, acknowledging no one. She only glanced up to see if Hope was at their usual spot – she wasn't. Probably for the best. She couldn't stand telling someone else that Baxter was going.

Ben texted, politely asking if he could come round at 2 p.m. She answered with a single 'OK.' She felt herself growing numb, again. It was better like this. Not to feel, not to take risks, not to be so wounded. She fed Baxter and sat with her arms around him until the doorbell went.

Ben stood outside in the pouring rain, his hair already soaked. She wouldn't ask him in.

'Here's his things,' she said like a robot, passing Ben a packed bag with more force than was strictly necessary. 'I'll get Baxter.'

She slammed the door in Ben's face. Petty, but it felt good.

'Come here, boy,' she whispered to Baxter, throwing her arms around him. 'I will never forget you. Never.'

She couldn't start crying again, or she'd never stop, and she didn't want to upset the dog. Baxter licked her face tenderly. She forced herself to get up and open the door and pass his leash to Ben.

'There you are. That's everything.'

'Do you . . . want to say goodbye?' Ben said falteringly.

Kathy stared at him, chin held high. 'No,' she said. 'No, I do not want to say goodbye. At least not to Baxter. But to you, definitely. You know, I was right the first time I met you.' Her chest heaved painfully, the words spilling out of her. She couldn't stop them. 'I thought you were careless. And yes, everyone thinks you're great and charming, but the truth is, you're just chaotic and careless. I should have known you'd end up hurting me.' And with that, she shut the door again.

She held her breath, waiting for the sound of retreating footsteps. She couldn't believe she'd said that. She put her eye to the keyhole. She saw Ben, his face fallen, his shoulders slumped. He looked like a broken man for a moment. Then he shook his head, pulled his shoulders back and walked off swiftly, Baxter at his feet.

*

It was a dark day. Kathy pulled a blanket over her on the sofa. She couldn't be bothered to make anything to eat; she had no appetite, anyway, and nothing appealed to her. She pulled out her laptop, the screensaver a photo of them all at the Muddy Dog Challenge the week before. How things could change. The rug swept from under your feet, just when you'd started to feel settled again.

She sent Freya an email saying she was sorry but she could no longer continue volunteering at Battersea, with no further explanation.

As she lay on the sofa, lost in her thoughts, she kept thinking back to the moment that she'd been in Ben's arms. She'd thought he understood her, in that moment. So why would he do this, hurt her like this? She cursed herself for those times she'd wondered about spending more time with him, all the times she'd noticed his green eyes or scruffy hair. He was careless. She should have listened to her instinct from the start when he let go of Harry. Whatever else people said about him, he was not to be trusted.

Chapter 16

Over the next two weeks, autumn truly took hold. The leaves crisped orange and started to fall. It rained almost every day, accompanied by a strong wind. Kathy was glad. It matched her dark mood. She'd had a concerned email back from Freya, asking if she was all right and if there was anything she could do. Kathy hadn't answered. She'd also ignored a message from Judith, suggesting a DIY rendezvous, and one from Asha, asking her for a coffee.

The only messages that brought a flicker of joy into her heart were from Jacqui, Alex and Becs. Jacqui in particular had surprised her by getting in touch in thoughtful ways. She checked in a few times a week – 'No pressure, hope you're doing OK?' – and Kathy would ask – and sympathise – about her pregnancy symptoms. Jacqui was often exhausted and nauseous. Kathy offered to come down for a weekend and help out around the house, and Jacqui accepted gratefully.

It was a relief to get out of the house, but it felt strange to be there without Baxter. She worried the awkwardness would come back, but it didn't. They were a family now.

'Maybe he brought us together and that was his work done, like Mary Poppins,' said Becs thoughtfully, and Kathy smiled and rumpled her hair. 'We'll find our dog, Nana. Don't worry.'

She went for a long walk with Alex, just the two of them.

'I can see you're hurting,' Alex said. 'I could see how much Baxter meant to you. I loved him, too.' He took her hand and squeezed it as they walked through the barren fields under a leaden sky.

They paused to look at the view and Kathy leant her head on his shoulder.

'Yes,' she said. 'That feeling of having someone you love who brings you so much joy, ripped away.' She was crying, she realised.

Alex wrapped his arms around her and didn't say a word. In the stillness and calmness of his embrace, Kathy realised how much of John still lived on in him. Alex had the same ability to calm her. She hugged him back tightly.

'You know,' said Alex, 'I'm sorry this happened, but I'm glad you're telling me about it. It's nice you're letting me in.' He swallowed. 'You know, that's what was so hard about . . . when I learnt about Dad's illness. That I'd been shut out.'

'I am so sorry,' said Kathy. 'Really. We thought we were doing the right thing.'

'I know,' said Alex. 'You don't have to apologise. And I also know how much you put into helping me recover. Maybe I've never said that. But you don't have to protect me any more.'

Kathy nodded. 'And I've felt that I don't want to be a burden on you, when you're building a life of your own.'

'You aren't,' said Alex. 'At all. I think I worry more when I don't know what's going on with you, as I just jump to the worst conclusions, or I go to the other extreme and think you don't need anyone or anything.'

'I think I'd like to be in the middle,' said Kathy. 'Not superwoman, but not swaddled in cotton wool, either.'

'Deal,' said Alex. 'That gives me such a weird mental image.'

'Me, too,' said Kathy, feeling laughter bubble up inside her for the first time since Baxter went.

*

Back in their living room, curled up on the sofa, Kathy's heart felt soothed. But once again, she found herself dreading going back to her home alone. It would feel so different, arriving back without Baxter by her side. She wondered where he was, if he was happy with his new owners, if they were looking after him like he needed.

Ben had said to trust her with his decision, but she couldn't help but worry.

She began to think seriously about moving – she could sell the house and head down to be nearer Alex, Jacqui and Becs, especially with a new baby on the way. That might be nice . . . Although she'd still need to have a life of her own. She sighed miserably. Just when she felt she'd been working out a new recipe for happiness, it was back to square one.

*

It was the second week after she'd left Battersea Dogs' Home and Kathy was staring out of the window at the back garden as the rain drizzled down, when she heard the doorbell ring. She frowned and went to open it.

There, on the doorstep, was Judith. And Hope. And Baxter.

Kathy's instant reaction was joy. Baxter wagged his tail frantically at seeing her and strained on his leash to get nearer her. Hope reached down and unclipped him, and he scampered towards Kathy, who crouched down to greet him. He licked her face, pressing himself against her, his tail batting against her legs.

'I think we've got some explaining to do,' said Judith nervously.

Kathy had been so caught up in the joy of seeing Baxter again that she hadn't taken in just how surreal this all was. What on earth were the three of them doing here together?

She invited them into the living room, where Judith and Hope sat down on the sofa, side by side.

'Hope, what on earth . . . ?' began Kathy.

'It's Jessica,' said the girl, looking at Kathy and then looking to Judith as if for reassurance.

Judith put a steadying hand on the girl's forearm.

Kathy blinked, staring at Hope again. She couldn't see a link between this thin young woman, her hair dark and sweeping over her face, and the chubby blonde girl she remembered. Her body language was completely different, as well. Even though Hope – Jessica – had grown in confidence over the summer, she still hunched her shoulders, still found it hard to make eye contact without nervously glancing away.

Kathy looked at Judith, and in that moment, saw a glimmer of resemblance between mother and daughter. There was something about the angle and the shape of their eyes that was undeniably similar. And the more she looked at Hope, the more she saw Jessica – the bright, talented child that she remembered.

'Jessica . . .' said Kathy. 'What . . . what happened? Why do you have Baxter? I don't . . . I don't understand.' She wondered if she was dreaming. She reached her hand down to Baxter's ears. There they were, furry and warm. Real.

Jessica sighed and looked down. 'When I saw you that morning on the common, I knew who you were straightaway. And I was terrified you'd recognise me; that's why I kept my head down. I was so relieved when you didn't.'

'Why?' said Kathy.

'Because I hated what I'd become,' Jessica said with vehemence. 'You remembered me as that little girl from school, always playing her violin, full of potential. And I couldn't bear for you to see me as I am now. Or as I was then.'

'What happened after school?'

'We moved down to the south-west,' said Jessica. 'And while I was there, I hurt my hand. It meant I couldn't play the violin. And I couldn't fit in with the new kids there. I was angry. I was hurting.

'I started hanging round with these older blokes and a few girls. Thought they were my friends.' She laughed bitterly. 'Mum tried to stop it, to keep me in line, but I wouldn't listen.

'She was out working all hours and I just ran wild. Drank. Smoked pot. Same old cliché. And once I'd started failing, getting in trouble at school, not turning up for exams – well, it just got harder and harder to sort myself out. And I hated myself for being so weak.'

It was hard to see her like this, Kathy thought, her head bowed, her forearms pale and so slender.

'I left home as soon as I was sixteen and I was just roughing it for a few years,' she said. 'Sometimes turning up back at Mum's, mostly on couches, working odd jobs. Partying.

'It wasn't a life. I had a lot of mental health problems. Things got pretty bad. I ended up in hospital. That was a wake-up call.'

'We started rebuilding things,' said Judith, taking over the story. 'We made the decision to move back to London. To get Jessica the treatment she needed here.'

Jessica nodded. 'I was an in-patient for a while, then I was in sheltered accommodation. That's when you first saw me in the park. And now I'm living with Mum. We've been working on our relationship and it's so different now.'

'It's good to have you home,' Judith said, looking at her daughter proudly.

Kathy remembered how evasive Judith had been when she'd asked her about Jessica, how she'd heard Judith crying behind the door when she'd returned from Alex's. Had that been a fight with Jessica, she wondered?

'Why didn't . . . why didn't you tell me?' she said. 'I wish I'd known. I would have helped, however I could.'

'I couldn't bear for you to think I'd failed as a mother,' said Judith. 'And Jessica, after she saw you on the common, she begged me not to tell you.'

'I didn't want to have disappointed you,' whispered Jessica. 'You were always so proud of me, being that star violinist.'

'And once the lie had started, how could we go back on it?' said Judith. 'You'd have thought we were mad.'

Kathy thought back to the little lie she'd told about Christmas and how things were with her family. Once the seed was planted, these stories took on a life of their own.

'I do understand it, believe it or not,' said Kathy. 'I'm sorry you didn't feel like you could confide in me. But, look, where does Baxter fit into this?'

Both women visibly squirmed.

'Kathy, I think I did the wrong thing,' Jessica began. 'When I saw you on the common with Baxter, initially I wanted to stay away and hide from you. But I kept coming back to how brave Baxter was, even though he'd had so much wrong. And there you were, helping him. It made me think maybe all wasn't lost.

'I remembered how much you'd encouraged me before, at school, and I wondered if maybe that could happen again. When we started training, it was the only thing I had going.

It made me feel like I could do things again, like I could be a positive influence in someone's life. I started to think maybe I was worth something, after all. Maybe I could be responsible and helpful.'

Kathy nodded, encouraging her to continue.

'And the more time I spent with you and Baxter, the more I felt certain I wanted to offer a dog a home. A second chance. I know from experience how hard it is getting a second chance and how people can judge you. A few missing years from your CV and you're bottom of the pile,' she grimaced.

'But why Baxter?'

'The thing was, I knew Baxter. I knew all about his ears and his skin and what he'd need. And you'd said you couldn't keep him – or didn't want to. And Mum said the same thing when I talked to her about it, that foster carers look after dogs temporarily before they find their forever homes. I thought that maybe I could give him a good home. I knew him, he knew me – it made sense.'

Kathy thought back to when Jessica had asked her if she wanted to keep Baxter on their last training session. She'd said no. How was Jessica expected to read her mind? She thought back to her discussion with Alex, where he'd said he sometimes felt shut out from what was going on. She rubbed her temples. Maybe people had a point. Maybe she could let them in more, especially when it came to being honest about how she really felt.

Jessica licked her lips nervously. 'Then when we saw him go up on the website, we contacted Battersea Dogs' Home and we met with Ben. And he seemed to understand me. He didn't judge me for my past, only what I could offer Baxter in the future.

'So, when he said we could take him home . . . it was the best moment I've had in years.'

Kathy noticed how Jessica smiled as she said this, her face lighting up so that she looked more and more like the child Kathy remembered.

'We were going to come and explain everything to you anyway, but I wanted to wait until my life was more in order and I had something to show for it. Then Ben told us how upset you were and we felt so awful that we'd caused it.

'Honestly, Kathy, if we'd known how much he meant to you, how much you also needed him, we never would have put the adoption in motion. So, I'm here to offer Baxter back. You can have him back, Kathy, and I'll completely understand.' Jessica finished speaking and sat back with a sigh.

Kathy's head was reeling. She struggled to comprehend that this young woman was Jessica and she felt awful at what she'd been through. She was turning over in her mind how Judith had kept the truth from her – and feeling guilty that she'd felt she couldn't confide in Kathy. She regretted not being more honest about her feelings earlier on. Then maybe they wouldn't have been in this mess. And most of all, she was thinking of how wonderful it was to have Baxter back in her home. How right it felt.

'I'm going to put the kettle on,' Kathy said, shaking her head. 'I think we all need a cup of tea.'

She went through to the kitchen, and heard mother and daughter murmuring together. My God, that couldn't have been easy, Kathy thought with respect. They didn't have to come round like this. She wondered about what Ben had said. He'd asked her to trust in his decision and now she could see why he'd made it – and she cringed at those awful things she'd said to him. She closed her eyes and wished she could take her words back. She was learning a sharp lesson in how she came across.

She arranged tea, mugs and biscuits on a tray, and took them through. The two women were waiting, poised, Jessica's eyes bright and shining with emotion. She had her hand on Baxter's head. Kathy thought back to how scared she'd been of him when she'd first seen him. What a difference! She poured them both tea and sat back with a mug herself.

She sighed and forced herself to speak. 'I admire you hugely for coming round. And of course I don't judge you for wanting him. Baxter is a dog that you just fall in love with, isn't he? And it's hard, because he brought my family together. Especially me and my . . . granddaughter.

'But maybe his work here is done.' She felt like she was going to cry. 'I can't take him away from you, Jessica, not when you need him so much. And when he needs you so much. So, he's yours. From the bottom of my heart.' She was crying now, tears rolling down her cheeks.

Jessica got up and embraced her. 'You're not losing him, you know. You'll see him all the time. I'll make sure of it.'

Kathy nodded, her heart banging on her ribs. She'd done the right thing.

'Let me say a proper goodbye to him. We didn't get the chance last time.' She crouched down and took Baxter's dear face in her hands. 'You brought us back together, angel dog. You bring love wherever you go. I am so lucky to have borrowed you for a little bit. I'll see you soon.' She lowered her face to his head, and breathed in his warm familiar scent.

Her heart felt glad, she realised. It was good to have closure. She knew he'd be cherished by Jessica and help her on her way.

She straightened up and smiled at them both.

'You know,' said Jessica, looking thoughtful. 'You say it's all him who brought you together. But I wonder if it was you. Think about it. If you hadn't reacted the way you did when I first met him, with patience and understanding, then I wouldn't have had this chance. I'm sure it's the same with your family, as well.'

And Kathy realised Jessica was right. It hadn't just been Baxter. It was her, too.

Once they'd gone, Kathy opened up her laptop, took a deep breath and replied to Freya's email. She didn't want to get into it all, but she explained she'd had a tricky few weeks and was feeling better now, and she'd love to come back and volunteer, if that was allowed.

A reply popped up quickly that said, 'WONDERFUL! We've missed you. See you Thursday!'

Kathy smiled. It felt like everything was coming right again. Apart from with Ben. She had to make it right with him. She had to trust in her own ability to sort it out. And that meant a big fat apology.

Chapter 17

When Kathy arrived back at the rescue centre, it almost felt like she'd never been away. She was straight back into action, meeting the new dogs that had come in and catching up with a few familiar faces who hadn't yet found their forever home. It was colder now, so she wrapped herself warmly in a scarf and hat to take the dogs out for their walks, and made sure that the finer-haired breeds were cosy in their Battersea coats.

At lunchtime, she took a deep breath and went to the rehoming office, to ask if Ben was around.

One of the rehomers named Sara shook her head. 'He doesn't work Thursdays any more. I can leave a message for him, if you like?'

'Oh, no, it's fine,' said Kathy, backing away.

So that was that. Had he changed his days specifically to avoid her? Her heart plunged at the thought. She did have his phone number, but she wanted to apologise face to face. Though a message would be a start.

She pulled out her phone and began typing, then stopped and deleted it, then started writing again. Her lunch break would be gone by the time she got round to a finished message!

She settled on: 'Ben, I'm very sorry for what I said. I wanted to apologise in person, but I hear you've changed your days?' And she sent it. Was that enough? She *had* wanted to see him in person with the hope of opening up their friendship again, that much was true.

Her phone buzzed.

'Thanks for the apology. I think it's best we're not in touch,' it said simply.

That was it. No, 'Accepted,' or response to her question. That was a clear message. He didn't want anything to do with her.

Kathy sighed, kicking herself. She should have said that she understood why he'd given Baxter to Jessica, that she'd seen him again, that she'd accepted his new home – and was glad about it. But it was too late. She'd blown it.

*

As autumn progressed, Kathy felt almost happy again. She'd been down to see her family a few times and Becs had come to stay with her. Jacqui's pregnancy sickness had settled down, thank goodness, and she even had a little bump. Kathy had cried happy tears when she'd seen the scan, the little nugget swooshing around in black and white.

She phoned Becs regularly, to check she was excited as well, and not feeling left out. But there was no need for concern. Jacqui had got her involved in choosing the décor for the baby's nursery. Alex had also come to visit on his own a few times and they'd carried on sorting out the photos into albums. There had been laughter and a lot of tears.

'You know,' she said to Alex one rainy Saturday, the photos spread out around them, 'I think I've been struggling with this idea of moving on, when I never wanted to move on from your dad.'

Alex regarded her for a moment, clearly thinking.

'The way I think of it is that we're just bringing the memories of him into the rest of our lives,' he said. 'It actually feels like he's more present with us now than he's been these last few years. When we didn't really talk about him.'

Kathy nodded. 'I like the way you put that. And actually, maybe you'd help me hang up a painting?'

They'd hung the painting John had bought for her in Barcelona on the upstairs landing, and Kathy remembered the warm sunshine every time she passed it. She'd allowed herself more and more good memories of John and felt them flow around the memories of his illness. She was more balanced now, she realised. She wasn't afraid of being bowled over by thinking about him; although, of course, there were still moments of deep pain. But now, she allowed herself a good cry and she invariably felt lighter after. She'd miss John for the rest of her life, of course she would, but she'd let other things in now.

And as for Baxter, Jessica was true to her word. She and Kathy went for their regular Wednesday walk most weeks. The change in Jessica was noticeable almost every time they met, her eyes bright, her laughter always ready. Baxter kept them both on their toes – he was so full of boisterous energy. They'd had to apologise to numerous people, still, for Baxter almost bowling them over, even though he was slightly better mannered than before. Jessica had also been taking him to dog agility classes to keep his mind busy.

'He loves it,' she explained to Kathy. 'It's like the training we did for the Muddy Dog, but even more full-on. It's the only thing that tires him out – and me, to be honest.'

It was another thing that made Kathy realise Ben had been right all along. She would never have been able to keep up at the dog agility classes. Baxter was boisterous and young, and needed someone to match his energy. She was thrilled to see them both thriving.

'And,' said Jessica shyly, 'I've met someone there. She's called Sam. It's early days, but she's great. She's got a very lively cocker spaniel, who Baxter adores. The two of them wouldn't leave each other alone, so we got talking and then . . .' She shrugged, embarrassed. 'We're taking it slowly, but it's going well so far. She even helped me clean Baxter up after he'd tried to eat a cow pat, so she must be a keeper, right?'

Kathy beamed. 'I'm so glad. No one deserves this more, Jess. And anyone who can deal with Baxter getting in a mess like that is worth their weight in gold, frankly.'

'What about Ben?' Jess said suddenly.

'What about him?' Kathy felt herself blush.

'I thought . . . maybe there could be something between the two of you.'

Jess' eyes were sparkling and Kathy allowed herself to feel caught up in the excitement for just a moment before coming back down to earth.

'He was so concerned for you, when you were upset after the adoption.'

Kathy cringed at how she'd treated him once again.

'I think we're just too different,' she said before adding, light-heartedly, 'but if you spot any handsome men of my age at your dog training, do pass them my way.'

Jess smiled and thankfully left it at that.

*

The days shortened, and Kathy realised it wasn't long until she'd be away in Thailand. Her enthusiasm for the trip had returned and she was looking forward to some adventures.

She felt far more confident about talking to strangers, thanks to all that time spent striking up conversations when she was walking the dogs and socialising with the volunteers, and it would be nice to come back with travellers' tales. You always appreciated home so much more after a stint away.

Then, one Monday morning, she received an email from Tom asking if she'd consider another foster dog. She rang him to hear more.

He explained they were looking for a foster home for a Jack Russell terrier who was frazzled in kennels.

'I'd be up for it,' she said. 'But remember, I'm off to Thailand mid-December, so I couldn't do something as long-term as Baxter.'

'We think it's all right,' Tom said. 'We have a nice history from his previous owners – they had to give him up due to their own ill-health. We want to see how he behaves in a home environment. Give him a chance to settle in. But we think he'll be able to find a home pretty quickly. Do you want to come and meet him?'

And so Kathy went in to be formally introduced to Archie. He was a middle-aged Jack Russell, a little grizzled around the mouth. Kathy smiled. She'd always had a soft spot for Jack Russells and this little guy was as handsome as they came, his head tan-coloured, bar a blaze of white down his nose, and his body white with a big patch of tan.

But he was stressed, no doubt about it. His body was rigid and his eyes bulged, his face set hard. He also barked at them as they approached and it took a while for him to settle so they could go into his pen. He was shivering, which was a sign of stress.

As soon as they were in a quieter room, Kathy saw a change come over the dog. He seemed much calmer, even coming to sniff her hand and sit politely by her side.

'Poor boy,' said Kathy. 'You can tell he's stressed. I'm sure he'll be fine with me.'

Archie gently licked her hand as if agreeing.

'That's great,' said Tom. 'His old owners said he could be a bit contrary and keeps you on your toes, but that he's a lovely character.'

And so Kathy found herself heading off with her third foster dog, thrilled all over again by the sound of his little paws pattering on the pavement beside her. Here, once more, was a chance to do good. To help this little dog transform however he needed to. She wouldn't make the mistake again of thinking of him as hers – that was how she'd been hurt with Baxter. For now, it was simply enough to be part of Archie's journey at Battersea Dogs & Cats Home.

*

If Archie was a person, Kathy thought to herself a few days later, he'd have an opinion on absolutely everything. Archie had settled in beautifully, visibly relaxing as soon as they got in the door. He wasn't shaking now, he had a healthy appetite and the barking had stopped – mostly. In so many ways, he was the model of good behaviour. He'd sit by the back door, indicating that he wanted to go out to the toilet. Kathy had been taken aback by his manners – he seemed almost human. She found herself adding, 'If you'd like?' or 'If you don't mind?' to her request for him to sit or come to her.

But he knew just how to wind her up. She'd come downstairs on the third morning with him, to find Archie gleefully chewing one of her woollen walking socks. How had he even found it? It had been annoying her for weeks that she had an odd one drifting around and she thought she'd looked everywhere. Evidently not everywhere a terrier could look.

'Drop that, Archie, please,' she said.

Archie paused in his chewing, looked at her with a side-eyed glance, and then picked up the sock and trotted off to elsewhere in the house.

Kathy followed. 'Archie, drop it.'

Again, the pause, the consideration, the trotting off, to just out of her way.

Kathy felt her frustration rising – but she had to admit, his comic timing was perfect. Each time she approached Archie, even with a treat in her hand to try to encourage him to drop the sock, he'd trot off at exactly the right moment and pace, his little hind legs working smartly, his tail wagging cheekily.

Eventually, Kathy gave up and decided to look at the Battersea website for more training tips on how to get a dog to drop things. She loaded up her laptop and began to read the advice.

Ah, so she shouldn't turn it into a fun game, which is what she'd been doing in chasing him around. She had the impression that Archie had been enjoying himself mightily. The first step would be to get him to associate the word 'drop' with food. She could work on that today.

Kathy felt something move on her foot. She looked down. Archie had placed the woollen sock carefully over her foot and had then put his paw out to attract her attention.

She looked down and burst out laughing at his butter-wouldn't-melt expression, as if he hadn't spent twenty minutes giving her the runaround just before!

*

One morning, she found Archie stood on the back of the armchair, staring out of the window, one paw raised in the air.

'What are you looking at, eh?'

She went over to him, and he glanced at her and wagged his tail. Then he hopped off the sofa, disappeared for a bit and returned with his lead clutched in his mouth, dropping it at her feet.

She was amazed. How had he got his lead? She struggled to remember where she'd put it – maybe it had been on the floor . . . But evidently, it was time for him to take her for a walk.

She loaded her pocket with treats, put on her coat, helped Archie into his little blue Battersea coat and then they were off. He strutted ahead of her and seemed to catch the attention of everyone they passed.

'What a smart dog!'

'He's so handsome!'

'What a cheeky little chap!'

Occasionally, Archie would let out a low woof in agreement. He was the model of good behaviour – sitting down by Kathy's feet when they came to cross any roads, glancing up at her when she started walking again.

'What are you up to, boy?' said Kathy. 'You're being suspiciously well-behaved.'

As soon as they got to Clapham Common, Archie dived to the ground and rolled in mud – and goodness knows what else. Kathy groaned. It was a completely normal part of doggy behaviour, but she'd have to clean him up when they got in. Archie glanced up at her, looking delighted, tail wagging.

'Come on then, monster,' Kathy said. 'Off we go.'

And then he was back to Mr Perfect, trotting along beside her, mud smeared all over his face.

Kathy had to laugh at his little foibles. Archie definitely knew his own mind.

She was very relieved to see that he behaved well with dogs who were off their leads. She held her breath when a young cockapoo scampered over and wanted to play – Archie was polite and friendly but put her in her place when she got a little too boisterous.

'Is he reminding her of her manners?' said the owner as he joined them.

'Yes, I think so,' said Kathy.

'She's only young. She needs a bit of guidance.'

She was a beautiful dog. She turned her attention to Kathy and started trying to jump up. Kathy straightened up and ignored her, turning side-on, and the dog quickly returned to all fours, earning her a 'good dog' and a treat from her owner.

'She's a fast learner,' Kathy said encouragingly. 'She got down pretty quickly then.'

Now that she was more settled, Archie re-approached her to say hello and she responded in a far calmer way, curving round and sniffing, her tail wagging, but without any of the dive-bombing or leaping around.

'There we go, Madge,' said her owner encouragingly. 'See, people are more likely to want to say hello if you're not jumping on their heads.'

'Words to live by,' added Kathy drily.

They exchanged a few more words before heading off in opposite directions. All continued calmly until Archie saw a puddle. Instantly, his body language changed. He stiffened his posture and stopped short, refusing to go any further. He even let out a tiny growl at the puddle.

'We don't have to go through it,' Kathy said. 'We can go round it.'

But it was no good. Even with her encouragement, he wouldn't go anywhere near the puddle. Kathy knew better than to push it. Who knew if he'd suffered some trauma in water before? It might be something she could work on, but she didn't want Archie to have any more bad experiences just as he was settling down. She wondered how she'd be able to wash him at home if this was the case.

They arrived back at her house. Kathy was lucky in having an outside tap and she'd left a towel nearby, so she could get the worst of the mud off his paws. He didn't mind her doing that, especially not when there were a few treats in store. But he was still rather stinky. She'd have to give him a proper wash.

She encouraged him upstairs and into the bathroom, where she turned the taps on, making sure the water was warm. She'd been afraid that this would spook Archie, but he seemed completely unfazed. Then, gently, she lifted him into the shallow water. She was ready for any signs of distress – but amazingly, Archie seemed to relax. He closed his eyes and looked dreamy. Tentatively, Kathy put a little more water on him. A tail wag.

'You are the most contradictory dog I think I've ever met,' she murmured.

She squirted out some dog shampoo and scrunched it into his fur. Archie let out a little groan of happiness, his eyes shut.

Kathy chuckled. 'Did you roll in that mud just to get a bath? You're a clever thing! And yes, I should have known you wouldn't fancy a nasty cold puddle when you could get the spa treatment here.'

It was nice to be able to treat him, she thought. He'd not had the easiest time in kennels, so it was good to help him relax. After a thorough shampoo, he was squeaky clean. Kathy lifted him into a towel and gently rubbed him dry. Of course, he helped by shaking himself vigorously, sending droplets flying in all directions. Because of his short coat, he'd dry quickly, but Kathy took no chances and turned the heating up a bit, to ensure he wouldn't catch a cold. They both returned downstairs, where Archie promptly conked out in front of the fire, his little flanks rising and falling.

Kathy watched him, feeling content. But then she caught herself. She couldn't bond with Archie, not to the extent where she'd start thinking of him as hers. That's where she'd got into trouble with Baxter and she wasn't going through that pain again. She switched on her laptop and began looking at a few outstanding details for her Thailand trip.

*

Kathy had never known a dog so contrary. He'd be good as gold for days, then decide to attack one of the cushions on her sofa, feathers flying everywhere. He'd been delighted by the vacuum cleaner emerging – bowing to it and pogoing around it, barking as Kathy hoovered up the feathers.

Next time they'd gone to the park, he'd barked at everything and everyone, and had happily splashed through a puddle with no nerves in sight. If he took against anything on their walk – a bush that somehow displeased him, even though he'd seen it before – he wouldn't budge. If he didn't want to go for a walk at all, he'd pick up his lead and hide under the bed with it.

On more than one occasion, Kathy had had to take ten deep breaths to keep her patience with him. This was particularly the case when Archie decided to howl along with the *EastEnders* theme tune. But then he'd charm her by hopping up next to her for a snuggle, his little head on her lap, his legs twitching as he dreamt. She could forgive him almost anything when he turned his big brown eyes on her and cocked his head to one side as if listening to whatever she said.

Becs and Jacqui came up to visit and fell in love with him instantly. He was soft as butter around Jacqui. Archie offered her a paw, politely, then settled down with his head on her feet, keeping one eye open as if watching over her.

'Oh, I could fall for this one, as well,' sighed Jacqui. 'I'm beginning to see why you're such a dog fan, Becs.'

'Finally,' said Becs, rolling her eyes, but her tone was warm, and she and Jacqui giggled together.

'You're not tempted by this one?' said Jacqui.

Kathy shook her head. 'Even if it wasn't for Thailand, I'm not sure I could cope with all his little quirks. You know, sometimes I think he knows exactly what I want him to do but then just makes up his mind as to whether it's worth his while. He really does have a mind of his own.'

Jacqui looked amused. 'Seems like you might have met your match in him. You're also someone who knows her own mind and sticks to it!'

'Rather like someone else I know,' said Kathy, nudging Jacqui.

The two of them now joked frequently about how stubborn they each were, how much they liked to organise and arrange. She couldn't have imagined enjoying Jacqui's company like this only a few months ago. Jacqui was a real rock, she realised. If she said she'd call, she'd call. If she said she'd bring Becs, she did. More and more, she understood why her son adored her like he did and she couldn't be happier that the two of them were growing their family together.

'You know, I'm really sorry you won't be with us for Christmas,' Jacqui said. 'We've got everything triply covered so we can take the day off. It'll be our last calm

Christmas before the little one arrives. You probably won't think of us at all, you'll be so busy enjoying a tropical paradise, but we will really miss you. It won't be the same without you.'

Kathy felt tears prick at her eyes at Jacqui's words. But there would be other years, she told herself. Other years to be at home for Christmas.

Kathy glanced around and noticed that Archie had disappeared. She was getting a sixth sense for when the little dog was up to something. A sort of suspicious quiet.

She got up and slipped out of the living room. There, in the kitchen, was little Archie, stood on his hind legs, paws perched on the open dishwasher, carefully licking every dirty plate within reach. Kathy groaned.

Archie popped down as soon as he saw her and trotted through her legs towards the living room. Kathy shut the dishwasher. He'd done an excellent job on the plates, she noted. They were squeaky clean. But it was lucky there hadn't been anything damaging to dogs left on the plates. Seemingly innocuous ingredients, like onion and garlic, could be extremely dangerous for them.

She went back through to the living room, where Archie was now reclining blissfully on the rug, the little Emperor, with Becs devotedly tickling his tummy. He had a knack of falling asleep on his back, with his paws up in the air.

'I caught him doing the washing-up,' Kathy said, raising her eyebrows. 'He was there on his hind legs, licking the plates in the dishwasher.'

'Oh, no!' said Becs. 'I must have left it open. I'm sorry.'

'No harm done,' said Kathy. 'This one is very wily, so you have to be extra careful with things like that.'

She was heeding her own words over the next few days, when Archie decided to get the hang of jumping for food on the work surfaces. She'd been cooking dinner, when he'd hopped onto the seat of a nearby chair – which Kathy had just used to get things down from the top cupboard – stood on his hind legs and delicately snaffled a strip of chicken before hopping down again, licking his lips.

Kathy knew there was no point scolding him. It was a dog's nature, after all, and she had to encourage him to behave in a different way instead. You couldn't impose a human system of 'good and bad' on a dog – they simply wouldn't understand it. She'd have to make doubly sure there was no food in sight and perhaps do some training on the 'down' command. But he was so quick, and smart! Whoever ended up rehoming him would have to be on their guard.

Chapter 18

Christmas was well and truly on its way. Even though it was just November, there was plenty of tinsel to be seen and Christmas songs on the radio. Even though Kathy rolled her eyes, she did love Christmas. She wondered what it would be like in Thailand. What would she be doing on Christmas Day?

She'd booked into a fancy hotel on one of the islands, so at least she could treat herself to a Jacuzzi. Some winter sun wouldn't go amiss – she thought about it every time she dragged herself awake in the dark for her volunteer day, or to take Archie out. Half the time, he was bleary with sleep as well, making funny little groaning sounds as he got out of his bed.

She hadn't seen or heard from Ben, but she thought about him often, and her ears pricked up if she heard his name. She couldn't shake how right it had felt to be in his arms after the Muddy Dog Challenge, or the sparks that had flown at the Thai restaurant – or how devastated he'd looked when she'd called him careless. She wished she'd known his reasons for rehoming Baxter with Jessica then. The two of them were going from strength to strength. Baxter was a very happy dog. He was training hard with Jess at the agility classes and was packed with muscle. He still had bags of energy, but he'd found the right owner to help him channel it into focus.

Kathy had tried to encourage Archie to weave in and out of a row of flowerpots in the garden, but he'd sat down and looked at her, then simply went round the side of them as if showing her there was a simpler way to do it. Kathy had found herself laughing and had gone the same route as him. He'd given her an encouraging woof – Kathy felt sure he'd have given her a treat and a pat on the head if he could. He really did think he was training her!

Still, he loved any form of mental puzzle. Kathy had taken to scattering his food, allowing him to hunt it down. He was so good at it she could even do it in the garden – it reminded her of setting Alex treasure hunts when he was little. She also liked to make him a 'destruction box', where she'd fill an old cardboard box with scrunched-up balls of paper and empty toilet roll holders, scatter in some of his dry food and let him loose on it. She'd videoed the last one and sent it to Becs, it was so funny. Archie adored tackling any objects that were larger than he was and he dragged the cardboard box around for all it was worth.

Another day, he'd somehow found an old, half-deflated ball of Alex's in the undergrowth and had wrestled it into submission around the garden, even though it was bigger than he was. Kathy found it less amusing when Archie insisted on picking up the biggest sticks he could find and carrying them all around the park. It was almost as if he were trying to trip her up, she thought, as the stick bashed against her ankles. But then she'd look down at Archie's determined little face and her heart would melt.

*

'What are you doing on Christmas Day?' said Jess as they walked round Battersea Park with the dogs. 'I was wondering if you wanted to come round. And Archie, too, if he's still with you. I'm going to cook at Mum's and I think Sam will come, too.' She blushed at this last bit. 'It'd be nice for you to meet her.'

'Oh, Jess,' said Kathy. 'I'm away, remember? The Thailand trip?'

'I'm an idiot,' said Jess, shaking her head. 'Of course, Mum's been telling me all about it. She's so excited for you. Next year!'

Kathy nodded, but she suddenly wished she was staying in London for Christmas. That was her second invite, and she was sure a Christmas with Jess and Judith and the dogs would be a lovely one, as well. And now she thought about it, Freya had asked her if she might be free to volunteer on Christmas Day, as she lived nearby. It was a wonderful day, she'd explained, full of Christmas cheer. So that was option number three.

But she couldn't back out of the trip now and lose all that money. Plus, what if Christmas wasn't as idyllic as she imagined it to be? She'd thought last year that she was going to organise the perfect Christmas. If something went wrong again, she'd kick herself for not sticking to her guns and heading off independently.

'You're coming to the Battersea carol concert, though?' said Jessica, giving Baxter a treat.

Kathy nodded. 'Wouldn't miss it for the world.'

The carol concert was a week or so before she'd head off for Thailand. It was held in St Luke's Church in Chelsea and some Battersea dogs even got to attend as a guard of honour. With that, and the volunteer Christmas party, and heading down to Alex's to help them decorate the tree, Kathy's December diary was looking fuller than it had for many years. She'd also had an invite from one of the volunteers to go round for New Year's Eve, which she'd regretfully declined.

Her phone now buzzed with notifications: from her family, from friends like Judith and Asha, from the volunteer WhatsApp group sharing funny, cute photos of the dogs. She remembered this feeling from before John had died. Of having a busy, fulfilled life. Of having a place in the world. Of being part of a community. And it was all thanks to the rescue centre and its special people – and dogs. Battersea would still be there when she got back from Thailand, she reassured herself. Everything she'd built wasn't just going to disappear.

*

Finally, it was December. The tinsel went up around Battersea Dogs & Cats Home and there were Christmas trees in reception. The radios were dominated by Christmas songs – Kathy loved the oldies but couldn't bear some of the newer stuff – and Becs was always sending her links to listen to, which Kathy politely described as 'not my cup of tea'. Archie was reassessed for rehoming and his little advert put on the website. Kathy hoped he'd get a home before Christmas, so she could head off to Thailand knowing he was all right, with someone who would understand and accept all his little quirks, who'd love them and not be driven mad by them, as she sometimes was.

It was a windy, wet Wednesday morning when they went out for Archie's walk, and still dark, really, even though it was after 8 a.m. He peered up at Kathy from his blue Battersea coat, sticking close to her legs.

'We won't be out long,' murmured Kathy. She decided to head to Battersea Park, so she could pop into Asha's café for a warming cup of tea afterwards.

A chilly drizzle had started up and she shivered even in her cosy coat.

They crossed into the park and began to walk round, although their spirits were dampened by the weather. It would be a day for curling up inside, thought Kathy. She'd look over her Thailand kit once again, although she was sure she had everything she needed. And she'd email Ben's friends and remind them of her exact dates.

Ben. Her mind wandered once more to him and she wondered if he'd be at the carol concert, and if he might thaw a little bit in his attitude to her – and then she was off daydreaming.

She glanced to the side and saw that Archie had darted after one of his enormous sticks, determined to pick it up and carry it with him. She smiled – and then her blood ran cold. Archie was whimpering and limping.

She crouched down beside him. His poor front leg was raised, blood dripping from his paw, and Kathy's heart dropped. She glanced around and saw the fragments of a glass beer bottle, smashed. She cursed herself – she'd been daydreaming, half asleep, and this had happened. And she was panicking. Cuts to dogs' feet could be dangerous, as there was a main artery there, and this looked to be bleeding profusely.

Her heart hammering in her chest, adrenaline flooding through her body, Kathy swept Archie up into her arms and began to run with him as quickly as she could. He licked her face and whimpered as she ran, and she thought her heart would break with worry. Her only thought was to get him to the rescue centre as soon as possible, where surely one of the vets would be able to help.

Gasping, she dashed out of the park and across the road. She could see the Battersea building up ahead – and who was that by the entrance? It was Ben.

She yelled his name. He turned round, frowning.

She sprinted across the road.

'Please, help me! It's Archie! He's hurt. His paw is bleeding!'

Ben took in the scene in an instant. He took Kathy's arm and pulled her through the gates, and together they ran down to the veterinary centre.

'His paw is badly cut,' Ben said to the nurse there, his voice urgent. 'Try and stay calm, Kathy; it'll keep him calm.'

Kathy was trembling all over. They were ushered quickly into the surgery, where Adam, one of Battersea's vets, took Archie from Kathy. He whimpered horribly. Kathy could hardly bring herself to listen. It was all her fault. She'd been so careless and now look what had happened. She should have spotted that broken glass and steered Archie well away.

The vet's voice was calm.

'We'll need to sedate him, so we can check there are no shards left in there and clean it out. This looks like it might need stitches.'

'Oh, God,' said Kathy, overcome with guilt.

Archie twisted his neck to look at her and twitched his tail – it could barely be described as a wag, it was so feeble.

'Good boy,' said Kathy, forcing her voice to be positive.

'Do you want to come and give him a cuddle before we start?' asked Adam.

Kathy nodded and went to stand by Archie's head, leaning close so she could kiss his ears.

'It's all right,' she soothed. 'You had a bit of a nasty accident. But you'll be safe and home before you know it, stealing chicken from the worktop right under my nose.'

He peered up at her, looking for reassurance, and licked her face. She'd never seen his eyes so wide and pleading. It was enough to break her heart.

'If you want to wait outside, I'll let you know when we're done,' said Adam.

Outside, she sank into a chair. Ben sat beside her.

'It's all my fault,' Kathy began, agonised. 'I should have looked where he was going, I should have been more careful.'

She felt ashamed. She was so used to thinking of Archie as an independent spirit, she should have looked after him more. She'd accused Ben of being careless and now look at her. She hung her head.

'Things like this happen,' said Ben. 'You can't control everything. And you got him here as fast as you could. And look, you're still hanging on to his stick.'

Kathy looked down and realised she was still clutching the stick Archie had been dragging around. She must have seized it instinctively.

'That's what I call love,' smiled Ben.

Kathy nodded, grateful for his kind words, but she was still convinced she could have done something to prevent him from being hurt. Archie needed her and she'd let him down.

'You saw him in there,' said Ben, 'how much he looked to you for comfort. He knows how much you'll look after him, once he's back at home with you. We can't control everything in life. It's how you fix it afterwards that counts.'

Kathy wondered, with a glimmer of hope, if his words could apply to her, as well. She opened her mouth to speak, but Ben spoke first.

'I've got to head off,' said Ben. 'But are you OK?'

'We'll be fine. Thank you so much, again,' said Kathy, looking at him.

Yet again, he'd helped her in her hour of need. How could she have misjudged him so badly? His gaze held hers for a moment, then he dropped eye contact and turned towards the door.

'Forgive yourself, Kathy,' he said. 'Nobody's perfect – you just have to do your best.'

*

Kathy arrived home with Archie later that day. She felt exhausted, like she'd been awake for days. Archie's paw was neatly bandaged, with a cone around his neck (to stop him from chewing at his paw) that gave him a surreal Elizabethan look. She'd carried him all the way home, kissing the top of his soft little head and giving thanks that things hadn't been worse. She'd heard horror stories of dogs with cut paws, where the main artery had been hit.

She got into the house and lit the fire, carefully laying Archie down on his blanket by the hearth. He was still groggy from the sedation. She even brought his stick in for him. Who cared if it got dirt on the carpets, if it made Archie feel comfortable? He leaned over and sniffed it, and thumped his tail once or twice.

'You must be the only dog in history to get his owner to play fetch,' Kathy murmured.

Owner. She'd used the magic word.

She made herself a tea with several sugars and went to lie on the sofa, easing back into it and closing her eyes.

She sensed something move and opened her eyes to see a dizzy Archie tentatively trying to stand up and come over to her. She went over and carefully picked him up, tucking him next to her so he could lie down and stretch out his paws.

Oh, dear Archie. He needed her, she realised. She couldn't let go of him. He'd come and made himself right at home here, from the very start. And she needed him, too.

Suddenly, she couldn't imagine anyone else looking after him, anyone else understanding his quirks. The vet had said

Archie's paw would take two or three weeks to recover fully and the dressing would need to be changed every two days for the first week or so. She couldn't leave him with anyone else to do that, not when he'd placed his trust in her.

Each day with Archie had been surprising. She never knew what the little dog was going to do next – and that's what she needed to learn. To embrace the chaos, the unpredictability of life, and rejoice in it. She would give adopting him her best shot.

The trouble over Baxter had started because she'd pretended that she was superwoman – tough, independent and not needing anyone. She'd learnt some sharp lessons this year about how she managed to convince everyone else that was true. She'd be honest sooner, this time. More open. If she still wasn't his forever home, at least she'd know she'd done everything possible.

*

Two days later and Kathy had filled in the form to register her interest in adopting Archie. She'd also spoken to the foster team about it. It still didn't feel like enough. She wanted to speak to Ben directly. His words rang in her ears: that it was about fixing things that counted. Not being perfect but doing your best. She dithered about, picking up the phone to him – it was after 7 p.m. now, so he'd be finished with work – but couldn't bring herself to do it.

'Oh, Archie, Archie, what am I like?' she muttered to the dog, who cocked his head and looked at her.

He picked up the stick that was still lying by the fireplace and carried it around the living room proudly, despite his limp. Kathy smiled to see his spirit returning. He was a brave little dog.

She should take a leaf out of Archie's book, too.

She glanced outside. Some delicate flakes of snow were falling. An idea struck her. If she was going to go, it had to be now.

'Come on, boy,' she said, putting Archie into his cosiest coat. 'We're going to pay someone a little visit.'

She wrapped herself up, glanced in the mirror at her reflection and left the house before she could change her mind, with Archie tucked into her coat. He couldn't put much weight on his paw, but she was sure he'd appreciate being outside. She walked briskly along, trying to stop her nerves from getting the best of her.

And then she was there, outside Ben's house. She knew the address from his WhatsApp message after they'd had their dinner. A warm light emitted through the threadbare curtains, so he must be in. She gulped, forcing herself to walk up the garden path, past the straggly hedge, and ring the bell. The sound made her jolt.

Deep breaths.

And then he was there, in the doorway, hair dishevelled, his jawline stubbly.

'Kathy?' He sounded surprised.

'And Archie,' she said, her voice a squeak.

She wasn't sure how dignified she looked with Archie's head, complete with cone, poking out of the top of her coat, but she'd give it her best shot.

'Do you want to come in?'

She shook her head. She just had to spit this out before she lost her nerve.

'No, thank you, I . . . I just have something to say. Apart from thank you, again, for helping us.' She took a deep breath. 'Ben, I've applied to adopt Archie. But I wanted to come and talk to you as well, to explain why, and because there are some things I want you to know.'

Archie licked the snowflakes off her cheeks.

'I'm so sorry for what I said to you after Baxter. From the bottom of my heart. There's no excusing it, but I wanted to explain, if I can. You see, my husband died five years ago.'

She paused. It was still hard to say the words. She was grateful that Ben didn't say or do anything, apart from tilt his head slightly to one side as if to listen even more intently.

'And since then, I've tried to control everything,' Kathy continued. 'I've tried to get my life back together and pretend everything is fine. Better than fine. Perfect. When in fact, I was lonely. I didn't know my place in the world. And through Baxter, I learnt that you can't just pretend everything is fine when it isn't. I learnt that you should be honest with people, and with yourself. But I still hadn't learnt that I can't control everything.'

Ben smiled softly at her.

'So, when I didn't adopt Baxter, I was so angry at you, at myself, for not managing everything perfectly. I thought everything had been ruined. I am so sorry for what I said. You're not careless, at all. You're caring and kind, and have given me more second chances than I deserved.'

'Everyone deserves a second chance,' murmured Ben. 'Especially you.'

Kathy felt her heart flutter.

'After Archie cut his paw and you said that you can't control everything – I'd heard those words before, but that was when they truly sank in. That life isn't perfect. Life is about loss, as well as love. And you have to embrace that chaos.

'It's Archie who's made me do that. Nine times out of ten, he'll do what I say and behave perfectly. But then it's that one time where he'll do exactly as he pleases – and it used to drive me mad, if I'm honest. But now it's what I love most about him. He's his own little spirit. And if I am lucky enough to give him his forever home, he'll be the happiest little dog in the world. Because I need him – and I think he might just need me, too.'

She finished speaking, her heart banging against her ribs. The night air seemed very still. She realised she was shivering.

Ben raised his eyebrows. 'Do you want to come in, now?'

Kathy laughed and shook her head. 'No. I've disturbed you enough and I'm sorry to intrude. But I just had to take a risk and come and speak with you.' Her heart felt light, she realised. She grinned at Ben. 'Let me know your decision as soon as you can, though. Because if this little guy comes home for Christmas, I won't go to Thailand, despite all my careful planning. We'll be staying put. Like you said, isn't it about going with the flow sometimes? You just can't plan how things will turn out.'

Ben nodded.

Kathy turned round and walked down to the gate. 'Goodnight!' she called, as he shut his front door.

Kathy knew she'd probably come across as a crazy lady, but she didn't care. She felt alive and her heart was light. She'd given it her absolute best. Now, she just had to hope it was good enough.

Chapter 19

'I think we're going to love this,' Kathy said to Becs as they approached St Luke's Church.

The beautiful building was spectacularly lit up for Christmas, and as they got nearer, they heard the occasional bark.

'Dogs?' said Becs, turning to Kathy, her face a picture of delight.

Kathy had kept this element a surprise. The Battersea dogs formed a guard of honour to welcome visitors to the church for the Christmas carol service. They looked so smart in their blue Battersea coats, each with a Battersea handler by their side, and Kathy was filled with love and pride.

'Isn't it wonderful!' said Kathy. 'Seeing these dogs – who have been treated like second-best, or worse – finally get their moment in the spotlight.'

Becs squeezed her arm. 'And knowing they're getting the help they need.'

'Absolutely. At Battersea, no one ever gives up on a dog in need.'

'And you're part of that,' said Becs. 'Just think of all the dogs you've helped.'

'Stop that or you'll have me in bits,' said Kathy, sniffing loudly and taking a deep breath.

They walked past the dogs, stopping to greet them and their handlers. Becs was in her element.

'As soon as I'm old enough, I'm volunteering, as well,' Becs said. 'And I've been thinking about career stuff. About being a vet. I've got to choose options soon and I think that might just be what I go for.'

Kathy beamed at her. 'You'd be fantastic!'

Then they were inside the church. Kathy took a moment to breathe in and savour the moment. That musty smell of stone, so reassuring, somehow, the beautiful vaulted ceiling, the creamy stone lit with golden candles, the organ music blazing out in welcome. There was a glittering Christmas tree at the front, with holly and ivy decorations on all the pews. The atmosphere bubbled with festive goodwill and excitement.

Kathy had been reading up on the history of the church and had discovered it was where Charles Dickens had got married. He was also one of Battersea Dogs & Cats Home's earliest supporters. She wished she could tell John about it – he loved those sorts of details. The impulse was tinged with sadness, of course, but more and more, she found she was able to remember the many good parts of her life with John and the memories brought her strength, not sadness.

Kathy caught sight of Jess and Judith, and waved. They were seated near the front, with Baxter. Jess looked nervous. She'd be doing a reading later, of her own Battersea story about Baxter. Kathy caught her eye and gave her a thumbs up. Jess smiled back at her and Kathy was glad she'd have Baxter by her side. He was such a confidence-giving dog. She waved to Freya and to some other familiar faces, keeping her eye out for Ben. She wasn't even sure if he was attending. She hadn't heard anything from him since her mad visit.

Then the service started. A chamber choir sang exquisite music that made Kathy's spine tingle. Then came an address from Battersea's executive officer about the work of the charity, thanking the public for their donations. She pressed home the point that Battersea receives no government funding, and everything is down to fundraising and donations from the general public.

Kathy was struck again by this fact. Battersea Dogs & Cats Home truly belonged to everyone and it was inspiring to see what people could do when they pulled together. Then Jess got up to read. She introduced Baxter and talked movingly about the positive effect he'd had on her.

'But before I met Baxter, there had been a whole team of people who had helped him on his journey. From the lost and found staff to the veterinary team, the kennel staff, and right down to his amazing foster carer.' Jess looked over and caught Kathy's eye.

Kathy blushed bright red as Becs said, 'This is her! It's you, Nan!' a little too loudly, and people turned and stared.

'Everything you did to help Baxter recover, and the love you showed him, was immense. I can't thank you enough for everything you did for us both.'

Kathy swallowed a lump in her throat and flapped her hand in front of her face to push away the tears. Baxter would always have a special place in her heart.

Then Jess finished speaking and they were on to carols, standing up and singing with all their might. Kathy felt full of Christmas spirit. They finished up with a rousing chorus of 'O Come, All Ye Faithful', and then it was time for a mince pie and a cup of mulled wine. Everyone chatted happily as they moved out of the church and into the frosty night air.

Kathy felt a tap on her shoulder and turned to see Ben. He looked serious.

'Can I speak to you for a second?'

Oh, God, this was it. She braced herself for the news. It would be fine either way, she told herself, but she was holding her breath.

'Kathy, I'm really sorry,' Ben said. 'You're now part of the Failed Foster Carer Club.'

Her heart sank. This must be to do with Archie's cut paw. They were taking him away and she could no longer foster. Then Ben was passing her some papers, on Battersea headed paper, and a pen.

'This makes it official,' he said, grinning. 'Archie will be coming home for Christmas. You join many of our wonderful other Failed Foster Carers, who've ended up adopting.'

'He's mine?' Kathy gasped.

Ben nodded.

She flung her arms around him. 'Oh, thank you, thank you!' The stars shone overhead and Kathy felt her heart soar at the prospect of having Archie in her life for good.

'It was clear to see the two of you belonged together,' Ben was saying. 'I like the fact that he's not afraid to give you a run for your money.'

'It'd probably be more appropriate if he signed my adoption papers!'

'What's going on?' said Becs, returning with a mince pie for each of them. 'Hi, Ben.'

'Archie's coming home for Christmas,' said Kathy, beaming. 'Which means I'm staying put. Do you think there's still room at the inn for the two of us?'

Becs squealed and almost dropped the mince pies as she hugged Kathy.

'This is the best news ever!'

Then Judith and Jess were surrounding her, keen to hear the news, hugging her with joy.

'Oh, but Thailand?' said Judith, her face falling. 'You won't get to go.'

Kathy shook her head. 'Not this year.' She glanced at Ben. 'But I've learnt that you sometimes have to change course. Go with the flow.'

'Well, I'm thrilled you're staying put,' said Jess. 'Means I have company for walks on those early grey January mornings!'

Kathy bent down to give Baxter a big kiss and cuddle. 'I owe you a lot, special dog,' she whispered to him. 'Thank you for opening my heart.'

They chatted excitedly about Christmas plans and presents and just how they were going to spoil their dogs on Christmas Day. Kathy looked round for Ben, but he'd disappeared. Oh! She'd wanted to talk to him more, but never mind. He'd made her Christmas wish come true.

Suddenly, all she wanted was to be back at home, to see Archie snoozing by the fireplace and know that he was there for good. To have Becs in the spare room and go to sleep knowing they'd be chatting away over breakfast. To ring Alex and tell him the good news. She and Becs said their farewells and walked home together.

Archie came to greet them as soon as they got in the door. He was still limping, but his spirits were clearly returning and his eyes were bright.

'Welcome home,' Kathy said, picking him up and kissing his head. 'Welcome home, forever.'

Chapter 20

Christmas Day grew closer. Alex had been delighted by the news that Kathy would be coming, after all. Jacqui had rung her separately, to discuss presents.

'We're so glad you're coming,' she'd said. 'He'd kill me for telling you this, but he was actually pretty glum about you missing Christmas. And this is going to be a good one, I can just feel it.'

Kathy felt it, too. She'd admittedly gone a bit mad buying presents for Archie – every time she'd gone in for a volunteer day, she'd been tempted by something new for him in the shop. A new collar, blue, in honour of his Battersea heritage, but studded with smart metal eyelets. A selection of toys, a new bed, some grooming brushes – well, now that he was here to stay, she may as well get everything they needed! She'd been looking up dog-friendly Christmas recipes, so he, too, could have a special meal on the day. Of course, she bought a few special toys for the Battersea residents, as well.

She felt full of Christmas joy, springing out of bed for her final volunteer day of the year and whizzing through her tasks. Christmas songs were playing on the radio and the kennels were festooned with tinsel. Even though it broke her heart that some of the dogs wouldn't have their new homes in time for Christmas, she also knew they'd be thoroughly spoiled by the volunteers who came in on Christmas Day.

Before she knew it, it was the twenty-third of December. She was packing the suitcase that had caused all the trouble the year before, ready to head off on the morning of Christmas Eve. It was funny, she'd had no problem picking out presents for her family this year. For Jacqui, she'd bought some colourful earrings that she just knew would suit her and a treat day at a spa. For Becs, a selection of books about dogs and a smart rucksack – just the right size to be an overnight bag for when she came to stay with Kathy. She'd also bought two tickets for Crufts, thinking they could go together. Becs would love seeing the dogs compete in the agility class. And for Alex, she'd wrapped up some cufflinks of John's – lovely silver ones, each in the shape of a dog. She'd poured herself a glass of wine as she'd wrapped them, and allowed the memories of her dear husband to surface. It felt right, to allow things to move on. She wouldn't forget him as she fulfilled her promise to keep living.

'Here's to you, John,' she murmured, lifting the glass.

Archie trotted over to her and pushed his head against her other hand. He was so bright and alert and attuned to her. If she ever had any low moments, he wouldn't push it – he was as good as gold. It was on her brighter days that he sometimes liked to test her patience.

Her phone rang. Alex.

'Hello, darling,' she said. 'How's it all going?'

'Hi, Mum.'

He sounded stressed. Oh, God. Here it was – they wouldn't be able to have Christmas together, after all. Kathy tensed and then relaxed. She'd have Archie's company on the day, whatever happened. She'd go and see Judith and Jess. It was funny, she didn't feel the same pressure to make everything absolutely perfect any more. She knew her family loved her, and she them. She would trust that they'd make up for Christmas Day another time.

'What's wrong?' she said.

'You're not going to believe this, but the boiler's gone at the house here. No heating, no hot water, and can't get anyone out to fix it this close to Christmas.' He hesitated. 'We were wondering . . . if we could come to you?'

'Of course!' Kathy said. 'There's plenty of room for you all here.'

'Thanks, Mum,' Alex said, relief in his voice. 'We'll bring everything foodwise, for starters and mains.'

'And I've got the Christmas pudding raring to go,' said Kathy. 'We'll have a great day. What matters most is that we're all together.'

'I'd better get packing up the car,' said Alex. 'We'll be with you tomorrow. Bye, Mum. Love you!'

'Love you, too,' said Kathy.

She hung up the phone and looked round at Archie. 'Christmas at home, after all, young man. I hope you're going to help me decorate.'

She hadn't gone overboard with decorations as she hadn't thought it was worth getting a tree if she was going to Thailand. Then, when her plans had changed and she was going to go and stay with Alex, it still hadn't seemed worth the trouble. She'd put a wreath up on the front door and some pretty white lights in the window, but she'd need to do better than that if the family were coming. Surely she could find a little tree tomorrow.

Humming to herself, she pulled the box of decorations out of the landing cupboard and set about finding the ones she wanted. She wasn't going to do the perfect colour scheme of last year, she decided. Instead, she reached for the old decorations with a history, ones that brought back sweet memories of decorating the tree with Alex and John.

She unwrapped one box in particular and had to giggle. It was a box of little dog-shaped decorations – three of them, in padded felt, with little Christmas hats and scarves. She remembered John buying them in the January sales, to cheer her up now that Christmas was over. He'd told her to look forward to when they could hang them on a new tree.

That was John, always looking forward to the future. And how strange – each little dog looked just like the ones she'd fostered this year. There was Milly, the elegant greyhound who had helped Kathy to grow in confidence. Baxter, with his heart of gold. And Archie, dear Archie, who was a whole world in himself. It really did look just like him, even down to the patches on his body. She felt the hairs stand up on her arm. Maybe she was being silly and it was just a coincidence, but sometimes she had the feeling that John was looking out for her still.

'It's you,' she said to Archie, showing him the decoration.

He cocked his head to one side, eyes bright.

'And it's not for eating.'

She messaged Judith to say she was staying in London, after all, and would she and Jessica be free for a post-lunch walk on Christmas Day. She had a little something she wanted to give Judith. Judith messaged back to confirm and say she'd have a few home-made mince pies at the ready, if they could fit anything else in. Kathy was going to have a busy day, she realised.

'I'm really happy we both get a rather different kind of Christmas this year,' Kathy typed back.

'Me too,' replied Judith. 'I think we deserve it!'

*

Christmas Eve was a busy one. Kathy got up early and made a list of everything she had to do – some habits would never change.

She made up the beds with fresh linen and hoovered the living room – with Archie dive-bombing the hoover and yapping the whole time. He had a complicated love-hate relationship with the machine, Kathy mused. Some days he couldn't stand it, other days he'd go up and attempt to play with it. Once, he'd even lain down in its path, tummy exposed, completely relaxed, making her laugh. He was so obvious when he felt he deserved attention. She'd tickled his belly with the hoover attachment (turned off, of course) and he'd closed his eyes with pleasure. But then the next day, he was back to seeing the Hoover as public enemy number one. Kathy was learning more about his little quirks each and every day.

Then she went to the shops to stock up on supplies. Yes, they were bringing Christmas lunch, but she needed to think about breakfast for four, nibbles and a few extra bottles of wine, plus what to have for supper that evening. Finally, she found a sweet little Christmas tree, only a few feet tall but perfectly proportioned and on sale cheap as it was Christmas Eve. She was glad to give it a home for Christmas Day.

She'd barely started decorating it when the doorbell rang. She glanced at her watch. It couldn't be that time already!

She answered the door to Alex, Jacqui and Becs, their arms brimming with supplies.

'Sorry we're a bit early, Mum,' said Alex. 'We made very good time.'

'And I'm dying for a pee,' said Jacqui, dashing off to the toilet. 'Sorry to barge past!'

Kathy welcomed them in and took a deep breath. Well, hadn't she told herself to embrace the chaos a bit more? So what if she wasn't perfectly ready?

'Thank you so much for having us, Nan,' said Becs earnestly. 'It was awful! The shower was freezing!'

The house was a hive of activity. They sorted out the food and Becs put on some Christmas music, while Archie patrolled them all, as if supervising that they were sticking to their tasks. Jacqui went upstairs for a lie-down and Kathy was glad to see her take some rest.

'What's next?' asked Becs once the food had been stashed away.

'Want to help me do the tree?'

'Definitely!'

With the fire on, Christmas carols playing, Archie asleep on his favoured cushion, chatting to her granddaughter, Kathy felt she might burst with happiness.

'This one's just like Archie!'

Becs had found the little Jack Russell decoration.

'John bought that one,' said Kathy, suddenly keen to share the memory. 'He loved buying me thoughtful little treats. I remember I was all glum because it was January and Christmas was over, when he pulled those little dogs out of his pocket to cheer me up.'

'I didn't know that story,' said Alex, coming in with a pot of tea. 'I do remember how good he was at surprises. This one time, when I was nervous about exams, he'd put a little note in my pocket saying good luck from Buddy.'

'I didn't know that one, either,' said Kathy.

'I have to confess, I still keep it in my wallet.' Alex looked down and blushed, and Kathy went to squeeze his shoulder.

'That's so lovely,' said Becs. 'Here, let's put this one somewhere where we can all see it. Isn't it a bit spooky it looks like Archie?'

She carefully hung the decoration right in the middle of the tree.

'Exactly the right spot,' said Kathy with a smile.

Alex brought through some sandwiches and slices of cake, and they munched on a sort of afternoon tea as they finished decorating the tree.

'I'm not sure it can take much more,' Kathy said, standing back and looking at it.

The little tree was covered in decorations, of all different colours, shapes and sizes. Right at the bottom of the box, they'd even found some old decorations that Alex had made at school – paper snowflakes, and silver bells made from egg cups and tinfoil.

'These have to go on!' Becs said, laughing.

Alex groaned. 'At the back, please. I don't think I want everyone commenting on my lack of artistic ability.'

'What's all this commotion?' said Jacqui, pushing open the living room door and coming in. Her hair was tousled, but she had more colour in her cheeks. 'Ooh, no one told me there was cake!' She picked up a slice and nibbled it. 'The tree looks gorgeous.'

She came closer to admire it. Archie had got up when she entered the room and insisted on staying near her heels, protectively. Kathy wondered if he instinctively knew she was pregnant and was on his best guard dog behaviour.

'My little guardian angel,' said Jacqui, looking down at him. 'Could I put something on the tree? If there's room?' She held out a delicately embroidered decoration. 'It's a koala. I know it seems silly, but my granny made it for me when I was little and it doesn't feel like Christmas unless it's up.'

'Of course,' said Kathy warmly. 'Christmas is a time for memories. Here, I reckon we can make a space right here . . .' She did a little bit of rearranging, so the koala could hang next to the Archie decoration.

'Thank you,' said Jacqui, hanging the decoration and looking sideways at Kathy. Her eyes were watery.

'It must be hard, being away,' Kathy sympathised. 'I tell you what, as soon as the baby is old enough, we'll plan a trip over there together. I need to put all the travel planning skills I learnt into action.'

'Any regrets about not being on a tropical beach right now, sipping a piña colada?' said Jacqui.

'I haven't even thought about it.' And it was true.

With the house prepared, they relaxed into a lazy Christmas Eve, watching *Carols from King's* and then some cheesy TV. Kathy prepared them a light supper – they'd be stuffing themselves the next day, after all – and they ate in the living room, plates on their knees, Archie circling to snaffle any dropped food. Then it was off to bed, all of them exhausted from a busy day.

As she lay in bed, Kathy found her mind turning once again to Ben. She imagined his house, the threadbare curtains, the hedge that needed trimming. She thought back to all the ways in which he'd helped her. Without him, she wouldn't even have thought of volunteering at Battersea and she would never have been led to Archie. And she thought of how little she knew about him: how he shut down questions about his past, but his expressive, beautiful paintings spoke of deep emotion.

'Merry Christmas, Ben,' she whispered.

Chapter 21

Christmas Day, and Kathy woke early. The house was dark and quiet. She savoured the cosiness of her warm bed for a moment before getting up quietly. She'd let them sleep for as long as they wanted.

She padded downstairs and into the kitchen. No Archie. His bed was empty. She frowned. That was strange.

She pushed open the door of the living room, to find the fire already lit and Becs in her pyjamas, cuddling Archie, who turned his head to look at Kathy, eyes woozy with the joy of being fussed so early in the morning.

'Happy Christmas!' Becs whispered. 'Look! He's been!'

Kathy glanced at the mantelpiece and beamed. There, underneath family photos old and new, was a stocking for Becs, one for Archie – small, but bulging with all sorts of goodies – and a third stocking with no name.

'Happy Christmas! And who's the other one for?' she whispered back.

Becs gave a proud smile and raised her eyebrows. 'Well, it might just be for you. Santa Paws says you've been a very good dog this year, with all your volunteering.'

'For *me*?'

Becs nodded. 'Yes. Everyone needs a Christmas surprise.'

Kathy hugged her. 'Thank you!'

'Oh, it was nothing to do with me and everything to do with Santa,' Becs said with a grin.

'Shall I get us some tea and we'll open these?' said Kathy. 'Then we could take Archie for a morning walk.'

Becs nodded excitedly and before long, the two of them were sat side by side, opening their stockings and encouraging Archie to snuffle at his presents. Kathy felt like a little girl again. She had cosy gloves, a fleecy headband for keeping her ears warm – she'd be putting that to immediate use – some posh hand cream and a funny little book of dog cartoons. Plus, some chocolate coins and satsumas. Each little gift was so beautifully wrapped, it warmed her heart.

'What have you got?' she asked Becs, who showed her some earrings ('I've been on at Mum to let me get my ears pierced forever, so I hope this means what I think it does'), some drawing pencils, pretty gold socks and a tinted lip balm.

Kathy offered her a chocolate coin and they nibbled a few with their tea.

'Shall we see what Santa has brought Archie?'

Kathy unpacked a beautiful new feeding bowl, with his name on, packets of dog-friendly Christmas treats and a colourful tug toy. Archie himself seemed more interested in shredding the paper into confetti, but then he picked up his new toy and paraded around with it happily.

'He's going to have the most presents out of us all,' Kathy laughed, thinking of the pile of gifts she had for him.

Oh, well – you only got one first Christmas in your new home; though she was fairly certain she'd spoil him in exactly the same way every year.

'There's one more thing in there,' said Becs.

Kathy pulled out an envelope and opened it. It was a printed-out certificate for a wellbeing kit to welcome other dogs into Battersea. The money would go towards toys, cosy blankets and soothing scents to help new arrivals settle in.

'Santa thought Archie might like to send something to help other dogs in the same position as he was,' said Becs, and Archie gave a little woof in agreement, sniffing the paper as if he were reading it.

'That's so thoughtful,' said Kathy. 'These are very kind and generous presents, and it's a total surprise. I haven't had a Christmas morning like this in years.'

Becs beamed.

'Let's get our shoes on and take Archie out.'

They bundled themselves quickly into any old clothes – there'd be time to shower and change later – and wrapped up warmly, heading out of the door with Archie, Becs holding the lead. They'd head out for another walk after lunch, with Judith, but Kathy loved to see the world waking up on Christmas morning.

The lights were already on in many windows, excited children no doubt tearing into their presents. But she spared a thought for people having a difficult Christmas Day. People who were alone, sad, missing someone, unhappy, or who simply wanted the day to be over. She wished them all well and prayed they'd find some comfort before next Christmas.

She and Becs did a quick circuit in the park, saying 'Happy Christmas' to whoever they passed. Archie for once didn't attempt to pick up an enormous stick, as if knowing there were presents galore for him at home.

They got back to the house to find Alex and Jacqui in the kitchen, making a start on breakfast. Christmas greetings and hugs were exchanged, and everyone tucked into scrambled eggs on toast.

'When do you want to do presents?' Jacqui asked Kathy.

'Whenever you like,' Kathy replied. 'When do you normally do them in Australia?'

'Actually, we tend to do them right after breakfast. We could never leave them alone when we were kids and it would mean we could perhaps Skype them for a bit. It'll be evening there now.'

'Absolutely,' said Kathy. 'Shall we go into the living room?'

'Fetch my laptop, love,' Jacqui said to Becs.

They all went into the living room, where Jacqui and Alex had put out presents under the tree.

Jacqui dialled her mum and dad and suddenly, the screen burst into life.

'Hi, love!' said a woman who had to be Jacqui's mother – the resemblance was so strong. 'Happy Christmas to you all!'

'Hi, Mum! Happy Christmas, too! Is Dad there?'

'Right here. And your brother, and Sal, and the kids.'

A whole host of beaming faces crowded into the screen.

'See how sunny it is?' Becs said to Kathy. 'I can't imagine Christmas being like that!'

'One year we should try it,' Kathy replied. 'It'd be an adventure!'

'Mum, Dad, I want you to meet Kathy.' Jacqui beckoned her forwards.

'Hi, Kathy! Happy Christmas!' The greetings rang out from the screen as introductions were made.

'We've heard so much about you,' said Isabel, Jacqui's mum. 'All the tales of the dogs you've rescued, the run in the park, the little Jack Russell – can we meet him, too?'

'Here he is,' said Kathy as Archie pressed his nose into the camera, his image filling up the screen and making everyone laugh.

'We know all about Battersea,' said Isabel. 'We love watching that Paul O'Grady show about it, although I tend to cry every week.'

'Oh, me too,' said Kathy. 'There's a Christmas special on tomorrow, by the way.'

Isabel scurried to make a note and Kathy flushed with pleasure that Jacqui's family already knew so much about her. It didn't feel like meeting strangers at all. And she realised she already knew a lot about them. About Isabel's pottery habit, her dad's love of surfing, her not-so-little brother's campsite business – 'although it's not really camping,' Jacqui had explained, 'the tents are way fancier than that, otherwise he knew he'd never get me to go.' So she felt quite able to ask questions about how their Christmas had been, and any presents they'd opened, and any plans they had for later in the day and New Year.

'And Jacqui said you'd chosen not to go on your trip to Thailand?' said Isabel. 'You'll just have to do it another time – and come and see us after!'

'It's a deal,' said Kathy.

Then it was time to open the box of presents that the family had sent over. There were coos as the girls unwrapped pretty shell necklaces, and some merino thermals for Alex.

'There's one for you, as well,' said Alex, handing Kathy a lumpy package.

'For me?' Once again, she was surprised – and happy – at how much she had been thought of and included. She tore open the wrapping paper to reveal a beautiful little pottery dish, perfect for holding a few items of jewellery. 'Oh! How lovely.'

'Mum made it,' said Jacqui, smiling.

'You're so talented,' Kathy said to Isabel. 'It's absolutely beautiful. That'll have pride of place.'

'She only gives us the really misshapen ones,' said Jacqui's brother cheekily, earning him a poke in the ribs from his mum.

'This is so sweet,' said Kathy, turning to Jacqui. 'I feel terrible about not sending anything.'

'Don't worry,' said Jacqui. 'We sent a box from all the family.'

All the family. She'd forgotten what it was like to have family to do things for you, that she didn't always have to be a solo player.

'Well, thank you for organising that,' she said warmly.

'We've managed to hold off opening it all day . . .' said Isabel.

Some small children scampered into view, a boy and a girl. Jacqui's niece and nephew, and Becs' cousins, eager to tear open their gifts. They each received a cuddly toy dog, squealing with delight.

'See, those were definitely inspired by you,' said Jacqui. 'Or should I say, Archie and Baxter.'

They'd also sent English tea and biscuits, a chiffon Liberty-print scarf that Isabel was delighted with, some posh toiletries and a cookbook from a British chef that couldn't be found in Australia.

'That took up most of the weight allowance, I'm afraid,' said Alex.

'It'll be well worth it,' said Jacqui's dad, leafing through it. 'I can't wait to try these!'

They chatted for a while longer, Isabel enquiring anxiously about how Jacqui was feeling, before saying their farewells.

Kathy glanced at her watch. Oh, Lord! They should think about getting lunch started, or it would never be ready in time. And maybe it was time to clear some of the breakfast things up – she stopped herself. Just relax and enjoy the day.

Becs was handing presents round, there were Christmas songs on the radio, and the atmosphere was warm and cosy.

She unwrapped a beautiful book on walks in the UK and a smart little day rucksack that would hold all the supplies she needed.

'I hope I did a bit better on the bag-and-book combo than last year,' said Jacqui, looking nervous.

'I was in a very different space last year,' Kathy said and hugged her. 'And these are just wonderful. I'll put them to immediate use.'

Jacqui was equally delighted with her spa day.

'Heavens! A whole day of being the customer, with my every whim tended to.'

Becs loved her gifts, especially the Crufts tickets.

Kathy passed Alex his present and held her breath when he opened the cufflinks.

'Oh, Mum,' he said. 'These are beautiful.'

'They were your dad's,' she said softly.

He smiled at her, looking so like John in that instant. 'I know. I used to spend hours fiddling about with them. I'd been wondering where they'd gone.'

'It's about time they were put to good use, not shut away in a drawer,' Kathy said, her voice wobbling.

Both she and Alex were a little emotional.

'Is this just a ploy to get Alex to wear a decent shirt for Christmas dinner?' Jacqui said, lightening the tone.

'Talking of Christmas dinner, we should get started,' Alex said. 'Mum, fancy helping?'

'Yes, Chef!' replied Kathy, following him into the kitchen.

'I just wanted a moment for us to remember Dad,' Alex said. 'Would you be up for a little toast?'

'Of course, love,' said Kathy.

Alex popped a bottle of cava and poured them each a glass. They toasted John, looking out on the garden.

'Do you remember the year we got him the electric car?' Kathy said, laughing.

'Yes, I do! After he was so bad at hogging mine the year before!'

That was all they needed. Just a little moment to remember him, with laughter and tears, before they turned to the question of Christmas lunch.

Alex opened the fridge, which was groaning with food.

'We might just have gone overboard,' he mused, 'especially with Becs not eating meat.'

Kathy's phone beeped. A message from Judith.

'Happy Christmas, Kathy and family! And Archie. Hope you're having a wonderful day. See you after lunch for a walk? We might be going hungry, as a certain Baxter managed to get the turkey onto the floor and scoff it . . .'

Oh, the poor things. Kathy stared at the amount of food they had in the fridge. Surely there was enough . . . The others approved of her idea instantly.

'The more the merrier!' said Becs. 'And we get to have Christmas with Baxter, after all!'

And so she invited Judith, Jess, Sam and Baxter over for Christmas lunch.

*

It was chaos. Wonderful, life-affirming chaos. Alex took over the kitchen, with Becs helping. Kathy and Jacqui welcomed their Christmas visitors in, bundling their coats upstairs and rushing to get them drinks. They'd brought all the food they could salvage and they laid it out on the dining room table – shutting the door firmly to avoid marauding dogs.

It suddenly occurred to Kathy that she hadn't even changed out of her scruffy dog walking clothes, but never mind. She put on the colourful necklace from Jess and Judith. How strange to think of putting it on a year ago, with no idea how these women would reappear in her life. She added the matching earrings, which instantly made her think of Ben.

Back downstairs, Alex was in full organising mode with the food.

'I think we're just going to lay it all out, buffet style,' said Alex, and Kathy agreed it would be easiest that way.

The house was noisy, full of life and colour. The two dogs played happily together, shredding wrapping paper into confetti and tumbling around in the joyful atmosphere. Baxter had been delighted to see them, loving being around so many people. It felt so right that he was here for Christmas, after all, thought Kathy.

Jess introduced Sam, who was lovely, and Becs was keen to chat to the older girls about agility training and what she could do to get involved.

'Just think, you could be being served cocktails on your sunlounger,' said Judith, red-faced from the heat in the kitchen as she and Kathy chopped vegetables side by side.

'I know,' smiled Kathy. 'I must be insane.'

'But it's so nice, isn't it?' said Judith. 'A Christmas like this.'

'It is,' agreed Kathy. 'I wouldn't have it any other way.'

It was so different to the organised, picture-perfect Christmas Kathy had planned the year before. It was a Christmas bursting with different people – a very different kind of family. A family completed by two very special dogs.

It was late by the time they sat down for lunch, chatting happily, each person piling their plate high with food. The dogs were scoffing their special Christmas lunch in the kitchen and Kathy just hoped they'd put any extra temptations out of the way. They pulled crackers, put on hats, told silly jokes and laughed, and they ate more than was sensible.

Kathy made herself take a moment to savour the scene.

What a difference a year made. She felt proud of how she'd changed and grateful to have these people – including the four-legged ones – in her life.

Lunch done, it was time to take the dogs for a walk – and the humans for some much-needed fresh air. Alex and Jacqui stayed behind, as Jacqui was keen to rest a little more before they drove home. The only disadvantage of them coming to Kathy's was that they had to return to the pub in time for Boxing Day. Their staff had covered Christmas Day admirably, according to the updates they'd received, and it would be Alex's turn to take over tomorrow. Even so, they'd had a wonderful Christmas Eve and Christmas Day, and Kathy knew she'd be glad to curl up with Archie in the quiet and digest all that had happened.

'Ready to go?' she asked Becs, Judith, Jess and Sam.

The five of them stepped out with the dogs and made their way to Battersea Park. The younger three went on ahead, skipping and jogging along with Baxter at their heels.

'I've no idea where they get the energy,' said Judith, and Kathy agreed.

Archie yawned by her heels and shook himself, as if he were drowsy, too.

'Yes, if I'd eaten another thing, you'd have had to roll me out the door.' She paused, drawing out an envelope. 'Judith, I wanted to give you this.'

Judith took it and pulled out a Christmas card.

'Open it,' said Kathy.

Judith took one look inside the card and burst into tears. 'I can't accept this. It's too much.'

'It isn't,' said Kathy. 'Really. I managed to get refunds on so many of the things I'd booked, so I didn't lose that much money in the end, but the plane ticket was non-refundable, only amendable. So, looks like you're going to Thailand!'

'But it was your trip,' said Judith, eyes bright. 'I wouldn't feel right doing all that stuff without you.'

'You helped me organise so much of it, though,' said Kathy. 'And you deserve it, truly. After all you went through with Jess, all that worry – you deserve a bit of an adventure of your own.'

Judith clasped the card to her heart and gave a wobbly smile. 'Are you sure?'

'Positive.'

Judith flung her arms around Kathy and squeezed her tightly. 'Thank you, thank you, thank you. This is a dream come true.'

Kathy laughed and hugged her back. It felt so good to surprise Judith like this. She'd had the money turned into flight vouchers, so Judith could book the trip for a time that suited her.

'You'll have to send me loads of updates. When do you think you'll go?'

'I'll be in touch every day!' Judith's eyes were shining. 'You know, it's quiet at work, so if I could get two weeks off soon . . . I'll go as soon as I can. Oh, Kathy, you don't know what this means to me. Imagine, I'll be seeing those temples! I'll be in that sea!'

Her enthusiasm was infectious. Kathy felt that exactly the right person was going on the trip.

They strolled on, arms linked.

'Hey, isn't that Ben?' said Judith, pointing to a figure on the path some way ahead, coming towards them.

Kathy's heart began to race.

It *was* Ben, with a dog called Phyllis walking beside him. They drew closer, and Kathy and Judith called out to him.

Ben looked up and raised a hand in greeting. He looked tired, Kathy thought. Sad. But he smiled as he reached them.

'Happy Christmas,' he said. 'Wondered if I might see you here. Same time next year?'

'You know,' said Judith, 'I'm just going to see where those girls have gone. I'll find you at the entrance, Kathy.'

Oh, blimey, it was just the two of them now. Well, four of them, as Archie and Phyllis introduced themselves.

'Happy Christmas,' said Kathy. 'How funny, bumping into you again on Christmas Day!' She scooped up Archie. 'We both have a lot to thank you for. If I hadn't bumped into you last Christmas and you hadn't mentioned the volunteering . . . well, I don't know where I'd be. Let alone little Archie. I can't imagine him anywhere else but here with me for Christmas. You started it all.'

Ben smiled. 'Things have a way of working themselves out. I didn't do much at all.'

'Oh, but you did,' said Kathy. Then she blushed. 'Are you volunteering today?'

He nodded. 'Yes.'

Was it just her, or did he seem more despondent than usual? More vulnerable, somehow. She saw him reach down and pet Phyllis' ears, as if for reassurance.

'And what are you doing afterwards?'

Ben looked down and shuffled his feet. 'I'll just head home, I think. Early night after a busy day.'

'Will you have company?'

Kathy knew she was prying. She thought of the photo she'd glimpsed in Ben's wallet at the summer party.

He shook his head. 'It's just me.'

Oh, that wouldn't do. Kathy couldn't bear to think of him heading home alone, with no one to keep him company. It wasn't that there was anything wrong with spending time alone, if that's what made you happy. It was that Ben seemed so sad.

'Won't you come by and have a drink and a mince pie?' she said, the words shooting out of her mouth. 'And some food. We've got so much left from lunch and it's so close to the rescue centre. It seems a shame for it to go to waste. No pressure, though, but Alex and co are heading off fairly soon and I'm not sure how long Judith will hang around for, but honestly, do come by.' Be quiet, Kathy, she told herself and thankfully, she stopped speaking.

Ben hesitated. 'Maybe, I'll have to see how it goes.'

That was a no, then. Ah well. She'd done her best.

She nodded. 'Give a big cuddle from me to all those dogs at Battersea. Tell them I'll be in soon.'

'Will do,' said Ben, and they parted ways.

She watched him go. She wasn't wrong. His shoulders were slumped, his head down. Should she text him? But no, she'd learnt the hard way – you couldn't control things. You couldn't help people if they didn't want your help. You had to let people go at their own pace.

Chapter 22

Back at home, they all slumped in front of the TV and watched an hour or so of Christmas telly, returning for just one last piece of Christmas cake, or some cheese, or a top-up of wine, over and over again. The two dogs lay down side by side and snored. Then all too soon, Jacqui was saying they should set off for the drive back.

'Yes, you get on your way,' said Kathy. 'You don't want to be back late and if you go now, it should be a clear drive. Do you feel tired, though?'

'I'm fine. Had a bit of a siesta when you were out walking. It's probably the most relaxing Christmas I've ever had!'

Kathy helped them carry their things to the car, pressing some Tupperware boxes of leftovers into their hands. She embraced each of them tightly.

'Thanks for the best Christmas ever!' said Becs. 'Until the next one, of course!'

Kathy laughed and said she'd see her soon.

Then they were in the car and driving away, tooting the horn in farewell. Kathy felt a little heartache as they drove off, then she looked down at Archie by her feet. She wasn't alone.

'Back inside, eh, boy?'

She made tea for everyone else and they chatted a little longer, on into early evening. It was well and truly dark outside now, the Christmas tree lights glowing cosily.

Judith yawned. 'You know, we should be getting back, as well. What a day! Thanks so much for having us over. And for the gift of a lifetime.'

They all said their farewells, and then it was just Kathy and Archie.

She shut the front door and went back into the living room, collapsing on the sofa, exhausted. Archie jumped up beside her and settled in for a cuddle. Kathy glanced around the room, which was a complete mess, despite Jacqui and Alex's efforts to tidy up while they'd been out on their walk. It could all wait. Right now, she just wanted to shut her eyes and drift off into the Christmas night for a moment or two. . .

Ding-dong.

Kathy woke with a start and checked her watch. Only half an hour had gone by, but she'd been so deeply asleep that it was a shock to wake up. Archie opened one eye and decided to go back to sleep again.

Had that been the doorbell?

It must be one of the girls, having left something behind.

She got up, glancing at herself in the mirror – her hair was a total bird's nest and she hadn't got changed out of her early morning dog walking clothes all day, it had been so hectic. She smiled to herself and flung open the door.

'Ben!'

There he was, standing on her doorstep, nervously clutching a box of chocolates.

'Hello,' he said. 'I can go, if it's not . . . I mean, if you don't . . .'

'Come in,' she said, standing aside to let him pass. 'It's freezing outside.'

'I couldn't find anywhere to get you a decent bottle of something, so I'm afraid these rather battered chocs will have to do.'

'Oh, don't worry. We've so much booze left over. Thank you for the chocolates.'

She took his coat from him and hung it up. The collar was frayed.

'Come on through to the living room. Can I get you a glass of something?'

'Just a glass of water, please.'

She nodded and went through to the kitchen. She could hear Ben greeting Archie, joy in his voice. She carried two glasses through – water for Ben, and a small glass of red for her, as a nightcap – and sat down next to Ben on the sofa.

It was a big sofa, but she was suddenly very aware of the distance between them. And the awkward silence. She heard Ben swallow. He looked at her and made eye contact, then looked down at Archie. She should have sat on one of the armchairs. Fortunately, Archie was seemingly immune to human awkwardness and he poked Ben with his paw, rolling onto his back for a tummy rub.

'So, how was your day at the dogs' home?'

'Oh, fine, fine. I always love being with the dogs.' He took a sip of water and turned to face her. 'Kathy.' He blew out his cheeks. 'Sorry. I can't find the words. It took a lot for me to come here. Christmas is . . . is hard for me.'

Kathy didn't say anything. She could see Ben was forcing himself to get the words out.

'A while back, when we had dinner, you asked about my past and I didn't want to tell you. Because it's painful.' He took a deep breath. 'I know what it's like to lose your partner. The same thing happened to me. I'd suspected it even before you told me. When I saw you, on that volunteer assessment day at Battersea, and you were looking at the memory wall in that way – I just knew you'd lost someone close to you. I knew how much you still hurt from it, because that hurt never goes away, does it?'

He looked at her then, eyes full of pain.

'My wife, Lydia, she had MS. She was diagnosed soon after we were married. For years and years, it was just about manageable. Hard, of course. But she had good spells and bad spells. We didn't have kids.' He sighed ruefully. 'It just seemed too much to cope with. She was the most wonderful woman. She was loving and kind and funny – so funny!'

'Is that the woman in your wallet?' Kathy asked.

Ben gave her a wry little smile. 'I knew you'd clocked that. Yes. And is that your husband?' He was looking at the mantelpiece.

'Yes, that's John. I'll tell you about him, in time. Tell me more about Lydia.'

Ben cleared his throat. 'I hardly ever talk about her. But . . . she went with the flow. You won't believe it, but she was always teasing *me* for being uptight, so organised. She changed me. And when the illness got worse, I learnt to let the little things go. So what if your shoelaces are undone, or you drop a glass in a restaurant? It's more important to enjoy yourself, to take each moment as it comes.

'That was another thing about MS, the unpredictability of it. Sometimes we'd have planned something lovely and she'd have a terrible day, so we couldn't do it. The disappointment and frustration of it, on top of the disease . . . So we learnt to go with the flow. Not to plan. Not to worry about controlling everything.

'So I changed. You were surprised about my old job, and I can't even imagine being in it now. I stuck at it when Lydia was alive because we needed the money.'

Kathy nodded. She didn't want to say anything, just listen.

'After she . . . died . . . I went to pieces. I was fired, if you really want the truth. I was drinking too much, a real state. And then I found something to help me put my life back together again. Lydia had had a service dog, Alfie.'

'The bench!' Kathy said.

Ben glanced at her. 'Eh?'

'Where you were sitting that time. It's their names, isn't it?'

He nodded. 'Yes. We loved that spot.'

In time, Kathy knew she'd tell him about a similar spot for she, John and Buddy in Windsor. There were so many parallels to their stories, but now was the moment to let Ben speak freely.

'What was Alfie like?' she asked.

'Oh, he was wonderful. He helped her with practical things, picking stuff up when she dropped it. He could even pick up a telephone and bring it to her. But more than that, he was just this constant source of love and goodwill and patience, and we both needed that.

'We knew that he'd come from Battersea before he was trained and given to us. He passed away a few months after Lydia and it was awful. It was like the last piece of her was gone. I figured I had to do something, or I'd lose myself, as well.'

Kathy reached out and took his hand, intertwining her fingers with his.

'It's awful, isn't it?' she said simply.

'Yes, it is. It breaks my heart that you've known the same pain.'

'Tell me what happened next.'

'Well, I started volunteering at Battersea. Once a week. When I say it saved my life, I don't think that's an exaggeration. I wanted to give something back to the place that had given Alfie a second chance, but it was me who ended up getting the most out of it, I think. Eventually, I worked my way up to becoming a rehomer there.'

'More second chances, every day,' Kathy said, and Ben nodded.

'It's a great feeling, when you match a dog and a person who really need each other.'

'And you're brilliant at it, clearly.'

'I'm glad you think so.' He squeezed her hand. 'I think my past is also why I chose for Baxter to go to Jess. I know what it's like when you need something else to build your world around, how powerful it is to be needed when you think you have nothing to offer. I didn't know how hurt you'd be. You're very good at putting a good spin on things. You seemed so confident, like you didn't need anyone.'

Kathy exhaled. 'Yes, I was a bit too good at putting a spin on things. But Baxter went to the right home. You made the right decision. One hundred per cent.'

Ben nodded. 'It means a lot to hear you say that. Those things you said to me . . . they cut deep. Because yes, I am chaotic, I know I can be. And I suppose it's how I coped with the illness, and afterwards. Not sweating the small stuff that everyone gets so worked up about.

'But when you said about me hurting you, by being careless . . . it hurt so much to think of myself like that. And I thought, maybe you were right. I'd been trying to pluck up the courage to tell you how I felt over the summer, but I kept chickening out.

'And then after Baxter, I thought maybe I'd just end up hurting you, so it was better to keep my distance.' He chuckled. 'But that was also annoying, as you're the first person since Lydia passed who I've even felt an inkling of something for.' His eyes met hers shyly.

'And you're the first after John,' replied Kathy softly.

She waited for a moment, to see how she felt, if she'd feel a lurch of guilt or grief. It all felt a bit strange, she concluded. But it didn't feel wrong. It simply felt new.

'What was he like?' said Ben. 'If you want to tell me.'

Kathy smiled. 'Oh, he was wonderful. He was kind and funny, too. He brought out the silly side of me, one that not many people could. And he loved Christmas.'

Ben nodded. 'Lydia, too. Any hint of doing Christmas decorations by half measures and she was not happy! She used to order me about to get the high decorations exactly as she wanted them. And I used to tease her about her artistic temperament.' Ben cleared his throat. 'God, sorry. I don't often talk about her these days.'

Kathy's heart went out to him. At least she had Alex to share her memories with.

'It's a funny mix, isn't it, talking about them? How it's possible to feel joy and sorrow in the same heartbeat.'

He nodded. 'Exactly that.'

'Life's complicated, isn't it?' Kathy murmured. 'No easy answers.'

They sat in a comfortable silence for a few minutes, each lost in their own thoughts, linked by their joined hands. Ben ran his thumb over Kathy's knuckles, over and over, and she found his touch soothing.

He turned to her. 'Look, Kathy. I just wondered . . . I know this is going to be new for both of us, and I'll need to take things slowly, and I'm not asking you to make any decisions quickly, but would you like to just . . . see more of each other? Get to know each other? Properly, now that we've both let our guard down a bit.'

He looked so nervous, his hair flopping over his face, that Kathy couldn't help but smile. She reached up with her other hand and pushed his hair back.

'I'd like that.'

Ben let out a sigh of relief. 'Phew! Haven't done that since I was about fourteen.' He reached over and held up his glass to her.

'To venturing down a new path!' Kathy said, clinking her glass against his.

They sat back again in a warm silence, broken only by Archie's gentle snoring.

'He enjoyed his first Christmas, then?'

'Oh, yes.'

And then she was telling him all about it, and about her family, and being honest about how difficult last Christmas had been. And Ben listened and asked her questions, and talked about how his day had been – and suddenly it was somehow 10 p.m. and Kathy was fuzzy from red wine and happiness.

'Oh, look at the time!' said Ben. 'I'm sorry, I only meant for this to be a quick visit.'

'It was lovely. But you must be exhausted.'

'Now that I know what time it is, I do feel tired.' He stood up. 'But let me help you tidy up a bit first.'

'Oh, no, don't worry, I'll—'

But Ben was already picking things up and carrying them through to the kitchen.

'Maybe I can prove to you that I wasn't always Mr Chaos,' he said with a smile.

They worked together, making the kitchen and living room decent enough to leave until Boxing Day.

'You've a ton of leftovers,' Ben said as he tried to wedge another Tupperware in the fridge.

'I know,' said Kathy. 'And this is after giving away as much as I could.'

Ben managed to wedge it in. 'See, how's that for organisation! Just the wine glasses to wash up now.'

'I thought I might leave those till the morning,' said Kathy. 'You know, live on the edge a bit.'

Ben laughed and Kathy felt like she was sparkling.

He walked to the front door and put on his coat.

'What time will Archie have you up for his morning walk?'

She groaned. 'I think about seven. I can't think about that now.'

'Good luck with that.'

Ben was bundled up in his coat now, the two of them standing near each other in the hallway.

'Well . . .' said Kathy, feeling like a teenager. 'Thank you for—'

'Happy Christmas,' said Ben, and he hesitated for a moment that seemed to go on forever, before he lowered his head and touched his lips to hers in a gentle, brief kiss.

Kathy placed her hands on his shoulders as he drew back. Her head was spinning.

'Happy Christmas,' she murmured, glad to see that Ben was blushing as furiously as she was.

He opened the front door and stepped out, turning back to smile shyly at her. Kathy was relieved to stand in the cold air for a few minutes, watching him walk to his car, allowing the freezing cold to cool her hot cheeks.

Ben had kissed her! And it had felt wonderful!

*

Exactly 7 a.m. on Boxing Day and Kathy was woken by a whining Archie, keen to be off. She groaned, her head fuzzy from the wine, although she was still thrilled at the thought of what had happened between her and Ben. Could she not just turn back over and roll back to sleep . . . ? No. She made herself get up and out of bed, shuffled into some warm layers and padded downstairs to find Archie, ready and waiting.

'Good morning, good morning!' she mumbled blearily, rubbing her eyes and putting him in his coat and on the lead. 'Let's be off, then.'

She opened the front door and Archie darted out with a woof. Enthusiastic, even for him. She fumbled with the keys, dropping them, and then her new fleecy headband slipped down over her eyes in the process of picking them up. She groaned.

'Looks like you could do with a cuppa.'

Ben!

She glanced up, to see him waiting for her just outside her garden gate. No wonder Archie had been keen to get out!

'I thought you might want some company on such an early morning walk,' he said. 'I've got a thermos of tea and some flapjacks. And we don't have to say very much at all, I promise. I'm terrible at conversation in the morning.'

Kathy stepped towards him and throwing caution to the wind, wrapped her arms around him and gave him a tight hug. It felt so good to be in his arms. His hair was tousled and messy, and she wouldn't change it for anything.

'I would like nothing more,' she said.

He offered her his arm and she wrapped her gloved hand around it, Archie's lead in the other.

'Let's be off, then,' Ben said.

'Where do you fancy going?'

'I thought,' he said carefully, 'that we might try a new route. If you're up for it?'

'Yes,' Kathy replied. 'Yes, I think I am.'

THE END

Acknowledgements

A huge thank you to Sam Eades and Phoebe Morgan, for their amazing creativity and wise counsel. Thank you also to Victoria Pepe, Claire Dean and Georgia Goodall for their insightful and thoughtful edits, which were so helpful.

I'd also like to thank the rest of the fabulous team at Orion, a full list of whom can be found in the back of the book, for their expert support of the project in so many different ways.

I'm indebted to the kind and generous team at Battersea Dogs and Cats Home for allowing me to visit (and meet a few residents!) and making me so welcome, and for answering all my questions about the work they do.

A very special thank you to Andrew Bram (and Alex the Staffie) and Fran White for talking to me about fostering and providing me with stories about the amazing dogs they have cared for.

Thanks too to Stephanie Butland and Harris the Greyhound, especially for an education in greyhound snoozing postures.

Thank you to Fiona Buchan, for her very helpful advice on treating cut paws.

A big thank you to my dear friends Rich Davies and Ollie Mann for talking to me about Madge and Minka (a dearly missed and greatly adored weirdo). I loved our conversation.

A thank you from the bottom of my heart to Madge for chewing my retainer, thus teaching us all how to live in the moment and relinquish material possessions with grace.

Finally, thank you to each and every reader for buying the book and helping support the vital work Battersea do.

Credits

Agent
Sarah Van Kirk

Editor
Sam Eades

Copy-editor
Claire Dean

Proofreader
Ilona Jasiewicz

Editorial Management
Georgia Goodall
Charlie Panayiotou

Audio
Paul Stark
Amber Bates

Contracts
Anne Goddard
Paul Bulos

Design
Lucie Stericker
Debbie Holmes

Finance
Jennifer Muchan
Jasdip Nandra
Rabale Mustafa
Elizabeth Beaumont
Ibukun Ademefun
Afeera Ahmed

Marketing
Amy Davies

Production
Claire Keep
Fiona McIntosh

Publicity
Patricia Deveer

Sales
Jennifer Wilson
Victoria Laws

Esther Waters
Lucy Brem
Frances Doyle
Ben Goddard
Georgina Cutler
Jack Hallam
Ellie Kyrke-Smith
Inês Figuiera
Barbara Ronan
Andrew Hally
Dominic Smith
Deborah Deyong
Lauren Buck
Maggy Park
Linda McGregor
Sinead White
Jemimah James
Rachel Jones
Jack Dennison
Nigel Andrews
Ian Williamson
Julia Benson
Declan Kyle
Robert Mackenzie
Imogen Clarke
Megan Smith
Charlotte Clay
Rebecca Cobbold

Operations
Jo Jacobs
Sharon Willis
Lisa Pryde

Rights
Susan Howe
Richard King
Krystyna Kujawinska
Jessica Purdue
Louise Henderson

Loved *Home for Christmas*?
Feeling bereft after saying goodbye to Kathy, Ben and Archie?

Keep on reading . . .

From Florence McNicoll comes another heartwarming novel of unexpected friendships, second chances . . . and furry friends.

The Nine Lives of Christmas

It's Christmas at Battersea Dogs and Cats Home and Laura is desperate to find a home for Felicia, a spiky, bad-tempered moggy with a heart of gold. Her boyfriend, Rob, can't understand why she's spending so much time at work but, for Laura, the animals aren't just a job – they're her life. She needs a partner who understands that – doesn't she?

As the December snow falls, Laura encounters nine people, all of whom need a little love in their lives and find it in new pets. Everyone needs somebody to curl up with at Christmas, and when the handsome Aaron walks in, he takes not just Felicia, but Laura's heart too . . .

The Nine Lives of Christmas

Florence McNicoll

Chapter 1

What would a cat do? thought Laura Summers blearily, through the beeps of her alarm clock. She reached out a hand to hit snooze, Rob grumbling beside her before he fell back asleep.

A cat certainly wouldn't be dragging herself out of bed at 6 a.m. on a cold, dark, winter morning. No, any cat worth her salt would curl right back up under the duvet and sleep until at least ten, probably eleven, before surfacing and demanding food and cuddles and finding the perfect spot by the radiator to keep cosy for the rest of the day.

Laura smiled. The thought of all the cats waiting for her at Battersea was more than enough to get her out of bed, pull on her dressing gown and pad through to the kitchen for a morning cup of tea, and to crack open the very first door on her chocolate advent calendar. Who said chocolate wasn't an acceptable breakfast? In Laura's book, in December, all normal dietary rules were off.

Mornings hadn't always been like this. When she'd been working as a PA at Nimbus, one of London's top advertising agencies, she'd often been lying awake already before the alarm went off, a tight knot of anxiety in her stomach, worrying about whether she'd sent off those invites, or booked her boss's taxi for the right time, or any number of other potential disasters. She'd left the agency about two years before, following a particularly vicious dressing-down from her boss after she'd asked if 'anyone needed a hug' in a tense client meeting. Pulling herself together in the office loos afterwards by watching some of her all-time favourite cat videos, Laura had seen an advert on Battersea's Facebook page for a welfare worker in the cattery. It had felt like a sign. Laura had decided she'd go somewhere where her talent for looking after people – well, cats, who were pretty much her favourite people anyway – would be appreciated. And she'd never looked back.

She'd loved her time in welfare, caring for the cats right from the moment they came in, ensuring that they were safe, well-fed, happy and healthy in preparation for their new homes. Just a month or so ago, she'd changed job and was now on the rehoming team, helping prospective owners find their perfect match, and the cats their forever homes. She'd spent time shadowing the rehoming interviews, before practising taking pictures of the cats for their online profiles, and answering phone and email enquiries. Her experience in the welfare team had been a great help, but it had still been a steep learning curve, and Laura was keen to prove herself in this new role – as well as being more than a little nervous. She'd always struggled with her confidence. She often felt like she was the one in the room who didn't have much of a presence, the one who wasn't heard, or who muttered and was asked to repeat things. It was one of the reasons she often felt more comfortable being around animals than humans – and, specifically, around cats. She never felt tongue-tied or silly when she was chatting to a cat. Their presence relaxed her, and the flick of a tail, the twitch of an ear, the rumble of a purr all assured her that she was listened to and understood.

Laura finished the last of her tea and tiptoed into the shower, hoping it wouldn't wake Rob. He'd got in late last night, slightly tipsy, having celebrated landing yet another new client. Rob was the one great thing she'd taken with her from her time at the ad agency. He was a hot-shot account director at Nimbus, charming, confident and completely gorgeous, with his blue eyes and dark-brown hair that flopped over his forehead in a way that still made her stomach flip. Laura had admired him from afar, their conversations generally extending only to him requesting meetings with her boss and sometimes asking her to arrange coffees – she'd always taken special care thinking what biscuits Rob might appreciate – and so she'd been amazed when he'd asked her out for a drink at the company's Halloween party two years ago, coming over to find her where she was standing in the corner, twisting her fingers and wondering how on earth everyone else found so much to say. Laura liked to think it had been because her biscuit offering that day – a zingy chocolate Bourbon and pink wafer combo – had finally convinced him they were meant to be together, but Rob said it was more to do with the Catwoman outfit she'd been wearing.

They'd been together pretty much ever since. She'd left the agency and joined Battersea shortly after they started seeing each other, which Rob had been supportive about. He thought she'd be happier in another role, and that it would be better for them not to work together if they were going to be serious. Then, about a year ago, she'd moved into his beautiful home, in fancy Chelsea. She felt like she'd hit the jackpot, really, especially when she'd been sharing a grotty flat in the outer reaches of north London with three other girls who were big on partying and low on tidying. Rob's place was an oasis of calm, exquisitely designed in an array of neutral colours.

After a boiling-hot shower and dressing proudly in her Battersea polo shirt and fleece, Laura slipped out of the house, shivering a little in the frosty air, hopped on a bus and began the journey to Battersea. She was determined to be a star rehomer in her new role. Insecurities couldn't get in the way. She couldn't bear to think of cats alone for Christmas – they would be well cared-for on Christmas Day by the amazing army of festive Battersea volunteers and staff, but nothing compared to knowing you were *home*, for good. And there was one particular cat she had in mind.

The bus pulled up outside Battersea's famous gates and Laura felt a thrill of pride as she buzzed her way in, waving hello to the security team and the receptionist. She crossed the courtyard, taking in the mix of old and new that she loved so much about Battersea. There was the old cattery building in the middle, named Whittington Lodge after the famous Dick Whittington and his cat, with its tiled roof and pretty blue staircase. It was a wonderful reminder of the history of the place. Laura always thought about the many feet – and paws – that had crossed this piece of ground since 1871. What stories they could tell! She got goose bumps at the thought of it.

It was just before eight, and Laura had enough time to pop up to the cattery before the morning meeting – the perfect representation of 'the new' in Battersea's history. The cattery was warm and cosy, with each cat living in an individual 'pod', large enough for a cat to exhibit its natural behaviours with lots of places for hiding – and they even had heated floors!

In anticipation of their breakfasts, most of the cats were now at the front mewing – the dawn chorus, as Laura liked to call it. She strolled past the pods, filled with cats of all colours, shapes, ages and personalities, to see the one cat she had a particular soft spot for. Laura's emotions rose up at the thought of Felicia. It was one of the most amazing, and most difficult, elements of working at Battersea – the emotional attachments you formed with the animals. And there Felicia was, running to the front of her pod as soon as she saw Laura. Laura couldn't resist opening the door and slipping inside, joy rising in her heart as she heard Felicia's loud purr of greeting. Laura sat down and Felicia clambered onto her knee for a cuddle.

Felicia had been one of the saddest cases during Laura's time in welfare. She'd been brought in emaciated and very sick, found by a dog walker in a nearby park. It had been touch and go on those first days as to whether she would survive, but thanks to the care of the veterinary team, Felicia had started to put on weight and recover physically from whatever ordeals she'd been through. Indeed, thought Laura as she held Felicia in her arms, they might have to start watching she didn't get a little *too* plump.

But the damage with animals was often so much more than physical. Felicia had been withdrawn and completely untrusting of humans, cowering at the back of her pod and responding with hisses and the occasional nip to those who came too close. Laura had been assigned as Felicia's 'consistent carer' when she was in welfare. Alongside the daily tasks of feeding and cleaning, Laura had started to build up Felicia's trust, working at the cat's pace, and often simply spending time sitting at the front of the pod, quietly reading or catching up on emails, to get her used to human company. Laura vividly remembered the day when she'd felt a touch on her leg, and had looked down to see Felicia's outstretched paw on her knee. The cat had blinked her golden eyes up at Laura, and Laura swallowed, a lump in her throat, elated and moved at this breakthrough moment.

From there, Felicia quickly gained in confidence and was soon climbing onto Laura's lap for cuddles, bumping her head against Laura's hand when she felt she was slacking off with the under-chin rubs. Laura would talk to her in a low voice and, even though she knew she'd sound crazy, she could have sworn Felicia understood. Occasionally, a playful side to Felicia would emerge – as an older cat at the ripe old age of eight, she was a rather stately lady most of the time, but she could be roused to action by a carefully twitched catnip mouse. Of course, other staff spent time with her too, but it was Laura she had a special bond with. Felicia took time to warm to people, that was for sure. Choosy, Laura thought, but she knew some would see it as unfriendliness if they didn't give her a chance. Then, one proud day, Felicia was assessed to be suitable for rehoming, and was moved to the first floor where she could meet her public.

'You're not tempted to take her yourself?' Jasmine had asked. Jasmine worked between intake and rehoming and was Laura's best friend at Battersea. Best friend full-stop, really.

Laura had shaken her head sadly. This was a major point of contention between her and Rob. He just didn't like cats, he didn't want one in the flat, using all his fancy mid-century furniture as a scratching post and getting hairs in the vinyl collection. Laura knew they could provide a perfect home for a cat – they had a small garden too – but Rob was adamant. He had a beautifully kept tank of tropical fish, and he'd said Laura could name a few of those. She hadn't had the heart to explain that it wasn't the same, much as she'd tried to bond with the newly christened Flotsam and Jetsam.

'How are you this morning, missy?' whispered Laura into Felicia's fur, receiving a louder purr in response. 'Ready for your breakfast?'

That received a small 'Miaow!' and Laura laughed, sure that Felicia understood. She put the cat back down and carefully let herself out of the pod, making her way to the morning meeting, where her team would go through all the cats on 'The List' who were currently up for adoption, as well as checking with the welfare team to see if there were new cats who were now ready to be rehomed. As it was 1 December, Laura made a mental note to get some Christmas decorations up in the cattery – Christmas songs had already been playing on the radio for weeks.

'Still no home for Felicia?' said Laura's boss, Sally, when they came to the cat's name during the meeting rundown.

Laura shook her head sadly. 'It'll have to be the right person. She's a special cat, she just needs someone to notice her, and who'll understand she needs the time and space to settle in. Plus someone who can cope with her medical needs.'

This was another element that had to be considered for Felicia. She'd tested positive for FIV – feline immunodeficiency virus. The virus was a slow-acting one, and many cats went on to enjoy normal lifespans with minimal health implications, but that wasn't always the case. There was the possibility that a FIV cat would have a weakened immune system, and be more prone to infections and other diseases. In order to protect other cats from contracting the virus, and an FIV cat from being exposed to illnesses from other cats, Battersea required that gardens were enclosed in any prospective new homes. This was simple to do with the right fencing, but understandably people could be reluctant to take on a cat with extra needs, and FIV cats took the longest to rehome. The staff always bonded with these cats, as they were in the cattery for so long, and when they finally did find their forever homes, they were given a special send-off with everyone gathered to say goodbye.

Sally nodded. 'Well, she'll be safe here with us for as long as it takes. But let's hope she finds her home soon. She's looking at being one of our longest-ever stays, poor girl.'

Laura did some mental arithmetic and realised that Felicia had been at Battersea for almost one hundred days. With cats counted as a 'long stay' after thirty days, she was already at more than three times that. Laura swallowed. Some cats just couldn't catch a break. Felicia was a bit older, and she was black and white – which for some reason proved to be an unpopular colour. As well as her FIV, she also had a heart murmur that could potentially lead to veterinary treatment, and people were understandably wary about extra costs, but Laura just knew the right match was out there. Felicia could bring someone a lot of joy. All Laura had to do was to keep believing and keep trying. This was to be her Christmas wish, then. Or, rather, her Christmas challenge: find Felicia her forever home, by Christmas Eve.

*

After the meeting, Laura was soon caught up in the flurry of emails and enquiries she received from potential rehomers. A huge part of the job was responding to these, as well as offering support and aftercare to new owners as the cats adjusted to their new homes, and the morning flew by. She hurried over to meet Jasmine for a quick sandwich in the on-site café.

'The first mince pie of the season!' Jasmine said, as they moved on to dessert. Last year, she and Jasmine had tasted pretty much every mince pie going from every major retailer, from the cheapest to the poshest, under the excuse of scientifically finding the best one. 'Shall I get the mince pie spreadsheet going again?'

'Absolutely,' said Laura, through a mouthful of pastry. 'The world needs to know the truth.'

'We're scientific pioneers, really,' said Jasmine.

'They should give us the Nobel Prize!'

'Nobel Pies!' said Jasmine, causing Laura to groan.

'Jas, we're not quite close enough to Christmas for me to cope with your cracker jokes just yet.'

Jasmine held up her hands in surrender. 'All right, all right. So, tell me how things are with you. How's rehoming?'

Laura took a breath. 'Well. I love it. I'm proud to be doing it. But I'm a bit nervous, I have to admit. The thought of doing a lot of interviews on my own – it's intimidating.'

'You will be completely fine,' said Jasmine. 'You've done all the shadowing and the training, and you won't be alone – you know we're a team effort and there will always be help if you need it.'

Laura nodded. It was easy for Jasmine to say – she could chat to absolutely everyone. She was just one of those people who lit up a room with her presence and her raucous laugh.

'I can tell you're stressing,' said Jasmine, reaching out a hand to pat Laura's arm. 'But don't. I've seen you with people – you've got that talent of getting people to open up to you, so you can find just the cat that suits them.'

Laura smiled. 'Thanks, Jas. That's really kind. What about you? Any hot gossip?'

'Not really. Just enjoying a bit of routine before the next foster rescue mission arrives.'

Jasmine was one of Battersea's foster carers, taking in cats who needed special care, or who were too stressed by life in the cattery.

'And are you ready for Christmas?'

Jasmine grimaced, and her face fell. 'As I'll ever be. Not my favourite time of year, I have to say. I've signed up to spend the day here, can't think of anywhere I'd rather be.' Laura knew that Jasmine had had a rough year, splitting up with her husband after she'd found out he was cheating on her last Christmas. She'd declared herself 'quite happy to be a crazy cat lady, thanks very much', but Laura knew this

Christmas would be a tough time for her. Jasmine was strong and proud, but Laura knew how deeply she'd been hurt.

'We can't tempt you to spend Christmas Day down here?' asked Jas. 'It is pretty amazing. Santa comes to visit, and there might even be a drop of prosecco at lunch.'

'I doubt Rob could be persuaded,' Laura said, with a sigh. They were scheduled to go to his parents in Surrey for Christmas, which she couldn't help but feel a little nervous about. Malcolm and Izzy were perfectly pleasant, but were from the Very Confident School of Life, just like Rob. They were a family that liked an occasion – there were many photos of Rob's boisterous childhood birthday parties in the house. He loved to reminisce about those days and how much fun they were, and Laura admittedly loved looking at the pictures of Rob as a cute kid, his delighted face smeared with chocolate cake, a grin from ear to ear. Christmas would be a noisy day of playing charades and commenting with great expertise on wines – just like last year. She'd struggled to recognise most of the films and plays that had come up in charades, and had overheard Izzy saying to Rob in the kitchen, 'She's as quiet as a little mouse!' 'Just give her time,' Rob had said, but the comment had thundered in her ears and she'd become even more quiet, retiring to bed as early as possible and wishing she was different.

'You know he's not keen on cats,' said Laura, breaking out of her reverie. 'So he's probably not going to be up for cleaning litter trays on Christmas Day.'

Laura had frequently tried to persuade Rob to come and see the cats at Battersea – she was convinced that if he'd just get to know the right one, he'd realise what a wonderful addition to their little household a cat would be.

'Ah yes, Mr Perfect,' grinned Jasmine. 'Apart from that one little oversight. What are you going to get him, then?'

'Not sure,' mused Laura. 'I want to get him something really special.'

'You two are just the perfect couple,' teased Jasmine, but when Laura didn't respond, her tone became more serious. 'Hey, I'm just messing about. Everything's okay, isn't it?'

'Yeah, it's fine,' Laura said. Why did she suddenly feel like everything *wasn't* okay with Rob? Why was she suddenly anxious about Christmas Day at his parents'? 'I suppose we're not seeing much of each other. He's so busy with work, so when we do spend time together, it's more collapsing on the sofa and staring at the telly rather than into each other's eyes.'

'Sounds completely normal to me,' said Jasmine, reaching over to squeeze her hand. 'What you need is to make time for each other a bit. Date nights! Do something fun, surprise each other. You'll get that spark back in no time.'

Laura nodded, liking this idea. Jasmine was right – she and Rob just needed to get that sparkle back. And what better time than in the run-up to Christmas? She remembered their first few months together: a whirlwind of romantic dinners, trips to the theatre, and lazy Sundays in bed. Then, as they'd become more established as a couple, endless holidays with Rob's glamorous friends, or freebie trips that Rob could somehow make happen through his advertising connections. He'd whisked her off for a night or two at the end of a shoot in some amazing location more times than she could remember, often refusing to tell her where she was going and simply saying what kind of wardrobe she needed to bring. She'd always buzzed with excitement to get to the airport and find out where she was going. Right then, that was mission number two – a little bit of Christmas magic.